LONGSHOT

A DESPERATE MISSION TO THE STARS

KEVIN J SIMINGTON

1

Mission Specialist Lieutenant Olivia Alvarez was getting impatient.

"We really need to go now, you two! We've got a shuttle to catch. Whatever important things you have to talk about will have to wait until we're on board."

Kelly Rearson was staring open-mouthed and with eyes agog at Daniel after his confession a moment before. He was apparently able to calculate the square root of 1081 to an impressive number of decimal places. Did this mean what she thought it did? Had the quantum enhancement of his brain actually worked?

"We're coming," said Daniel. He took Kelly's arm and gently guided her toward the pod door, whispering to her, "I'll explain later."

"You'd better!"

They were in a transparent tether lift pod, 1000 kilometres above the Earth, docked to Hubble Station, a transit station for Luna shuttles and ships to other destinations around the solar system. Below their feet, the Earth hung motionless, a beautiful globe of blue and white swirls. Olivia Alvarez, tall and slender and impeccably dressed in her ANSA officer's uniform, stood impatiently waiting for them to exit the pod and join her in the docking tube. Daniel and Kelly caught up with her and the three of them made the brief transit through the docking tube into the station.

"Follow me," Alvarez said. "We haven't got any time for gawking; we're on a tight timeline. And watch your step in the low gravity. It takes a little while to get used to."

Because Hubble Station was only 1,000 kilometres up the tether lift cable, and not at the geosynchronous orbital height of the anchoring asteroid, at 35,786 kilometres, their relatively low orbital velocity at this height meant that they were not in free fall and, therefore, not weightless. But they still had enough orbital velocity to offset some of the pull of Earth's gravity. They weighed about two thirds what they weighed at sea level, but their mass and inertia remained the same, which sometimes led to mildly amusing accidents for first timers.

They emerged into a short corridor which led them to a central circular concourse. There were people hurrying across the concourse and disappearing down corridors leading off in different directions, each signposted with its own designation: STL, FTL, Earth Orbit, Inner Sol, Outer Sol.

"This way," said Alvarez as she led them across the concourse to the FTL corridor. She explained as she went, "We could take the Slow Transit Luna Shuttle, which only accelerates at 1G, but I need to get back as soon as possible. So, if you don't mind, we're going to take the Fast Transit Lunar Shuttle. With a constant acceleration of 3G it's not as comfortable, but it's a hell of a lot quicker. We'll be at Armstrong Base in only three hours."

As they followed Alvarez, Kelly asked her, "Remind me again about this 1G and 3G business? I'm a microbiologist, not an astrophysicist."

"1G refers to the acceleration rate of 9.8 metres per second squared, which equates to the force of gravity you experience on the Earth's surface. It's the acceleration force of one normal Earth gravity. 3G means that our rate of acceleration will be three times Earth's gravity: 29.4 meters per second squared."

Daniel chipped in, "It means you'll be squished back into your chair as if you weigh three times your normal weight."

"That sounds like fun. I can't wait."

The corridor ended in an open airlock door revealing the short docking connector leading to the open shuttle door at its end. A sign above the airlock door read, Alliance of Nations Space Agency, Fast Luna Transit. A man in ANSA uniform stood by the open airlock door ready to scan the ID chips of passengers. When he saw Lieutenant Alvarez approaching, he snapped to attention.

"At ease, private," said Sylvia.

"Thank you, ma'am. I've been holding the shuttle for you."

"Who have we got on board today?" she asked as he scanned their wrists.

"Two honeymoon couples and an older couple headed for Starlight Casino, a handful of scientists for Armstrong Research Facility and three ANSA personnel who will be transferring to Longshot Base."

"Who's today's pilot?"

"Carmody."

Alvarez shrugged. "Don't know him."

"He's new to the Luna run, ma'am. Been working the Mars run for 18 months. Pretty smooth on the flips, so I hear."

"We'll see," she said, noncommittally.

A few moments later they were seated and strapped in, having grabbed three seats together toward the front.

"Do you know much about these FTLs?" asked Alvarez.

"A bit," said Kelly, but Daniel admitted that he knew almost nothing.

"They're impressive," began Alvarez. "Direct Fusion Drive. The DFD engine converts the Helium-3 isotope that we harvest from the Moon directly to plasma, resulting in a maximum exhaust velocity of 12,00 kilometres per second. Not that we'll ever need all that power. A Fast Transit Luna shuttle accelerates at 3G for 90 minutes and then, at the midway point, flips and decelerates for another 90 minutes. Three hours and you're on the Moon."

"Impressive," said Daniel.

"I need to warn you that three hours of 3G can be tiring. Actually, I'm surprised that the couples heading for the Casino didn't take the STL – the Slow Lunar Transit shuttle."

"Maybe the honeymooners are impatient to get to their happy ending," said Kelly with a sly smile.

"What about the older couple?" asked Daniel.

"Maybe they didn't read the fine print," said Kelly. "They might think FTL stands for Fun Time Landing."

"Friendly Travel for Lovers?" suggested Daniel.

"Find The Loo?" countered Kelly.

Alvarez merely shook her head and ignored their flippancy. "For some people, the hardest part of the flight is the drop."

"What's the drop?" asked Kelly.

As if in answer to her question, a voice came over the cabin speakers. "This is Captain Arvan Carmody. Welcome aboard FTL2. Flight time will be approximately three hours with a mid-flight flip after 90 minutes. We're about to drop from Hubble now and once we're clear, our direct fusion drive will kick in and we'll be accelerating at 3G. For those who experience motion sickness, particularly during the drop and the flip, there are sick bags located in your armrest. Enjoy the flight."

A moment later there was a grinding noise conveyed to them through the hull, followed by a loud pop and then they were falling. Daniel's stomach went straight to his mouth and there was a scream from the older woman who was seated a few rows back. The fall only lasted a few seconds, and then they were suddenly thrust deeply into the back rests of their seats as the powerful engine kicked in, bringing another muffled scream from the same woman.

"I hope she doesn't lose her lunch," said Daniel.

"Maybe FTL stands for 'Find The Lunch'?" said Kelly. Then she turned to Alvarez. "So, why doesn't the shuttle just float away from the station when we undock?"

"Because Hubble Station is only orbiting the Earth at about one kilometre per second. To be in a stable free-fall orbit at this height, we would need to be orbiting at about seven kilometres per second. The only reason Hubble Station doesn't fall to Earth is because it's attached to the tether cable. So as soon as the shuttle detaches, we drop."

"What's the formula for calculating orbital velocities?" asked Daniel.

"If I remember correctly from officer training school, it's V =the square root of GMe over R, where G is the gravitational constant, Me is the mass of the Earth and R is the radius of the orbit."

Daniel blinked and said, "7.244167765."

"Sorry?" said Alvarez.

"Hubble Station is at a height of exactly 1,000 kilometres, and assuming that the mass of the Earth and the gravitational constant haven't changed since I read about them last night, then using the formula you just described, the space station would need to be travelling at a velocity of 7.244167765 kilometres per second to be in a stable orbit."

Kelly and Alvarez stared at him.

"How the hell did you work that out so fast?" asked Alvarez.

Kelly looked uncomfortable. "Umm ... Daniel has a ..."

"I had a brain injury," interrupted Daniel, giving Kelly a subtle shake of his head. "When I woke up, I found I was really fast at math."

Alvarez shook her head in amazement. "That could actually come in handy."

"Yes," agreed Daniel. "If the fate of the whole universe ever depends upon knowing the value of pi to 700 decimal places, I'm your man."

"Actually, you're *my* man," said Kelly, reaching out and taking his hand. "And don't you forget it." Then she leaned closer and whispered, "And you owe me a BIG explanation for this!"

2

———

The first half of the flight to the Moon was punctuated by occasional groans from the elderly woman a few rows back, who was clearly struggling with the 3G acceleration. Mission Specialist Olivia Alvarez spent almost the entire time on comm calls. Eventually, however, she finished her calls and Daniel engaged her in conversation.

"What is the captain of Longshot like?" he asked.

"Captain Anderson is one of the best officers I've ever worked under. He's a good leader and he really cares about his crew."

"Have you known him long?"

"We've worked together for years. I've been with him on the Longshot team from the very beginning, and before that he was my captain on board SS Clarion. I was the systems analyst – the computer specialist."

"But now you're the mission specialist?" asked Kelly.

"Yes. I got a promotion. And speaking of the mission, let me bring you up to speed with a few details. As your inclusion on the mission team was ... shall we say, rushed ... you probably don't know much about the Longshot mission."

"Very little," agreed Daniel.

"Let me just say that the only reason we agreed to accept you at such a late stage is that you both have skills that we deemed to be valuable. Ultimately, it was my call as Mission Specialist to accept you."

"We really appreciate that," said Kelly.

Alvarez merely nodded. "Dr Rearson, your expertise in microbiology and in the newly developing field of bio-coding was seen as an extremely valuable contribution to the science team. Daniel, your expertise as a Senior Investigator with JUDAN, the Justice Department of the Alliance of Nations, is of special significance to us."

"Really?" said Daniel. "I would have thought that people with my skills were low down your priority list."

"Until recently, they were. But over the last few months there have been some ... shall we say, developments."

"That doesn't sound good," said Kelly.

"No. Not good at all," agreed Alvarez. "Let me fill you in. It's taken over 50 years to build Longshot, mankind's first starship, and it was in the planning stages for nearly 100 years before that. You'll get a whole lot of info about that during your crash briefings upon arrival."

"Daniel's already really good at crashing," said Kelly, helpfully.

"I'm never gonna live that down, am I?" said Daniel.

"Nope."

"Anyway," continued Alvarez, "the point is that for most of those 50 years, we didn't have a specific destination chosen, because we were still searching for a habitable world. Since the development of the VAR drive which makes interstellar travel possible ..."

"Vacuum to Antimatter Reactor drive," added Daniel. "I've been reading about it."

"Yes. Since we developed the VAR drive, we've been sending out probes to likely solar systems. One of the probes we sent out, 110 years ago, was to the Tama system, 37 lightyears away. 12 years ago, we started receiving images and data from that probe, and discovered our first and, so far, only habitable exoplanet. And that's when the whole ballgame got real. We finally had a destination, and we started ramping up our preparations. I say, 'we', but in reality, most of us on the final team have only been involved for a few years. We definitely stand on the shoulders of those who have gone before us."

"I still don't see how my skill set is valuable to the mission," said Daniel.

"I'm getting to that. Longshot is not the only starship currently under construction. Another one is being built on Mars by the Republic as part of their RISSE program."

"The Republic of Independent States Space Expansion program?" asked Daniel.

"Yes. And they are in direct competition with is. At least that's how they see it. They are determined to get to the Tama system first and, according to our best intel, they plan to claim the whole planet for themselves."

"They can't do that!" exclaimed Kelly.

"We believe they will definitely try that move, and they will almost certainly be prepared to use force to defend their newly claimed world if they get there first. The Alliance, on the other hand, is more than willing to share the new world with the Republic if we get there first."

"I still don't see ..." began Daniel.

"The point I'm getting to," continued Alvarez, talking over the top of him, "is that the Republic are determined to get there first at all costs, and part of their strategy is to try to slow down or, if possible, compromise the construction of Longshot."

"They've tried sabotage?" asked Daniel.

"Not just tried. Succeeded. Over the last few months there have been several incidents – accidents, unexplained system failures and one instance where a bomb came close to being successfully detonated – and we believe the Republic were behind it all. Daniel, JUDAN have informed us that you have some recent experience dealing with RISC – the Republic of Independent States Commissariat – their secret service?"

"Yes, a little."

"More than just a little, I think. Your file says you recently foiled a serious attempt by them to infiltrate a research laboratory and steal valuable research data."

"Yes, I played a role in that."

"That's why we were very keen to welcome you to the team. Security is going to be absolutely vital during these final few weeks before launch. The Republic's starship is still at least two months from completion, and we suspect that they will be doing everything they can to delay our launch. We are appointing you as the 2IC in our security department, working under our Head of Security, George Cullen."

"What's he like?" asked Daniel.

"I won't lie. You'll have to win him over. He doesn't have a high opinion of JUDAN, and he wasn't in favour of your late inclusion on the mission team. He's a tough but fair man. If you prove your worth, he'll back you."

Daniel raised his eyebrows. "Okay. At least I know where I stand."

A soft chime sounded, and the captain's voice addressed them. "Folks, we've reached the half-way point and we're about to execute our flip. Acceleration will be cancelled momentarily, and we will quickly spin the shuttle on its axis to line our engine up with the Moon. Then we'll commence deceleration. I remind you that sick bags are located in the armrest of your chair. Thank you."

A moment later, the passengers all lurched forward as acceleration was cancelled. Daniel and Kelly experienced true weightlessness for the first time and Daniel laughed out loud when he glanced at Kelly.

"What's so funny?" she asked.

"Your hair! It's everywhere."

Kelly put her hand to her head and felt her mass of floating hair that made her look like a mad scientist. "Note to self," she said. "Must put hair in ponytail when in zero gravity."

The stars in view through the porthole windows spun crazily as the shuttle was quickly flipped through 180 degrees and Daniel felt a wave of dizziness. There were more groans from the woman behind them. The shuttle stabilised and, for several moments, the pilot made small corrections with manoeuvering thrusters as he aligned them precisely with the Moon. Then they were all thrust deeply back into their seats as the engines fired up again. Behind them, Daniel and Kelly heard the sound of retching as the elderly woman apparently lost her fight with vertigo.

"There goes her lunch," said Kelly. "I hope she grabbed the sick bag in time."

As they settled into the second half of their journey, Olivia Alvarez continued to describe the current mission status.

"As you know, there are a total of 200 colonists plus a crew of 40 ANSA personnel who have been selected for this mission and who will be making their home on the new world. There were hundreds within the Alliance of Nations Space Agency who volunteered for the mission, but only 40 were chosen. The 200 colonists have been in training for several years; a combination of online education and regular APITs – Astronaut Physical Intensive Training. Two months ago, they said farewell to Earth and have been living at Longshot Base, on the northern edge of Sinus Iridum, on the Moon. They have two more weeks of intensive training there before finally transferring to Longshot itself, which is in orbit, undergoing final testing of its systems."

"In terms of your roles on the mission, both of you will have a seat on the mission team. This is a group of eight key people, now ten with your inclusion, who are effectively the leadership team for the mission. The seven currently on the team apart from myself are the captain, first officer, and the heads of departments; science, logistics, engineering, security and psych."

"Why do we get a place on the leadership team?" asked Kelly.

"Daniel is included because we are very concerned about the current threat level and his experience in dealing with RISC will be invaluable. You are included because, quite frankly, you are now the most highly qualified microbiologist on the mission and your skills will be extremely important, particularly once we reach the new world."

"I just don't want people to resent our late arrival," said Kelly.

Alvarez nodded. "I understand. And, yes, there was some

pushback from our science officer about your inclusion on the team. As in Daniel's case, you will also need to win her over, as you will be technically working under her leadership. But I'm sure you will sort it out." Alvarez glanced at the flight display on the front bulkhead wall, above the door to the pilot's cabin. The display showed their position in relation to the Moon, which was looming closer. "After we land at Armstrong Base, we will transfer to a hopper for the 20-minute flight to Longshot Base."

"We're not staying overnight at Armstrong?" asked Kelly.

"No. Time is precious. You're going to need every minute you can get at Longshot for your intensive training."

"That's a shame. I was hoping to see the casino and the observatory."

"Depending on the departure time of the hopper, there may be some time for you to have a quick look around."

As it turned out, they didn't even make it to Armstrong Base.

3

The shuttle was in Luna orbit. The window portholes on one side of the spacecraft revealed a spectacular view of the Moon, while the flight display on the bulkhead wall showed them coming up on Armstrong Base.

"We're about to undergo a de-orbit burn," said Alvarez, looking at the display. "We'll be on the ground at Armstrong in less than 10 minutes."

Kelly and Daniel watched the flight display in fascination as the icon representing the shuttle drew closer to the icon for Armstrong Base and gradually overlapped it and then, finally, left it behind.

"That's strange," said Alvarez, frowning. "The pilot must have missed the window. Damn it! We're going to have to do another orbit."

As she said this the flight display screen went blank and the shuttle altered course. They were pushed into their seats as their craft veered toward the north and angled steeply down. Alvarez's frown deepened. She unbuckled herself and moved from her seat in the front row to the door of the pilot's cabin, having to work hard against the acceleration that was trying to force her backward. She tried the door, but it was locked.

"Pilot, open the door!" she called, knocking as she did so. When there was no response, she called out again, "Open the door! This is Lieutenant Olivia Alvarez." The door remained stubbornly closed. As she was considering what to do, her comm chimed and she quickly answered. Daniel and Kelly couldn't hear the other side of the conversation, but Alvarez's comments were enough to concern them deeply.

"Yes?"

PAUSE.

"What? When?"

PAUSE.

"Oh my God!"

PAUSE.

"No. I'm not armed."

PAUSE.

Alvarez looked around the passenger compartment. "There are six civilians, four scientists, three ANSA personnel and our two new team members."

PAUSE.

"No! Don't fire until it's the last resort. We'll try to take control."

She disconnected and stood to her feet.

"What's happening?" asked Kelly.

"ANSA personnel to me!" called Alvarez. Two men and a woman in ANSA uniforms made their way clumsily to her as she clung to her seat, struggling against zero gravity and the slight acceleration of the shuttle. "Starship Longshot is under attack in orbit! The pilot of our shuttle isn't answering calls from ground crew and our trajectory looks set to impact Longshot base. It looks like he's planning to turn us into a missile. Does anyone have a weapon?" They all shook their heads. "Even so," continued Alvarez, "we need to get into the cockpit and regain control of the shuttle. We've got about two minutes before ground lasers open fire on us! Follow me!"

Daniel started to get up, but Alvarez shouted at him, "Sit down and leave this to us!"

The four ANSA personnel made their way to the cockpit door and found it locked, which was expected. "Break it down!" commanded Alvarez. The man grabbed the vertical handhold bars on the bulkhead wall on either side of the door and began smashing his legs into the door. It was only a flimsy, inward opening door, not made to withstand such an attack, but even so, the zero gravity made the man's leverage relatively weak. Nevertheless, his pounding began to take effect. The door started to buckle in the middle and, after about 30 seconds, it smashed open with a splintering and tearing sound.

There was the sizzle of a laser blast, and the man was blown backward with a smoking hole in his chest. A female ANSA officer immediately behind him was knocked backward as well and they both tumbled back through the shuttle, bouncing off seats under the influence of the shuttle's acceleration.

"We'll rush him together!" said Alvarez to the remaining woman. "One, two, three!"

They both propelled themselves through the open doorway and more laser fire ensued. There were cries of pain and Alvarez ended up on the floor just inside the door, with the woman on top of her. The woman, a corporal, was missing a part of her head. As Alvarez tried to free herself, she saw a carry-on bag come flying through the air. The pilot swung his pistol up and fired instinctively, but as he did so, an arm appeared in Alvarez's peripheral vision, and she heard a loud gunshot.

The pilot convulsed and seemed to pass out. Alvarez pushed the dead corporal off her and saw Daniel propped in the doorway with a tiny pistol in his hand.

"It's a neural disruptor gun," Daniel explained. He nodded toward the pilot. "He'll be out for a few minutes."

"Help me get him out of the seat!" said Alvarez. She had been hit in her right shoulder and was in a lot of pain.

Together they pulled him clear and threw him into the passenger compartment. "Secure him somehow, private!" shouted Alvarez to the ANSA woman who had returned to the front. Alvarez flopped into the pilot's seat and told Daniel, "Get rid of him, too!"

The co-pilot had a neat hole drilled through his head. Daniel struggled and dragged him from his chair, while Alvarez opened up the main comm channel.

"This is Lieutenant Alvarez on FTL2 to Longshot Base, do you read me? Over."

"We read you, Lieutenant."

"We've disabled the pilot and have taken command of the cockpit."

"Roger, FTL2. You need to abort your current trajectory immediately. You are on a direct collision course with the base."

"Damn it!" said Alvarez as she flicked a number of switches ineffectively. "I think he's somehow locked the controls." She turned and spoke over her shoulder. "Private! Have you had any pilot training?"

"No, ma'am."

"Bugger!" She activated the comm again. "Longshot Base, the controls appear to be locked and we don't have a pilot up here. Any suggestions?"

"Wait for instructions," came the reply.

Alvarez turned to Daniel. "I don't suppose you've got any pilot experience?"

"I crash landed a flitter about a week ago."

"More crash than landing," said Kelly who had propelled herself forward to float just behind them. In the passenger cabin behind her, they could hear sobbing and hysterical cries coming from several passengers.

"That'll do. Jump into the co-pilot's seat, Daniel, and strap in. I'm gonna need your help. My right arm is useless. Kelly, you and the private get back there and make sure everyone is strapped in tight. You might be about to experience your second crash landing in a week."

The comm came to life again. "Lieutenant Alvarez, on the far right of the front console there is a small screen with the initials, ANSI – Automatic Navigation System Interface."

"I see it!"

"Touch the screen. You should see an option appear, 'Disable ANSI'. Select yes."

Alvarez did as instructed and then swore. "It's asking me for a password."

"That doesn't make sense. There shouldn't be a password on that system. It must have been tampered with."

"You don't say!" said Alvarez. "Give me something, please!"

"Is there an emergency over-ride option on the screen?"

"Negative."

There was a pause. "Lieutenant, we don't have a solution to hand. But if you don't alter course within 60 seconds, our ground lasers will have no option but to open fire. I'm sorry."

"Bugger!" said Alvarez. She tried several more buttons and screens but had no luck activating the controls.

"Here, try this," said Daniel, handing her the pilot's laser that he had picked up from the floor.

"What do you want me to do with it?"

"Shoot the crap out of the ANSI," he replied.

"You're joking!" She looked at him incredulously.

"Have you got any better ideas?"

They stared at each other for a few moments.

The comm came to life again. "30 seconds, Lieutenant. I'm sorry."

"I can't believe I'm about to do this," said Alvarez. She grabbed the laser out of Daniel's hand and, without pausing to think any further, fired into the ANSI screen. A sizzling, blue laser bolt smashed into the panel, causing an eruption of sparks. The pungent smell of burnt metal and plastic filled the cabin and a fire alarm started beeping insistently.

Daniel had his hands on the co-pilot's flight controls. "The controls are responding!" he cried. He had pulled the control column back, and manoeuvering thrusters had fired from the nose of the shuttle, altering their pitch.

"FTL2, we can see that your trajectory has altered. Well done! You are now going to overshoot the base. Our laser crews are still on standby, but the fire order has been suspended."

"Roger, Longshot Base," said Alvarez. "We're going to attempt a landing. We have three deceased and at least one injured on board and will require immediate assistance."

"Roger FTL2. We have already mobilised our rescue team. We will track your course and get to you ASAP. Good luck."

"Roger." She turned to Daniel. "I can't operate the flight control with one arm, so you're going to have to do it."

"Okay," he said, grimacing and gripping the controls more tightly.

"I'm engaging reverse thrust now," she said.

Armstrong Base flashed past underneath them as they streaked downward. Daniel was thrown forward against his restraining straps as reverse thrust kicked in, slowing their forward momentum.

"We're coming in way too hot. Pull up on your controls more!"

Daniel pulled back violently, and there were more screams from behind as the shuttle's pitch shifted violently.

"Not that much!" said Alvarez.

Daniel eased off again.

"Keep the attitude indicator guide just above the blue horizon line," she said, indicating the screen in question.

"Okay."

Alvarez scanned the instrument readouts and said, "We're still coming in too hot! I'm pushing our reverse thrusters to full!"

Daniel felt the straps dig deeply into his shoulders and his eyes blurred, with dark forming around the edges of his vision. There were even more screams from behind.

"Squeeze your core, Daniel! Don't black out on me!"

Daniel squeezed and his eyes cleared a little. Another alarm sounded, along with a recorded verbal warning. "Pull up! Impact warning! Pull up! Impact warning!"

"Do it, Daniel! Pull up!" yelled Alvarez.

He pulled back on the control column and the nose tilted up again. A moment later they hit the ground with a violent impact and Daniel lost consciousness.

4

———

Daniel opened his eyes. He wasn't sure how long he'd been unconscious, but it seemed like only a few seconds. There was noise everywhere. People behind him were moaning and crying and there were two sets of alarms blaring constantly.

He looked toward Alvarez and saw that she was unconscious. There was a lump on her forehead and some blood trickling down her face. He looked at the controls on the cabin ceiling and saw two red flashing alarm indicators. One said, 'impact alert'.

"No kidding," Daniel muttered. He switched it off and one of the alarms ceased. The second said, 'hull breach'. "That's not good," he said to himself. He switched it off and the second alarm stopped. He unstrapped himself and swivelled around in his seat.

"Quiet! Everyone!" Several people kept crying. "Shut up! NOW!" he yelled again, and this time, he got the silence he needed. "Everyone stay quiet! I need to listen for escaping air!"

There was silence now, and Daniel could hear the high-pitched whistling of escaping air. "Bugger! That's definitely not good."

"It's coming from somewhere in the cockpit," said Kelly, who had joined him.

"Are you okay?" he asked.

"Yeah. But there are a few injuries back there."

"We'll deal with those later. Right now, we've got a bigger problem."

Looking around, Daniel saw a scorch mark on the ceiling, just above the cabin door. He put his ear to it. "It's coming from here! It's from the laser blast when the pilot shot at the bag I threw in. It must only be a tiny pinprick of a hole, otherwise we'd all be unconscious by now."

He looked more carefully at the damage. The laser had scorched a section of the cabin ceiling, melting the plasticarb lining and scorching a gouge through to the outer hull. There were no instrument panels in that section of the ceiling, so there had been nothing much to stop the blast from reaching the hull. He could only dimly see the hull through the gouge in the inner ceiling lining, and he couldn't see any hole.

A new indicator on the ceiling started flashing red and an automated message announced, *"Warning. Cabin pressure dropping. Cabin pressure at 90 percent."*

"We need to find the hole and seal it," said Daniel.

"But how?" asked Kelly.

Daniel picked up the laser from the floor near Alvarez's feet. "These things should have a setting for ... yes, here it is." He dialled the power setting down to low and quickly fired it at the cabin door to test it. It didn't immediately burn through. He swivelled and aimed it at the ceiling.

"What are you doing?" asked the ANSA private, whose nametag read, Jenkins.

Daniel spoke as he started firing and cutting. "I'm cutting a section of this ceiling panel away so I can see the outer hull."

It only took a few seconds to cut a large square, and the piece of plasticarb obediently fell out, revealing a section of the hull, along with a variety of conduits. Several of the conduits had been severed. There was a burnt gouge across the outer hull, about 20 centimetres long. Daniel examined the gouge carefully but couldn't see any obvious hole, yet the hissing sound continued to originate from that spot.

"Warning: Cabin pressure falling. Cabin pressure at 80 percent."

"There must be microcracks along the gouge," said Private Jenkins, with panic in her voice.

"Does the shuttle have an emergency hull breach kit?" asked Daniel.

"I'm sorry, I don't know. I work in communications."

"Get on the comms and ask someone, while I try to make a temporary patch."

As Jenkins squeezed into his vacated seat and tried to make contact with Longshot Base, Daniel examined the laser pistol and found the aperture setting. He adjusted the pistol to its widest aperture and checked that the power setting was still on low. He pointed the gun at the door again and fired. The wide laser beam hit the door but didn't cut into it. Instead, the plasticarb material of the door began to melt.

"It might work," he said.

"Warning: Cabin pressure falling. Cabin pressure at 70 percent."

"The comms aren't working!" said Jenkins.

"Great! The hits just keep on coming," replied Daniel. He picked up the square of ceiling that he had cut out and held a corner of it against the start of the burnt groove in the outer hull.

"What are you doing?" asked Kelly.

"This plasticarb material contains high tensile carbon fibre nanotubes. I read about it last night. If I can melt it into the groove in the hull it might provide a temporary seal. The cold of space coming through the microcracks should solidify some of it quickly enough to stop all of it dripping down."

He aimed the laser at the corner of the piece in his hand and opened fire. The corner of the plasticarb material slowly melted into the groove. When it began to drip down, he stopped firing and examined the result. Some of the plasticarb material had already solidified again and was staying in place.

"Warning: Cabin pressure falling. Cabin pressure at 60 percent."

"Let's just hope this is the only breach," said Daniel, as he placed the edge of the ceiling panel against the next section of the groove and opened fire again. For the next few minutes, he worked as fast as he could, punctuated by two more warning messages from the cabin pressure monitor. Finally, he stepped back and looked at the ugly mess he had made. He listened carefully and asked Jenkins and Kelly, "Can you guys hear any hissing?"

They were all silent for a few moments.

"I think you've done it!" said Kelly.

"Cabin pressure stabilised at 38 percent. Warning. Cabin pressure low."

They were all gasping for breath now.

"How long can we last like this?" asked Kelly, breathlessly.

"The top of Mount Everest is about 30 percent of sea level air pressure," replied Daniel. "We can survive like this for a while, but it won't be pleasant. Are there pull-down oxygen masks on this shuttle?"

"I've already looked," replied Kelly. "There's nothing. I guess the designers figured that loss of cabin pressure in space is usually catastrophic. Oxygen masks won't save you in that situation."

They went back to the passenger cabin and began to attend to the injured. The older lady had a back injury and had lost a tooth when her head hit the seat in front on impact. Several others had bruises and minor cuts, but nothing serious. The renegade pilot was dead, his neck broken during the impact, as he hadn't been strapped into a seat. Alvarez had regained consciousness but seemed concussed and confused.

"Now what do we do?" asked Kelly.

"Now we wait and hope they find us in time," said Daniel, sitting beside her. He reached out and held her hand and they sat together listening to the laboured breathing of their fellow passengers, waiting to be rescued.

5

———

It took another 20 minutes for their rescuers to arrive, and for many of the passengers on the crashed shuttle, it was the longest 20 minutes of their lives. The low cabin pressure meant that every breath was an effort and several people lapsed in and out of consciousness toward the end.

The rescuers arrived in a hopper, a simplified shuttle for flying short distances on the Moon. Emergency air was pumped into the shuttle via an external intake valve and normal cabin pressure was quickly restored. An emergency docking tunnel was then attached, linking it to the hopper, and a medical team was soon dispensing first aid to the survivors.

A sergeant named Davenport was in charge of the rescue team and, after ensuring that the injured were being attended to, he reported to the injured Lieutenant Olivia Alvarez, who was being treated by a medic.

"Commander Decker sends his apologies, ma'am. He would have been here, himself, but he and the captain are dealing with the situation on board Longshot."

"What happened up there?" Alvarez asked.

"There was a hostile takeover attempt. Fortunately, it was unsuccessful, but several of our crew were injured in the process."

The medic treating Alvarez said, "Your shoulder is going to require surgery, ma'am. The laser has done some damage to your clavicle and some tendons."

"Get her on board the hopper, doc," said Sergeant Davenport. He turned to the rest of his rescue team. "We're evacuating now, people! Let's get everyone out! We don't know how much longer this cabin pressure will hold."

As they strapped themselves into their seats on board the hopper shortly afterward, Kelly said to Daniel, "That was the best crash landing you've done so far. You're getting better!"

"Thank you. But let's face it, I couldn't possibly get any worse."

"True," she admitted. "The previous one was 99 percent crash and one percent landing. I'm giving this one a 60/40 split."

"I was hoping for 50/50," said Daniel.

"I would have scored it as 50/50, but I had to deduct points off the landing for your subsequent destruction of the cabin door and ceiling."

"That's a bit harsh. Destroying those things is what kept us all breathing!"

Kelly shrugged. "Sorry, but the judging rules aren't open for negotiation."

The hopper took off and flew them back to Longshot Base, a cluster of domed structures surrounding a large circular tarmac, about 500 metres in diameter. The tarmac had four circular landing pads, each delineated by a painted white circle. The shuttle landed on one of the circular pads. A few moments later the pad descended to an underground bay and a roof closed over the top of them. Once the roof was sealed and air pressure was normalised, the hatch opened and everyone disembarked. Everyone from the shuttle was taken immediately to the medical bay for assessment and treatment. Lieutenant Alvarez was taken directly into surgery and the others who were injured were triaged and treated promptly. Daniel and Kelly were placed on oxygen for 30 minutes and their saturation levels were monitored. They were soon assessed as not requiring any further treatment and were cleared to leave.

A private then led them out of the medical bay, explaining as he went. "The captain sends his apologies. He was going to be here to welcome you himself, but he is still dealing with things on board Longshot. We're giving you rooms in our officers' quarters for the time being, as the captain wants to speak with you prior to your insertion into the training program."

He guided them to a lift and as they descended to the next level down, the private asked, "How are you coping with the lower gravity? The Moon's gravity is only one sixth of Earth's."

"It's very strange," said Kelly. "I keep feeling like I'm about to lose my footing."

"Yes, it takes a bit of getting used to," agreed the private. As they emerged from the lift, he explained, "Most of Longshot Base is underground, in hollow lava tubes, similar to the construction of Armstrong Base. We simply enlarged the pre-existing lava tubes and caves. This level is the officers' and crew's quarters. The next level down is hydroponics and the water harvesting plant. The base is situated over a huge subterranean reservoir of water ice. We harvest some of the water for drinking and some for splitting into oxygen for our air supply and hydrogen for rocket fuel."

"And where is the base's power plant?" asked Daniel.

"In Dome 4. It's a fusion reactor powered by the helium-3 isotope which is in abundance on the Moon. There are six domes located around the perimeter of the central tarmac above us. Each dome has at least one underground level, and there is a tunnel system linking all the domes. In the event of a security breach or a failure of the life support system, each dome can be sealed off from the rest of the base."

He stopped outside two doors, side by side. "We've given you adjoining rooms. Yours is the one on the left, Dr Rearson. You might like to freshen up and rest. Your bags have already been brought here and flight suits in your sizes are on your beds. These rooms are reserved for special guests because they both have a private shower and toilet. Dinner will be in an hour, at 1800 sharp in the officers' mess. Just follow this corridor – you can't miss it. If there's anything you need in the meantime, press the comm button in your room and speak to the person on watch duty." With that he turned and left them to slide open their doors and explore their temporary accommodation.

There wasn't much to them. A tiny cubicle with a single bed and an adjoining cubicle with a shower, toilet and wash basin. It took all of 30 seconds for them to explore their rooms, after which Kelly stuck her head into Daniel's room.

"Okay, here's the plan," she said. "15 minutes to shower and change, then you're going to give me that explanation you owe me!"

"Yes, ma'am."

15 minutes later, they were sitting on Daniel's bed. Kelly had one leg tucked underneath her as she faced him.

"Now, tell me! You owe me, Daniel Newman!"

"Yes, I guess I do."

"There's no guessing about it! The quantum system works, and you hid it from everyone!"

"Yes. I'm sorry. I did."

Daniel had been the victim of an unlawful experiment by an unscrupulous researcher. In the race to develop the world's first quantum enhanced biological sentience (QEBS), a long chain molecule had been developed that could provide the perfect environment for the world's first room temperature quantum computer. The molecule, with its functioning quantum qubits had been injected into his brain, along with nanobots that were programmed to form the quantum molecules into micron-thin filaments that had permeated his brain, attaching themselves to individual neurons. The theory was that once the quantum system was initialised, the quantum processing system would enhance his mental abilities exponentially.

"When the system was initialised," continued Kelly, "I saw the initial results. The monitors showed the system coming alive, and the microscopic transceivers built into the filaments were sending a stream of information. Then it all suddenly shut down."

"Yes," he agreed. "I did that. It took me a few seconds to map and analyse the millions of filaments in my brain. I isolated the ones that were acting as transceivers and I shut them down."

"Because you didn't want to be a freak show for the rest of your life?"

He nodded. "Uh huh. If people knew the system was working, I would have been poked and prodded – and probably hounded and chased – for the rest of my life. I just want a normal life."

"You do realise that 'normal' isn't going to be a word that easily applies to you from here on?"

Daniel didn't say anything.

"So, tell me!" continued Kelly. "What is it like? What can you do?"

"I'm still learning to live with it," he replied. "I can shut it down or – I don't know – kind of disconnect it when I want to. But when I connect to it consciously, I can read and remember things incredibly quickly. I've spent the last few nights reading and absorbing huge amounts of information from Solnet."

"Plus, you can do math like an absolute nerd," said Kelly.

"Yes, I can think faster and more clearly than I ever thought possible. Answers to difficult calculations just seem so ... easy now."

"And there is no pain? No discomfort?"

"No. None."

She reached out and took his hand. "I'm glad, Daniel. For a while there, I thought I was going to lose you." Her eyes welled up with tears.

Daniel reached out and caressed her cheek, tenderly. "I thought I was going to lose you, too."

She leaned forward and kissed him briefly. "You're stuck with me now, Daniel Newman," she said, wrapping her arms around his neck and drawing him to her. They kissed again, this time much longer and more passionately. She continued to kiss him deeply as she lay back on the bed and drew him down on top of her.

"Do you think the Moon qualifies us for the mile-high club?" she murmured through her kiss.

"We might miss dinner," he replied.

"To hell with dinner."

They made it to dinner, albeit a little late.

The officers' mess was a self-service buffet-styled eatery. There were about 30 officers scattered around the tables, all eating and talking with their colleagues. As they entered, Kelly and Daniel looked around and could not recognise anyone. Several heads turned their way and gave them curious glances, then quickly lost interest in them. They made their way to the buffet servery, dished themselves two plates of food and then found a table to themselves. The food was tasty without being exceptional: some kind of stew with rice.

While they ate Kelly asked a question that had puzzled her but which, up until now, she had not had a chance to ask.

"I've been meaning to ask. How did you end up with that neural disruptor gun in your possession? We were scanned for weapons at Tether Lift Terminal at Quito."

"George slipped it to me when he called me back to speak to me when we were about to board the tether lift pod. He said he hoped I would never have to use it again."

"Well, that turned out to be a forlorn hope."

"Yes. But let's hope that's the last time it gets used."

After dinner they went back to their rooms. As they stood outside Kelly's door, she turned and enveloped Daniel in an embrace and gave him a long, lingering kiss. "I'm curious to compare my bed to yours," she said.

"How curious?" he asked.

"Very," she said, continuing to kiss him.

"Well, I think we'd better find out, then. We can't leave you in this state, can we?"

"Absolutely not." She murmured through her kiss. "A true gentleman would never leave a woman in a state of unsatisfied curiosity."

"I'm at your service, ma'am," he said as they opened the door and stumbled into her room.

6

───────────

Sergeant Davenport, the same sergeant who had shown them to their rooms, came to get them the next morning. They had eaten breakfast in the officers' mess at 0700 and were just wondering what to do when Davenport knocked on their doors. He was momentarily surprised to find them in the same room but did not comment.

"Captain Anderson sends his compliments. There is a meeting of the mission team in the wardroom at 0800 and the captain would like to see you in his office beforehand."

Daniel and Kelly looked at each other and nodded. "We're ready now," said Daniel.

"Good. If you'll just follow me."

He led them to the lifts, then up one level, along a corridor and into a spacious office. Captain Nash Anderson was sitting at a tidy desk, tapping at a data interface, with a scowl on his face. He looked up as they entered, and his face cleared into a welcoming smile. He stood and came around from behind the desk, offering his hand to them both.

"Nash Anderson. You must be Dr Rearson."

"Please, call me Kelly,"

"And Mr Newman," he said grasping Daniel's hand.

"Daniel is fine, Captain."

"Welcome to both of you," Anderson said. He invited them to sit in the two visitors' chairs, while he resumed his chair behind the desk. Daniel regarded him carefully, realising that this was the man who would be responsible for his future welfare for the foreseeable future. Nash Anderson was in his late 50s or early 60s. Fair skinned, pure white hair and matching trim white beard. He had deep crinkle lines around his eyes, as if he smiled a lot. Daniel thought that if he put on some additional weight, he could pass for a reasonable Santa Claus. He looked Scandinavian or Norwegian and spoke with an accent to match. "I'm sorry that neither my first officer nor I were here to greet you yesterday. As you are well aware, yesterday was ... extremely difficult."

"It certainly was," agreed Daniel. "Is everything under control again on board Longshot?"

"Yes, to a certain extent. I'll go into that in detail at our mission team meeting, shortly. But my reason for meeting with you beforehand is that I wanted to express my gratitude for your heroic efforts yesterday."

"There wasn't much heroism involved," replied Daniel. "We were just trying to stay alive."

"Well, your actions saved a lot of innocent lives. And, I have to say, your quick thinking and ingenuity was quite remarkable. Using a wide-beam laser to melt plasticarb into the hull breach was brilliant. I'm not sure I would have thought of it."

Daniel shrugged. "How is Lieutenant Alvarez?"

"She was operated on yesterday afternoon and is doing remarkably well. She has a titanium clavicle now, and the combined stem cell infusion and nanobot therapy is hastening her healing remarkably quickly. In fact, she insists on attending our forthcoming meeting. Which brings me to my second reason for seeing you briefly now."

He paused and gathered his thoughts. "I want you to know that I consider you both to be very valuable additions to our mission team. Kelly, your qualifications and experience as a microbiologist and bio-coder will be extremely valuable to us, particularly once we get to the new world. And Daniel, your arrival here at this time is fortuitous. We are in considerable need of additional security advice and assistance. Despite the fact that you have only just arrived, I want you both to feel completely free to contribute to our discussions and decisions. Your input will be very welcome."

"Is there a 'but' coming?" asked Daniel.

"You are perceptive. The heads of both your departments are good people. Competent, articulate, level-headed. But they are ... shall we say ... wary of the addition of newcomers to our mission team. You will need to foster those relationships carefully."

"I understand," said Daniel.

Anderson continued. "My Executive Officer, Commander Bryce Decker, has also been known to be somewhat impatient with non-military personnel. I have spoken to him and given him instructions that you are to be treated with the same respect as everyone else on the team. If you feel that is not happening, I would appreciate being informed."

"Thank you, Captain," said Daniel. "I appreciate the heads up. I'm sure we'll be able to navigate the relationships sensitively."

Anderson nodded. "Good. I'm glad you understand." He paused again to gather his thoughts. "There's another reason why I wanted to speak with you prior to the meeting. Over the last few months there have been several attempts to slow our preparations and delay our mission, including attempted sabotage. Without going into the specific details of each incident, the cumulative evidence of all these incidents has led me to believe that there is a traitor in our midst, possibly at the highest level."

"Someone working for RISC?" asked Daniel.

"Yes. The Republic of Independent States Commissariat. I believe you recently uncovered a RISC agent placed very high within JUDAN?"

"Yes. It was ... shocking ... because I had come to regard him as a friend."

Anderson nodded, sympathetically. "I'm sure it was very diffi-cult for you. In the same way, I am currently having to face the very real possibility that someone I regard as a trusted colleague is actually working against us."

"Someone on the mission team?" asked Kelly.

"That is a very strong possibility. The one person I can now rule out is Lieutenant Olivia Alvarez. If she was a RISC agent she wouldn't have acted as she did yesterday in helping to neutralise the rogue shuttle pilot. But everyone else on the mission team must now be regarded as a suspect."

"And you want us to see what we can uncover?" asked Daniel.

"I do. You are both obviously above suspicion because of your heroic efforts yesterday, so I know I can trust the two of you. And you, Daniel, have recent experience in uncovering a RISC agent. That is why I was so keen to accept you onto our team. I want you to be my eyes and ears. Perhaps, with your fresh perspective, you might be able to see things that I am missing."

"I understand," said Daniel.

"I can't stress how important this is, Daniel. If there is a rogue agent in our midst, our whole mission and the lives of every person involved are in great jeopardy. We must find whoever it is and neutralise them before they destroy the mission and possibly all of us in the process."

"I see," said Daniel.

"It's not exactly the position you expected to find yourself in here, is it?" asked Anderson.

"To be honest, no. I thought I'd just left behind all that kind of stuff. I was kind of hoping for a more peaceful life."

"Me, too," said Kelly. "It looks like it's a case of out of the frying pan, into the fire."

Anderson continued. "You'll report directly to me on this issue. If you have any concerns at all, even the slightest doubts about someone, I want to hear about it, ASAP. Is that clear?"

"Yes, Captain. You can count on us," said Daniel.

Anderson stood up. "Good. Now, let's get this meeting started."

7

Captain Nash Anderson called the meeting to order. The ten members of the mission team were seated around a large oval table with a hollow centre. Daniel looked around the table and felt under-dressed. He and Kelly were in flight suits – one-piece grey jump suits with navy blue piping and ANSA insignia on the left breast – while most of the others were in officers' uniform. The only exception was a slim, short, olive-skinned man who spoke with an almost comical Pakistani accent who had introduced himself upon entering as Rajish Patel. He was wearing civilian clothes, and his warm, friendly greeting contrasted with the cool indifference that Daniel felt emanating from several of the others around the table.

Daniel and Kelly had been shown to the meeting room by a private while Captain Anderson made a last minute comm call. Now, as Anderson entered, everyone stood to their feet and snapped to attention.

"At ease everyone. Take a seat. Let's get started. We have some important decisions to make. But first, some introductions are in order. Let me introduce our two additions to the mission team. Dr Kelly Rearson is a highly qualified microbiologist whose training and experience are going to be invaluable to us once we arrive at the new world."

Kelly nodded and smiled, and was greeted by blank expressions from the others, except for Rajish Patel and a middle-aged woman with frizzy, grey-streaked hair, both of whom gave her warm smiles.

"And this is Daniel Newman. Daniel is a Special Investigator with JUDAN, the Department of Justice of the Alliance of Nations. Daniel has been brought onto the team because of his recent involvement in thwarting an undercover operation by RISC agents in Quito recently. Undercover agents of the Republic of Independent States Commissariat attempted to steal valuable research data, and Daniel's actions single-handedly foiled their attempt. Furthermore, his heroic actions yesterday saved not only the lives of everyone on the shuttle, but also, as is about to be explained, probably the lives of everyone on this base. I expect you all to treat both Dr Rearson and Mr Newman with the respect they deserve."

Daniel smiled at the faces around the table but drew a similar blank response from most people, except for the frizzy-haired woman and Rajish Patel.

Captain Anderson continued. "To that end, I am hereby appointing both Dr Rearson and Mr Anderson to the rank of Warrant Officer." He turned to them both. "Your uniforms will be in your rooms when you return."

Daniel was shocked but said nothing. He wondered why Anderson had not mentioned this to them in their private meeting with him.

"Now, it would be easiest if each of you could briefly introduce yourselves. Let's start with you, XO," he said, speaking to the grim-faced man on his left.

"Executive Officer, Commander Bryce Decker," he said. He was tall with dark hair and steely blue eyes. There was not even the hint of a smile on his face.

The officer next to Decker spoke next. "Lieutenant Maria Vargas, Science Officer." She was diminutive and slim, with short dark hair, brown eyes, olive skin and a figure that looked as if it had been carefully sculpted in a gym.

Kelly looked at the beautiful Latino woman with interest, realising that they would be working closely together. Significantly, Vargas did not meet her eyes, maintaining a look of cool indifference.

"Warrant Officer George Cullen, Security Chief." Cullen was a bald, nuggety, aggressive-looking man with a gruff voice. Daniel looked at him and sized him up. Cullen stared back at him with a dour expression but nodded politely, perhaps more in deference to the captain's request than out of genuine warmth.

"Rajish Patel, Systems Analyst. I look after all the programming and computer systems," he said, smiling. "It is most wonderful to welcome you both to our team." The slightly built man of Indian or Pakistani extraction beamed at them and wobbled his head as he spoke.

"Warrant Officer, Angus Fraser. Engineering." Fraser was a freckle-faced Scotsman with a broad accent and a mop of the reddest hair Daniel had ever seen. Fraser nodded politely and managed a brief smile. Daniel felt that he was a no-nonsense character who was probably more at home with machinery than people."

"Lieutenant Dara Bernstein, Welfare Officer. Welcome to you both." Bernstein had already warmly welcomed them as she had arrived. She was a middle-aged woman of African American heritage, with short, dark, frizzy hair that was in the early stages of turning grey. Her dark eyes were crinkled with smile lines. Daniel felt instinctively that she was going to be a warm, friendly colleague.

"Mission Specialist, Lieutenant Olivia Alvarez. We've already met, and I owe Daniel my life. Thank you, Daniel." Alvarez was sitting immediately to Daniel and Kelly's left, between them and the captain. The tall, dark-haired woman had her arm in a sling, and she looked pale, despite her olive skin.

"Lieutenant Alvarez should still be in the medical bay, but she insisted on being here," said Captain Anderson.

"I'm okay, Captain. Pain blockers are a wonderful thing."

Anderson grunted. "Well, that's all of us. Now let's get down to business. Firstly, the attempted attack on this base. The trajectory of the shuttle indicates that it had locked onto the fusion reactor. A direct impact on the reactor would have blown a crater in the moon two kilometres wide. Those of us who were on-base yesterday wouldn't be here talking this morning if that had happened. We owe our lives to the brave actions of Lieutenant Alvarez and Mr Newman."

He paused. "The pilot was clearly a RISC operative and had just transferred from the Mars run. As you know, Mars is the location of the Republic's major off-world base, where they are nearing construction of their starship, the Shengli – the Victory. It was a kamikaze mission, and the pilot was apparently determined to die in the process of wiping out our base." He paused and looked around the table. "The intention was clearly to wipe out the colonists and as many of the crew as possible, all of whom are undergoing final training here on the base. If that had been successful it would have set the mission back by at least 18 months."

Anderson continued. "At the same time, an attempt was made to seize control of the starship itself. An unauthorised shuttle docked with Longshot in orbit. They gave the correct ID code for yesterday, but their story seemed suspicious, and they were initially denied access. They claimed to be a team of engineers sent by me to upgrade some components of the life support system. The duty officer on board Longshot was immediately suspicious and placed an electronic lock on the inner airlock door while she contacted me. When I didn't corroborate the story, she mobilised a security team who were sent to the airlock. By the time they got there, the invaders had breached the door. A laser battle ensued. There were twelve invaders and only six guards on board Longshot. Sadly, we lost two good people, and another two were injured. But the invaders were boxed in, having only just breached the airlock, and our team had the advantage of crossfire.

Six of the invaders were killed. The remaining six retreated to the shuttle and left."

Anderson paused to let the seriousness of the situation sink in, before continuing. "By then, both Longshot and the departing shuttle were roughly over Copernicus Military Base. The shuttle adopted an aggressive trajectory, aiming directly toward our military base there, no doubt hoping to succeed where the other shuttle had failed. After several warnings, and after consultation with me, the Commander of Copernicus Base ordered the launch of two guided missiles. They destroyed the shuttle in mid-flight."

"Where did the shuttle come from?" asked Daniel.

"The Republic of Independent States has a military research base here on the Moon. No doubt, it came from there."

"In that case, why did they commandeer our shuttle for the original attempted destruction of the base?" Daniel persisted.

"No doubt to give them some kind of plausible deniability. Perhaps they might have claimed that the pilot suffered a medical episode. Or they may have claimed that he was a rogue individual with a bee in his bonnet about something – nothing to do with them."

"Could just twelve people have taken over the ship?" asked Lieutenant Maria Vargas.

"Easily," answered Commander Decker. "We only had six guards and probably about 20 unarmed personnel working on various systems. Once the armed guards had been dealt with, the rest would have been easy to subdue."

"Yes, but could such a small number have flown the ship?" persisted Vargas.

"We're not sure what their intentions were from that point," said Anderson. "They may have been planning to crash it into the Moon. Or they may have attempted to fly it to their base on Mars. If it was the latter, they would only have needed about six people to do so."

The Chief Security Officer, George Cullen, shook his head. "Outrageous! Their audacity is ... well, it's unbelievable. I wish I'd been there to drill some of those bastards myself!"

"Where were you, chief? If you don't mind me asking," said Daniel.

Cullen glared at Daniel for a few moments, then glanced quickly at the captain before deciding to answer. "I was on Armstrong Base, on a four-day break. We work ten days and then get four off."

"Which is where I was, as well," said Commander Decker. "The chief and I were planning to share the same hopper that you and Lieutenant Alvarez were supposed to catch from Armstrong to here."

Daniel merely nodded and filed that information away for later.

"Are we out of danger now?" asked Welfare Officer, Dara Bernstein.

The captain shook his head. "Sadly, no. In fact, we may be in very grave danger indeed. Because, as a result of yesterday's events, the Republic and the Alliance look like they're heading for all-out war."

8

———

"We're about to go to war?" asked George Cullen, his bald head creased with concern.

Captain Nash Anderson nodded. "Yesterday's attack on Longshot and the attempted destruction of this base has incensed the Alliance of Nations. Of course, the Republic of Independent States is denying that they had anything to do with it, but no one believes them. The Alliance Senate had an emergency meeting overnight and we have gone to Alert Level 5. All military personnel have been ordered back from leave, and every base and asset in the solar system is on high alert."

He paused, to allow the seriousness of their situation to sink in.

"What implications does that have for our mission?" asked Commander Decker.

"If war breaks out before we have a chance to depart, there's a good chance we will never leave. Longshot Base and Longshot herself will be primary targets. We will probably be destroyed in the first wave of attacks." He looked around the table. "For that reason, General Petersen, the Chief of our Armed Forces, has ordered our immediate departure."

There was stunned silence.

"Immediate?" asked Decker.

"As soon as we can," replied Anderson. He looked around the table again. "So, talk to me, people! How soon can we go?" He looked at Fraser. "Engineering?"

Engineering Chief, Angus Fraser, answered in his broad Scottish accent. "You'll have no problems with engineering, Captain. We've been ready to go for the last month. We're fully fuelled and all systems have been tested to within an inch of their life."

"Good. Science?"

The diminutive Brazilian, Maria Vargas, considered her reply. "All of our equipment is installed, sir, but we are a few days away from bringing the forward scanners completely online. If we worked around the clock, we could get them operational within 48 hours. Hydroponics is another matter. It is still ramping up and won't be able to supply us with enough fresh food for another couple of weeks. The yeast processors can be brought up to speed within 48 hours, so we won't starve. We've got a limited supply of fresh food, so we might need to subsist on yeast mush for a short time."

"Get your team ramping up food production and working overtime on the forward sensors. What about cryogenics?"

"Good to go, sir," replied Vargas.

Anderson nodded and looked at his Chief of Security, George Cullen. "Chief? How are we with security?"

"Good to go, as well, sir. In fact, it will be a hell of a lot easier trying to keep just the starship secure instead of spreading ourselves thin guarding the base as well."

"Understood." He looked at his XO, Bryce Decker. "Commander, what about stores and mission equipment?"

"All the large machinery and building materials for the new settlement have been in place for over a month. We are still awaiting the last supply vessel to finish stocking up on dried food and other non-perishables. The last supply vessel is due to dock with us tomorrow."

"Good. Lieutenant Alvarez, how quickly could we transfer all the colonists to Longshot?"

"With two shuttles operating continuously, we can have them all up there within 24 hours, sir. But the logistics of transferring them is not the main challenge. The next two weeks of training here on the base were going to be important for their preparation. Without that final training and familiarisation some of the colonists might struggle with conditions on board Longshot, particularly prior to acceleration and the establishment of normal gravity."

"That can't be helped, Lieutenant. They'll just have to cope as best they can. Make it happen."

"Yes, sir."

"Lieutenant Bernstein, how is the morale among the colonists?"

Dara Bernstein, the Welfare Officer, spoke confidently. "On the whole, they are in good shape, psychologically. There are a small number who have been struggling with adapting to life in space, and two have had to be sent home because they weren't coping. But the vast majority have trained for this for years and are brimming with enthusiasm."

"Good." He looked around the table. "Anything I haven't thought of?"

No one spoke, and several shook their heads.

The captain nodded. "Very well. As of this moment, we are initiating an emergency departure of Longshot. Get everyone on board and bring all systems online and fully operational as quickly as possible. Work around the clock if you need to. We will depart as soon as we can. I want to fire up our main drive within 48 hours." He stood. "Let's go people! Make it happen! Mr Newman and Dr Rearson, can you remain behind for a moment?"

The meeting broke up and people left, almost at a run. When they were alone, Captain Anderson asked Daniel, "Well? What did you think?"

"I found it interesting that Decker and Cullen were completely off base at the time of the attacks. If there is a highly placed RISC agent among us, it would make sense for them to be safely off base while the attacks occur."

"Yes, I had thought of that, myself," conceded Anderson.

"Which members of the mission team were here on base, and which were on Longshot in orbit?" asked Daniel.

"The only two who were here at Longshot Base were Welfare Officer Lieutenant Dara Bernstein and Systems Analyst Rajish Patel. The rest were on Longshot."

"So, logic would seem to suggest that anyone one here on the base yesterday is unlikely to be our traitor, because the traitor would have known to stay clear," said Daniel. "Which means that Bernstein and Patel can be crossed off our list."

"Unless," suggested Kelly, "one of them is the traitor and wasn't told of the attack. Maybe the agent-in-place was considered to be expendable."

"Perhaps," admitted Daniel, "but less likely than the traitor knowing about it and staying clear. So, perhaps we don't rule them out entirely, but they are definitely at the bottom of my list of suspects."

"I agree," said Captain Anderson. "And sadly, Commander Decker and Warrant Officer Cullen have been at the top of my list for some time."

"How did the invaders manage to get through the airlock after it had been electronically locked?" asked Daniel.

"That's one of the puzzling things," answered Anderson. "They didn't break the door down or cut through it. They somehow managed to open it without using force. Which leads to only one conclusion."

"They knew the door code?" asked Kelly, thinking ahead.

"Just so," agreed Anderson.

"How many people know that code?" asked Daniel.

"The duty officers on the bridge."

"And who among the mission team would know the code?" persisted Daniel.

Anderson gave Daniel a piercing look, then sighed and said, "Just Commander Decker and George Cullen."

Daniel nodded while he took that information in.

Anderson changed the subject. "For the rest of today, I want you both to get up to speed with some basic knowledge of the starship and our mission. I've organised for you to spend the day in our cinema room here on the base, watching instructional videos. It's important that you have a basic understanding of our mission. You'll transfer to Longshot first thing in the morning with the last of our crew. Everyone else on the mission team will be up there today, but there's really no point in you being on board Longshot before tomorrow, because today is going to be chaotic. There will only be a handful of personnel left to transfer up tomorrow."

He picked up two wrist communicators from his desk and handed them to Kelly and Daniel. "Wear these on your left wrist. They will pair with your ID chips. Only the mission team have these. If you want to place a private call to anyone on the mission team, just say their name when you press the activation button, and only they will receive your call. If you want to speak to everyone, just start speaking."

They placed them on their wrists, and Anderson said, "I've assigned Corporal Carmichael to supervise your video sessions and to answer any of your questions. She can fill you in on any details you are unclear about." He stood. "I'll see you tomorrow, on board Longshot."

9

The base was swarming with activity. Final preparations for launch, which were meant to have taken another two weeks, were now being crammed into two days. People were running everywhere and the whole base was in upheaval. Daniel and Kelly were taken to a cinema room that could easily seat 200 people but which they had all to themselves. Corporal Carmichael showed them to their seats and said, "I'll just be in the next room if you need me, sir and ma'am."

"No need to call us that," said Daniel. "Daniel and Kelly is fine."

"No, sir. Sorry, sir. That isn't acceptable. You are both warrant officers, and you are to be addressed respectfully by lower ranks."

Kelly and Daniel were now wearing their new uniforms and were still getting used to their elevated status. Daniel sighed. "Very well. Thank you, Corporal. Continue."

"I'll return and answer any questions you might have after the first video is finished. If you need anything before that, just press the comm button on your armrest."

As she walked out the door, the lights dimmed and a video commenced.

"Here we go," said Kelly, sliding down in her chair. "Did you get the popcorn."

"I thought you were supposed to bring it," said Daniel with a smile.

A diagram image of Longshot appeared on the screen and a voice-over began.

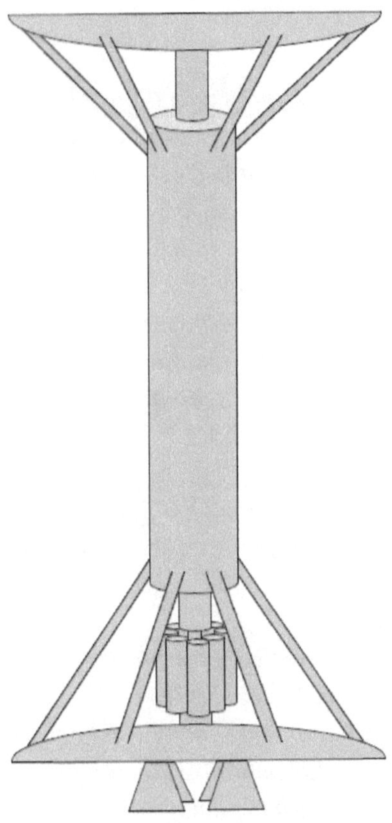

"Longshot is mankind's first starship. It has taken over 50 years to build and was in the planning stages for over 100 years before that. Arguably the biggest hurdle for travelling to another solar system is distance. The universe is unimaginably vast. The nearest star to our own, Alpha Centauri, is 4.2 light years away. That might not sound far, but a bullet, travelling at 2,000 kilometres per hour, would take 2.3 million years to get there. Until recently, the fastest spacecraft we have

ever built, travelling at twenty times the speed of a bullet, would still take 115,000 years to get there. And that is just our closest neighbour! Some stars are many millions of times further away. That is why, until now, we have been constrained to stay within our own solar system."

"And that's why, until now, I have been constrained to stay home, watch movies and eat chocolate," said Kelly.

"I didn't think you needed any excuse to eat chocolate," said Daniel.

"True."

"But everything has changed with the development of the VAR drive. The vacuum to antimatter reactor drive allows Longshot to accelerate continuously for the entire first half of its journey and decelerate for the entire second half, without needing to carry vast amounts of fuel. That is because the particles of hydrogen and antihydrogen necessary to form the ongoing explosion within the reactor can be harvested from space itself. The 200-metre diameter deflector dish at the front of the spacecraft harvests hydrogen atoms from space and a laser annihilation field will convert some of the hydrogen to antimatter."

"Do you think there's such a thing as anti-chocolate?" asked Kelly.

"Some people are anti-chocolate," replied Daniel.

"Really? Does that mean that if you put them together with chocolate, they explode?"

"I guess it must."

"The Longshot, powered by the incredible VAR drive, will achieve a velocity of 99 percent of the speed of light after only 10 months of acceleration. This means that instead of taking 113,000 years to travel to our nearest star, it would take only take 5 years 3 months. The VAR drive has made it possible to reach the stars!"

"I wish this video would hurry up and achieve light speed! I already feel like I've been here for years," said Kelly.

"Let's have a detailed look at Longshot, now, and introduce you to your new home for the next few years. The main body of the spacecraft is essentially a very tall cylinder standing on its end, with a 200-metre diameter concave deflector shield protruding from the top, and a VAR drive unit with four huge jet nozzles at the bottom, mounted within a

duplicate concave deflector dish. This is because the starship will be travelling backwards for the second half of its journey, as it decelerates. The two concave deflector shields serve two purposes. Firstly, they collect hydrogen atoms from space for fuel and, secondly, they protect the starship from collision with high-speed microparticles. This becomes increasingly important as the spacecraft approaches the speed of light because, at that speed, even the tiniest particles of dust could tear through the hull of the ship. For this reason, the deflectors are made of an impenetrable composite of maranium and carbon nanotubes – the toughest material known to mankind. The outer edges of the shields also produce a constant LAF across the surface of the shields – a Laser Anni-hilation Field which instantly reduces any particles to their constituent atoms."

"The cylindrical main body of the starship is 400 metres tall and 80 metres in diameter and has 74 levels. The floor of each level is in the direction of the VAR engine which will provide constant acceleration to simulate gravity. A bank of lifts provide access to all levels."

"It looks like an elongated can of beans," said Kelly.

"Or asparagus," said Daniel. "In limiting it to just beans you are guilty of vegetable stereotyping."

"The levels are set out from top to bottom on your screen, with Level 74 at the top:

74. Command Centre

73. Science

72. Medical

71. Dining

70. Lounge 1

69. Lounge 2

68. Recreation 1

67. Recreation 2

66. Crews' Quarters

65. Colonists' Quarters 1

64. Colonists' Quarters 2

63. Hydroponics 1

62. Hydroponics 2

61. Yeast Farm

60 - 59. Fusion reactor

58. Engineering and maintenance

57. Life Support Systems

56. Cryogenics 1

55. Cryogenics 2

54 – 51. Shuttle Bays 1 to 4

50 – 1. Storage Bays 1 to 50

"*The fusion reactor provides power for the internal workings of the entire starship and is quite independent from the VAR drive. The VAR drive is a separate module that is attached to the underside of the central cylinder's base and provides power for the starship's main jets as well as the LAF – laser annihilation field. The VAR drive will provide normal Earth gravity to the starship by accelerating at a constant 1G, or 9.8 metres per second squared, which is the acceleration force of gravity experienced on the surface of the Earth.*"

"*While you will spend the majority of your voyage to the new world in cryogenic stasis, it is anticipated that you will be awake for the first two weeks of the voyage and a month or more at the end, while you are in orbit around the new planet prior to transferring to the surface. It is for this reason that a lot of thought has gone into designing the living quarters on board Longshot. The recreations decks offer a range of exercise facilities, including two gymnasiums, jogging tracks and several squash courts.*"

"Does this mean I'm going to have to get fit?" asked Kelly. "I hate exercise."

"You don't have to actually do it," said Daniel, helpfully. "You can just go there and watch other people do it."

"Excellent! I'm a big fan of vicarious exercise."

"*The two lounge decks offer informal seating for relaxing and mingling, along with large viewing windows. The sleeping accommodation is basic and compact. Each room consists of just a double bunk and a small cupboard for storing personal effects.*"

"No double beds?" asked Kelly. "Who designed this starship? Monks?"

"I'm sure we can make do," said Daniel, and Kelly reached out and held his hand.

"During the awake phases of your voyage, automated food dispensers located around the dining deck will provide nutritious, if somewhat limited meals, derived primarily from Longshot's hydroponics and yeast farms, with some supplementation from dried and frozen food that has been stored on board. The hydroponics and yeast farms are fully automated with robotics and will be activated one month prior to you being woken from cryogenic stasis."

"There are 50 storage levels on Longshot. These contain essential equipment and supplies necessary for the establishment of a viable colony on the new world. This includes farm machinery, construction materials, portable fusion generators, tools and solar powered vehicles, as well as seeds for a huge variety of plants and trees. Longshot is also taking an extensive range of frozen embryos of animals to breed as a food source."

The video continued for another 30 minutes, providing detailed descriptions of each feature of the starship. By the end Daniel and Kelly were ready for a break. Corporal Carmichael entered the room and brightened the lights as the video finished.

"Do you have any questions, sir and ma'am?"

"Yes," said Kelly. "Where's the loo?"

"And I could use a coffee," said Daniel.

"Certainly, sir and ma'am. Follow me."

10

Daniel and Kelly arrived in the officers' mess a little late for lunch and found it only half full. Those who were already eating were doing so quickly and departing as soon as they finished. Daniel and Kelly filled their plates and looked for a table. George Cullen, the security chief was seated on his own and Daniel decided to take the opportunity to get to know him a little better.

"Do you mind if we join you?" he asked as they arrived at the round table.

Cullen shrugged and said, "Help yourself."

Kelly raised her eyebrows at Daniel in response to the less-than-enthusiastic reception, but Daniel was undeterred.

He sat down opposite Cullen, with Kelly alongside him. "It looks like we'll be working closely together," Daniel said as he loaded his fork with beans.

"So it seems."

"And I recognise that I have a lot to get my head around," he continued.

"That's an understatement."

Daniel took a sip of coffee to wash the beans down, then sat back and looked at Cullen. The bald-headed, nuggety warrant officer was exuding an aura of constrained hostility.

"How do you see my role as 2IC working?" asked Daniel, and immediately regretted asking it, as it gave Cullen the opportunity to voice the obvious response.

"I don't, quite frankly. You don't know my people. You don't know the starship. You've had no training for space, and you've got no experience in ANSA. The captain may have put a uniform on you, but that doesn't mean you're qualified to do the job. The lowest private on my team has more training and experience than you."

"Doesn't Daniel's experience in law enforcement count for anything?" asked Kelly.

"I don't have a lot of time for JUDAN. They're a bunch of pencil pushers. Pieces of paper don't get the job done in the space corps. What's needed is action."

"The kind of action that Daniel did yesterday?" asked Kelly, with some heat in her voice.

Cullen nodded, thoughtfully, then looked at Daniel. "You did alright, yesterday, I'll give you that. So, maybe there's hope. But you've still got a lot to learn."

"Look George, I get that you aren't exactly waving a welcome flag at my arrival. But we're going to be stuck together inside a spaceship for years and we have to learn to work together. I'll do everything I can to get up to speed as quickly as possible, but it would sure help if I had your support and your respect."

"I'll give you some support. But respect is another thing. You've got to earn that."

"So yesterday doesn't count at all?" asked Kelly, exasperation now edging her voice.

"It's a start. We'll see how he goes from here on." Cullen stood and picked up his empty plate. "Security team meeting at 11:00 tomorrow, in the briefing room on Longshot. Be there." He turned and walked away, leaving Kelly shaking her head in exasperation.

"Wow! What a tool!" she said.

Daniel shook his head. "No. I get where he's coming from. He's got a tough job to do and he's under enormous pressure. And right now, the last thing he needs is a novice like me coming along and getting in the way."

"That's assuming he's not the traitor we're looking for. His aggression toward you could be because he sees you as a threat to his mission."

Daniel nodded. "Yeah. That's certainly another possibility."

"Do you guys mind if I sit with you?" They looked up and saw the Welfare Officer, Dara Bernstein, holding a plate of food and smiling at them.

"Please! Be our guest," said Kelly. "You can't possibly be as grumpy as our previous meal companion."

"Oh, don't mind George. He's all bark and no bite. He likes to put up a tough exterior, but underneath I sense he's quite insecure."

"If his gruffness is all an act, he's very good at it," said Daniel.

Bernstein chuckled. "How are you guys settling in?"

"There's certainly a lot to learn," said Kelly, "and I'm still getting used to people calling me ma'am."

"Welcome to the space corps. You'll get used to it. And you shouldn't feel as though your officer status is unwarranted. From what I hear, you both thoroughly deserve it."

"Thank you, that's very kind," said Kelly.

"I assume that you have some kind of expertise in the area of human behaviour?" asked Daniel.

"Master's degree in psychology. Not that that means much. There are a lot of people out there with letters after their name who are still as clueless about human behaviour as when they first began their studies."

"How are the colonists coping with current events?" asked Daniel.

"There is a lot of excitement, rather than fear. You have to remember that the kind of person who volunteers for a mission such as this, has a high threshold for dealing with risk and danger. While yesterday's events are very concerning, most of the colonists are extremely resilient and are just keen to get going. They've trained for this mission for years, and they are extremely motivated to board Longshot and launch."

"How are the shuttle transfers going?" asked Kelly.

"Very well. By 17:00 today, all the colonists will be on board. Tomorrow morning, the last of the crew, including yourselves, will transfer up. Then it will be a simple matter of receiving the last of the supplies before we launch. Can I ask, how you are both feeling?"

"We've got a lot to learn in a very short space of time, but we're getting there," said Daniel.

Bernstein smiled and gave him an appraising look. "That's not exactly what I asked. I asked how you are feeling."

"Ah, yes! Feelings. I've heard about them. I'm sure I've got some, somewhere," Daniel said light-heartedly.

Bernstein looked at Kelly and asked, "Is he always this evasive about his feelings?"

"I don't know. I'm still getting to know him." Kelly tilted her head and gave Daniel a discerning look. "He's probably as much of a blockhead about his feelings as most men. I'm probably going to have to tell him how he's feeling most of the time."

Bernstein laughed and said to Kelly, "I think you and I are going to be good friends."

"I think so, too."

11

———

After lunch, Daniel and Kelly returned to the cinema room and were shown another video, this one providing background and details for the mission itself.

An image of deep space, filled with stars, appeared on the screen, and the voice-over began.

"Mankind has been searching the stars for habitable exoplanets for nearly four hundred years. In the early days, that search involved radio telescopes with limited range and capabilities. 150 years ago, the VAR drive was invented – the vacuum to antimatter reactor drive – and we began launching probes to star systems, starting with the closest ones first. Thousands of planets have been studied and catalogued over the years, but none of them proved to be habitable. Until Tama-B."

"Tama is a star 37 light years distant from Earth. A probe was launched to that system 110 years ago. Being one of the early model probes, it only reached 60 percent of the speed of light, so it took 61 years to reach its destination. It began transmitting data immediately but that data, travelling at the speed of light, took 37 years to reach us, meaning that it took 98 years from the time of the probe's launch until we received the first data. The first image, received 12 years ago now, sent the scientific world into a frenzy. We had found our first and, to date, only habitable exoplanet."

"Tama is a spectral K-type main sequence star, also known as an orange dwarf. These stars are smaller than our own sun (which is a G-Type yellow dwarf) and they are somewhat cooler. This means they emit less harmful UV radiation and tend toward the infrared spectrum. Because they are cooler, the habitable zone for life-sustaining planets orbiting a K-type star is much closer than the distance that Earth orbits our sun. Tama is one of the larger K-type stars that we have discovered, being about 80 percent of our sun's mass. This is desirable because it means that a planet orbiting within its habitable zone won't be so close that it will be tidally locked – with the same side of the planet perpetually facing the sun as it orbits."

"My brain is hurting," said Kelly. "Will there be a test on this? Because if there is, I'm sure I'm gonna flunk!"

Daniel smiled. "Don't worry, I'll pass you the answers."

"Tama has three planets orbiting around it, currently named Tama-A, Tama-B, ..."

"Don't tell me!" said Kelly. "I think I can guess!"

"...and Tama-C."

"Darn it! I was going to say Jupiter 2!"

"Tama-B, the second planet from the star, turns out to be a beautiful, pristine, habitable world, very like Earth." A screen shot of Tama-B appeared on the screen: a stunning blue/green world with swirling white clouds and a thin blue atmosphere band surrounding it.

"Wow! That really is beautiful," said Kelly, her previous flippancy forgotten.

"There's our new home," said Daniel, his eyes gleaming with hope.

"Tama-B is about 90 percent of Earth's mass, so gravity will be slightly lower than on Earth. It orbits its sun, Tama, considerably closer than Earth orbits our own sun, so it completes a full orbit in just nine Earth months. It has a rotational period of 22 Earth hours and an axial tilt that is two degrees less than that of Earth, meaning that the climate fluctuations between summer and winter will be more subtle than on Earth. Tama-B's distance from its sun is such that it will enjoy a temperate average climate that is reminiscent of Earth in the early 1900s, before climate change accelerated out of control. Its atmosphere

has been analysed by the probe to be extremely similar to Earth, with one percent less oxygen and two percent more nitrogen. To this point, no harmful elements have been detected in the atmosphere. Tama-B also has a greater percentage of its surface as ocean – 78 percent – and this assists in keeping the planet's temperature stable."

"Maybe I should have packed a bikini," said Kelly.

Daniel's eyebrows went up. "I'm sure I can fashion a bikini top for you from a couple of coconuts."

"Your journey to Tama-B will take 38 Earth years, although due to the time dilation effects of general relativity as a result of travelling at near-light speed, Longshot will only experience the passing of seven years. For most of that time, you will be in cryogenic stasis, and when you are finally woken by the automated ship's systems, you will already be at your new home. Upon arrival, Longshot will spend at least a month in stable orbit around the planet, undertaking final tests to ensure that the planet is safe for human habitation and examining potential sites for the new settlement. Following this, colonists and light materials will be transferred to the surface via the ship's shuttles, and large or heavy equipment will be transferred via drop boxes – large heat shielded boxes with orbit retarding rockets and parachutes."

The rest of the video described materials and structures that would be available to the colonists and proposed an orderly time-line for the establishment of buildings and infrastructure. By the end of the presentation, Kelly's mind was spinning, and they declined further discussion with the private who arrived to ask if they had any questions. A break for a cup of coffee was followed by another video outlining ship protocols and safety procedures.

By the end of the day, Kelly had reached her limit and Daniel was ready for a break as well. By now, the base felt empty, with much fewer people walking through the corridors. All the colonists were, by now, safely on board Longshot, and only a skeleton staff and key supervising officers were left on the base.

Daniel and Kelly took advantage of the scarcity of other personnel to monopolise the officers' gym. They changed into PTs in their rooms and spent an hour working out with the specialised equipment designed for low gravity. Kelly complained most of the time and spent more time than was necessary sitting and drinking from a water bottle, but Daniel encouraged her, and she managed to work up a decent sweat in the end.

Later that night, as they cuddled up together in Kelly's bed, they spoke of the surreal nature of their situation, realising that this would be the last night they would spend on the ground within their solar system.

"We're about to spend 38 years in a spaceship," Kelly said.

"Starship," corrected Daniel.

"Alright, smarty pants." Then she sighed. "What if my cryogenic pod thingy doesn't work properly and when we wake up, you still look like this, and I look like a wrinkled old hag?"

"Don't worry about that," he replied, kissing her on the cheek. "If that happens, there'll be plenty of other pretty young women for me to choose from."

He was rubbing his arm for several minutes afterward.

12

———

They woke in the middle of the night to the strident sound of an alarm ringing throughout the base. Daniel had gone back to his own room to sleep, and it took him a few moments to orient himself. He quickly dressed and ran to Kelly's room and met her as she was opening her door.

"What's happening?" she asked, raising her voice over the alarm that was echoing down the corridor.

"I don't know, but it can't be good."

As he spoke, a message began broadcasting. "All base personnel report to action stations. All remaining Longshot mission personnel evacuate the base immediately. Longshot mission personnel make your way to Hangar I."

The message began repeating and Daniel turned to Kelly. "Grab your carry bag! We're leaving now!"

A few moments later, they were running down the corridor as fast as they could in the low gravity, their feet slipping out from underneath them as they occasionally lost traction. They reached the lift and squeezed on with four other personnel.

"What's happening?" asked Daniel.

"No idea, sir," said a corporal.

A moment later the lift opened onto the underground hangar,

and they saw personnel in various states of dress emerging from corridors and lifts surrounding the hanger. There was a white circle painted on the tarmac with a shuttle parked in the middle.

A sergeant was yelling instructions. "Make your way onto the shuttle as quickly as possible! Hurry people!"

"What's happening, sergeant?" asked Daniel.

"We're at war, sir. The Republic has declared war against the Alliance. The captain has ordered the immediate departure of Longshot. That's all I know."

"Is the base under attack?"

"There's nothing obvious yet, sir. But the Republic of Independent States has a military research base 1200 clicks from here and we're pretty sure they have missiles. They also have lunar satellites that have laser capabilities. If we are at war, this base and the starship would be very high on their target list. You need to get into this shuttle now, sir. A second shuttle, loaded with supplies, is also about to lift off from Hangar 2." He turned away and began yelling instructions to new arrivals.

Daniel and Kelly boarded the shuttle and strapped themselves into seats in the front row. The shuttle could seat about 50 people, but Captain Anderson had mentioned that there would only be a handful of people left to transfer up to Longshot today. The back of the shuttle was piled with supplies and only the front half was available for seating, but even so, not all the seats were taken. They waited a few more minutes while the base alarms continued to sound, and the sergeant could be heard issuing instructions. Several more people boarded the shuttle, then the sergeant stuck his head through the door and yelled to the pilot who was already warming the engines, "I think that's all. You're good to go!"

"Thanks, sergeant. Good luck!" called the pilot.

The shuttle steps folded into the fuselage and the door swung closed. Daniel looked through the porthole window and saw the remaining base personnel clear the area and, shortly after, the airlock doors into the corridors all sealed. They sat for a while as the air was pumped out of the underground hangar and then they waited while the roof above their circular landing pad slid open.

The pad began rising, lifting them toward the tarmac on the surface. The pilot had left the cockpit door open, and Daniel heard the comm come to life with an incoming call.

"Shuttle's 1 and 2! We have multiple missiles inbound! ETA 40 seconds! Get clear as soon as you can!"

Daniel heard the pilot swear and say to her co-pilot, "We're gonna have to punch it!"

Their pad continued to rise agonisingly slowly, and Daniel heard the pilot muttering to herself, "Come on, come on!"

Their slowly rising pad was still a couple of metres below ground level when she said, "We're not waiting any longer!"

"Are you sure? It's a tight fit," said the co-pilot.

"Shut up and give me power now!"

The engine note intensified, transmitted to the passengers through the hull, and the shuttle rose vertically while the pad was still in motion. There was a grinding sound as a part of the shuttle scraped against the outer rim of the hole in the tarmac, the pilot not having executed a perfectly vertical ascent.

"Oopsy. Sorry about the paintwork," muttered the pilot.

A moment later, they were clear. They rose vertically for a few more moments and then the pilot exclaimed, "Crap! There are the missiles! Punch it!" They were all thrust deeply back into their seats as the shuttle accelerated forward and upward at steep angle. They had barely begun to accelerate, however, when it felt as though they were hit from behind and the view through the side portholes and the front screen spun and tumbled crazily.

"Arrrgh ..." groaned the pilot as she fought the controls. "Blast wave!"

Daniel's eyesight narrowed and dimmed as he started to red-out from the centrifugal G-forces. He glanced at Kelly and saw that she had already passed out, her head swinging from side to side as they continued to tumble and spin. Daniel tightened his core and fought to stay conscious while he listened to the pilot's groans as she continued to fight for control. Gradually the tumbling and spinning stopped and but their final alignment had them powering straight down toward the Moon's surface again. Kelly regained consciousness and blinked in confusion, trying to work out where she was and what was happening.

"Hang on back there, people!" yelled the pilot as she hauled back on her flight controls and rammed her throttle to full power. The shuttle's dive bottomed out with barely metres to spare as the engine screamed, and they swooped back upwards with G forces that had Kelly slumping into unconsciousness again. Daniel squeezed his core as hard as he could, forcing blood upward into his brain and barely hung onto consciousness, his vision darkening until he was looking through a small tunnel of light almost totally enveloped in blackness. Slowly his vision cleared as the pilot backed off the power and the G forces dropped.

Daniel breathed a sigh of relief and looked at Kelly, whose head had slumped forward. He reached over and lifted her chin to clear her airways. He held her like that until her eyelids started to flutter and she gave several big sighs, finally opening her eyes to gaze around her in confusion.

"Welcome back, sleepy head," he said.

"What happened?"

"The blast wave from a missile impact threw us around a bit. You passed out. Twice."

She groaned. "I've changed my mind. I'd like to go back home now, please."

"Sorry. No refunds permitted. You can't get off until the ride is finished."

"Hey! You back there! Come and give me a hand!" The pilot was looking over her shoulder at Daniel.

"Who? Me?"

"Yes. You! Get up here."

Daniel unbuckled and moved forward, pulling himself against the force of acceleration.

"My co-pilot is unconscious. Must have hit his head. His legs are wedged against the nose thruster controls. I'm fighting against them the whole time. Unclip him and drag his guts out of that chair!"

Daniel looked around into the cockpit. The co-pilot had

slumped forward and there was blood across one side of his face. Daniel pulled his upper torso back toward the seat and unbuckled him. He grabbed him under his closest arm and heaved him up and out of the seat. The acceleration of the shuttle helped, as it was currently mimicking a gravity environment, and the man slid out of his seat and lay across the cramped access walkway to the cockpit.

"Drag him to your seat back there and strap him in, then get back up here. Congratulations, you're my new co-pilot."

13

Daniel dragged the unconscious co-pilot back to the passenger compartment and Kelly helped to strap him in. "So, you're going to have another go in the cockpit?" she asked. "You're making a habit of this."

"It's not something I aspire to," he assured her.

"It's not something you're particularly good at either. Try not to crash this time!"

"I'll do my best."

"I swear if you crash and we all die, I'll never speak to you again."

Ninety seconds later, Daniel climbed clumsily into the co-pilot's seat and buckled himself in.

"You did well back there," the pilot said. "You're the only passenger who didn't pass out."

"How did you ...?"

She pointed at a small video screen, showing the passenger compartment.

"Oh," Daniel said. He looked around the cockpit with its complicated instrumentation. "What do you want me to do?"

"Absolutely nothing. Don't touch a thing. You're only here in case something drastic happens and I need help."

He looked closely at her. Short dark hair, spiky on one side and shaved close to her scalp on the other. Several rings through her nose and dark eyeliner around her eyes. Daniel was surprised, as he didn't think that kind of thing was permitted in the space corps. He noted that she was a sergeant and also saw that she had both a pilot's patch and a security patch on her shoulder.

"You're on the security team?" he asked.

"Yeah. A lot of us on the mission have dual roles. MRP."

"MRP?"

"Multiple Redundancy Protocol."

"I'm Daniel Newman," he offered.

"I know who you are."

"And you are ...?"

"Trying to save our lives."

She was about to say something else when a comm call came through. "SS Longshot to Shuttles 1 and 2. Do you copy?"

The pilot replied, "This is Shuttle 1. I copy."

"SS Longshot to Shuttle 2. Do you copy?"

There was no reply.

Longshot repeated their query, with the same result.

The pilot spoke again. "This is Shuttle 1. I don't think Shuttle 2 made it. The base was hit by at least one missile just as we were launching."

"Copy. We have reports of two missile strikes on the base." There was a pause and then the voice continued. "Shuttle 1, we have had to take evasive action to avoid coming into range of the Republic's military base. We have left orbit and are under acceleration in a direct line away from the Moon."

"Roger. I see you on my screens, Longshot. What is your rate of acceleration?"

"We are currently under emergency acceleration of 3Gs."

"Crap!" said the pilot to herself, then punched a button and said, "Oops. Forgot to mute the comm." She took a few moments to scan the readouts which showed Longshot moving further away from them at an alarming rate. Daniel watched her as she stared at the screen, her lips moving silently as she calculated in her head.

She unmuted her comm and said, "Longshot, we are going to try to catch you."

"Roger Shuttle 1. We can see you on our screens. The Captain wishes you god-speed but says he is unwilling to risk the starship by slowing down."

"Roger Longshot. Out." She turned to Daniel. "Gird your loins, dude, things are about to get gnarly."

She thrust her throttle forward and the shuttle leapt forward as if it had been hit from behind. Daniel was forced far back into his seat, and he heard groans from those in the passenger compartment. Through gritted teeth, he asked. "How ... fast ... are ... we ... accelerating?"

"6G," she replied, her voice straining as she strained her core.

"How ... long ...?" asked Daniel.

"We're gaining. About ten minutes."

He groaned. "I ... don't ... think ... I ... can ..."

"Yeah. You're right," she said. "Ten minutes is too long." She reached out and pushed the throttle further forward, and Daniel felt the pressure increase even further. "7Gs now. Just six minutes to go."

Daniel's eyes fluttered and his head slumped forward.

"Sweet dreams, dude," said the pilot.

14

Daniel opened his eyes and looked around him, trying to work out where he was.

"Congrats, dude. You're the first to wake up," said the pilot, indicating the video screen showing everyone in the passenger compartment still unconscious. "You're a natural. We should train you as a pilot."

He groaned. "I've already crashed one flitter and one shuttle."

"On second thoughts, cancel that last idea."

"Aren't you supposed to call me 'sir'?"

"I promise I'll start calling you 'sir' when I've finished saving your life."

"What's your name?"

"Jordan."

"Is that your first name or your surname?"

"Both. I only have one name."

"You only have one name?"

"Look, dude, we can do the whole 'getting to know you' thing later, if you like. But right now, I'm still trying to save your life."

"You still haven't saved it? What's wrong with you, Sergeant Jordan? You need to lift your game."

She looked at him and smiled, saying, "I think I preferred you when you were unconscious."

Daniel turned ask checked on Kelly. She was conscious again and was groaning a little. "Are you okay?" he asked.

"Never felt better," she said, groaning again. She looked out the window at the stars. "You didn't crash us this time."

"No. Crashing all the time was getting boring."

"You've ruined your perfect record," she replied with a strained smile.

Jordan called back to Kelly, "How's my co-pilot doing?"

Kelly looked at the co-pilot who was now strapped into the seat beside her. "He's drifting in and out of consciousness and groaning a lot. The sooner we can get him some medical help, the better."

Daniel asked Jordan. "What's our situation? How close are we?" They were still being pressed into their seats but not quite as deeply as before

"Coming up on Longshot. Two clicks. We flipped and decelerated for a while and then flipped again. Now we're nudging up on them at 3.1Gs acceleration. They're still under 3G acceleration."

The comm light lit up. "Longshot calling Shuttle 1."

"Copy, Longshot," said Jordan.

"The captain sends his congratulations. A nice bit of flying."

"It was a cakewalk. You should see what I can do when I'm really trying."

There was laughter on the other end. "Roger that. What's your status?"

"All systems in the green. We have one known head injury. Others may need medical attention following prolonged loss of consciousness."

"Roger. We'll have med teams standing by. The captain believes we are out of immediate danger now. Prepare to cancel acceleration on my mark."

"Roger, Longshot. One moment please." She muted the comm. "Okay, as a reward for being such a good sport, I'm going to let you cancel our main thrusters."

"Really? That's nice of you."

"Yeah, but don't get all gushy on me or I'll change my mind."

"What do I do?"

"See that big, glowing, orange button directly in front of you, that says 'Main Thruster Shutoff'?"

"Yep."

"Just punch that button, on Longshot's mark."

"Cool."

She nodded and unmuted the comms. "Ready when you are, Longshot."

"Roger. Cancel acceleration in three, two, one, mark."

Daniel punched the button and there was instant relief as the force pressing them back into their seats was cancelled. "Ah! That feels so good," Daniel said as his arms started to float free.

Longshot was visible in their front window now, slowly growing in size as they approached at a slightly higher velocity.

"Shuttle 1, we are opening Shuttle Bay Door 8, on the starboard side from your perspective."

"Roger, I see it. Stand by." She spent the next few minutes making slight adjustments to their velocity and orientation, using the manoeuvering thrusters.

Finally, they were floating alongside a large open shuttle bay. Up this close, Longshot was enormous. Their tiny shuttle was now floating near the base of the starship, perpendicular to Longshot's long axis. The central cylinder of the spacecraft towered far above them, disappearing from sight above their front window. To their left, the open shuttle bay was a brightly lit rectangle in the gloom of space. The opening looked about 40 meters wide and 10 metres high, and Daniel could see docking clamps on the floor ready to lock down the shuttle.

"Longshot we are in position."

"Roger, Shuttle 1. Please lock on to the docking telemetry signal."

"Roger." Jordan tapped a screen a few times and then sat back, taking her hands off all controls. "Shuttle 1 is locked on. You have control, Longshot."

"Roger, Shuttle 1. Longshot has control. Out."

"That's it?" said Daniel, disappointed. "We pay you the big bucks and you just sit there and do nothing now?"

"What did you expect? This isn't a Star Wars movie, dude. The sphincter police don't want us hotshot jocks scratching their nice new paintwork."

"I seem to remember you've already put a few scratches on the paintwork," Daniel said.

"I won't say anything if you don't," said Jordan.

Daniel smiled. "Deal."

15

A medic was attending to the co-pilot, who was now conscious but suffering from a concussion. Several other passengers from the shuttle needed some assistance after the arduous acceleration they had endured in catching up to the starship and they were taken to the med bay for assessment. As soon as the shuttle had been secured in the shuttle bay, Longshot had fired up its main thrusters and began accelerating again, this time at a more comfortable 1G, thereby establishing normal gravity throughout the starship.

While shuttle bay personnel continued to secure the shuttle, Jordan – the pilot – along with Daniel, Kelly and four other passengers walked across the brightly lit shuttle bay toward the bank of lifts. Daniel glanced at Jordan as they walked. Her short spiky hair, almost completely shaved on one side, along with her nose rings and dark eyeliner, made her look like a retro punk rocker from the 20th century.

A private greeted them and addressed Daniel and Kelly. "Sir and ma'am, Captain Anderson has requested your presence in the wardroom on Level 74. He has called an emergency mission team meeting. If you'll step this way, we'll take this express lift straight to the top."

"Sure," said Daniel. "Just a moment." He turned to Jordan. "We owe you our lives, Jordan. Thank you." He held out his hand.

Jordan stared at his hand. "Us enlisted plebs aren't supposed to shake hands with officers."

"I don't give a crap," said Daniel, his hand still held out, waiting.

Jordan nodded. She reached and shook hands. "You know, for a warrant officer, you're actually a half-decent human being."

"Wow," said Daniel. "Try not to get too effusive with your praise."

"I won't. Most officers are bastards," she said as she walked toward a different elevator.

The private who was waiting to accompany them to the wardroom opened her eyes wide in disbelief at Jordan's insolence, but Daniel merely chuckled. As they walked toward their own lift, he said to Kelly, "You know, she reminds me a lot of you."

"Really? In what way?"

"Irreverent, unconventional and annoying as hell, but in a surprisingly appealing way."

"Aww, you're so sweet. You're so good with compliments. Have you ever thought about writing greeting cards for a living?"

The elevator whisked them up to the top level in a matter of moments. They walked out into the expansive command centre which was buzzing with activity. Even though it was technically the middle of the night, the current crisis meant that all crew members were on duty and at action stations.

The control centre took up the entire top level of the starship and, like all other levels, was completely circular, nearly 80 metres in diameter. The elevators were situated against the wall and opened onto a five-metre-long corridor which led out into the huge central area. The walls of the lift corridor also served as the walls for the wardroom to the right and the Captain's day cabin to the left.

Daniel and Kelly stood at the end of the corridor and gazed at the scene before them. The circular wall was 10 metres high and the section of wall immediately opposite them comprised a series of huge screens, some of them revealing views into surrounding space and others with readouts and various graphs. The central area of the command centre was taken up with dozens of consoles, in a scene that looked surprisingly like the flight control centre of a rocket launch facility. On this side of the circular room, the corridor from the lifts opened onto a raised platform that followed the curve of the wall and which looked down onto the consoles in the centre of the floor. The captain's chair was situated on this platform which Daniel realised must be the bridge.

The XO, Commander Decker, was in the centre of the floor, giving instructions to a variety of people, his steely blue eyes focused and determined. Captain Nash Anderson was in deep discussion with someone beside him, but when he saw Daniel and Kelly, he broke off and came over to them.

"Daniel and Kelly! I can't tell you how glad I am that you made it. The decision to leave orbit and potentially leave you and several others behind was one of the most difficult of my career. But it was absolutely necessary for the safety of this ship and her crew."

"I totally understand, Captain," said Daniel. "You don't have to explain. What's happened back at the base?"

"That's part of what I'm about to discuss with the mission team. It's time to get the meeting started." He turned and called to Decker, "Commander! The wardroom, now please." Turning back to Daniel and Kelly, he said, "Follow me."

The wardroom was about five metres by eight and had a duplicate oval table to the one on Longshot Base. The rest of the mission team were already there, mostly already seated, but the slightly built systems analyst, Rajish Patel, made a point of standing and greeting Daniel and Kelly effusively.

"Dr Rearson and Mr Newman! How very wonderful to see you!" He shook hands with both of them as he greeted them. "I was extremely worried for you and have prayed to God for your safe arrival. And look! Here you are!"

"We are, indeed," said Kelly, smiling. "And that's very kind of you."

"It is God who has looked after you and brought you safely to us. Of that, I am sure!"

The captain called the meeting to order and began with these dire words, "Ladies and Gentlemen, we are now at war, and Longshot is in terrible danger."

16

The other nine people around the oval table in the Longshot wardroom gave Captain Nash Anderson their full attention and there was silence as his words hung in the air.

"Firstly, let me brief you on developments to this point. Yesterday's failed attack on Longshot Base and the simultaneous failed attempted takeover of this starship set in motion a series of rapidly escalating events. A strongly worded denunciation was issued to President Haito Bismati, the president of the Republic of Independent Nations. The Alliance of Nations also placed immediate trade embargoes on several of the Republic's biggest exports. The Republic responded by withdrawing ambassadors from all Alliance nations and arresting dozens of Alliance diplomats in several countries. When news came in that the Alliance base on Mars, Lovell Research Facility, had been taken over by hostile Republic forces from the Republic's own base on Mars, the Alliance issued an ultimatum: withdraw from Lovell Base and release our diplomats within two hours, or the Alliance would retaliate in force. When that time elapsed without any capitulation, the Alliance Cruiser, SS Sydney, in orbit around Mars, fired upon the Republican Base and destroyed several buildings, but was, in turn, destroyed by missiles launched from the almost complete starship, Shengli, in Mars orbit.

"War was declared by both parties immediately following that incident and things have continued to escalate. Back on Earth, dozens, perhaps hundreds of ICBMs have been launched and the satellite defence systems of both parties have only managed to destroy about 70 percent of those before they reached their targets. The Earth is a seething mess right now. Many satellites and space stations have also been destroyed, including Hubble Station."

Nash Anderson took a deep breath, then ploughed on. "On the Moon, two missile strikes caused serious damage to Longshot Base, but it appears they deliberately avoided striking the fusion reactor. My guess is that they wanted to take the base for themselves. Our military base on the Moon, Copernicus Military Base, some 800 clicks to the southeast of Longshot Base, also came under heavy missile fire, but our laser interceptor system destroyed the Republican missiles mid-flight. These missiles all originated from Xian Xing; the Republican Base 1200 clicks East of Longshot Base. In response, the Alliance cruiser, SS Charon, in orbit around the Moon at the time, fired upon Xian Xing, with deadly consequences. Their laser canons utterly destroyed the Republican base."

Anderson paused, to let all that sink in. "I made the decision to launch Longshot and execute an emergency departure from the Moon. At that stage, Xian Xing, the Republican military base, was still in play and our orbit would have placed us within range of their missiles within another 30 minutes. I have no doubt that had we not executed an emergency departure burn, we would not be alive now."

"That brings us to our current predicament. Our emergency burn has set us on a course that is taking us in completely the opposite direction to our destination, Tama-B. We could, of course, pivot Longshot on its longitudinal axis and start firing our VAR drive in the right direction. But we are already travelling at considerable velocity, and it would take the best part of a day, at 1 G acceleration, to bring us to a relative standstill so that we could being accelerating in the right direction. The main problem with that scenario is that we would become a sitting duck for the Republic, which, as you know, is determined to destroy or capture Longshot to ensure that their own starship gets to Tama-B first. Hubble Base, shortly before it was destroyed, reported that the Republican cruiser, Hand of God, had left Earth orbit and was plotting an intercept course with us."

"Taking all that into consideration, I believe that our safest course of action is to keep on our current trajectory. With a slight alteration to our current flight path, we can slingshot around Venus and use it to correct our course and, in the process, avoid a potential conflict with any Republican forces that may be actively seeking us."

"But there is a catch. The Republic have a small orbital base at Venus. We believe it is primarily a research base, in orbit around the planet, but the Alliance has never been able to ascertain whether it has weapons. Knowing the Republic's love of weaponry, there is a possibility they may have lasers, and a very slim chance that they have missiles. It is also a complete unknown where the Republican station will be in its orbit when we execute our sling-shot fly-by. It could be on the other side of the planet and pose no threat to us at all. These are all factors that we have to consider, but most of them are just guesses."

Anderson looked around the table. "I'm open to comments and suggestions, ladies and gentlemen."

"It seems to me that we don't have a choice," said Mission Specialist Olivia Alvarez. "A Venus fly-by is the safest course."

"I agree," said Science Officer, Maria Vargas. "The Republican orbital station at Venus, which I believe is called 'Altair' – the flying eagle – is definitely a scientific base, not a military one. A Venus fly-by seems the safest option."

"How are we provisioned?" Daniel asked Anderson. "You mentioned yesterday that we were scheduled to receive a final supply shipment from Earth today. Plus, there was the shuttle that was loaded with supplies from the Moon base that didn't make it tonight."

Anderson nodded. "Yes. We will miss those supplies, but my understanding is that they were not essential. Is that right, Commander?"

The XO, Bryce Decker, nodded. "Yes, sir. The shipment from Earth that we missed out on consisted of additional luxury items and some dry goods, and the items in the shuttle from the base were last minute things that were thrown in for good measure – additional clothing and that sort of thing. Nothing that we missed out on receiving today will significantly impair our mission or prevent us from leaving."

"Good to know," said Anderson.

"Pardon my ignorance," said Daniel, "but does Longshot have weapons?"

"None," said Anderson. "No missiles and no laser canons. We have laser annihilation fields that energise our deflector shields during flight for the purposes of neutralising potentially damaging particles and small objects, but they can't be focused or directed away from the ship. Our shuttles have laser firing capabilities, but that doesn't do us much good when they're parked in the shuttle bays. In terms of defence, we have a plasma infused magnochromatic shield that is designed to be powered up during Longshot's flip manoeuvre at the midway point of our journey to Tama. The shield is designed to absorb and destroy any fast-moving particles that might collide with the side of the ship during our flip. Theoretically, the shield could absorb limited laser fire, but it's not what it is designed for. The bottom line is that this is a colony starship, not a military cruiser. Hence why we are running and not fighting."

Anderson looked around at everyone. "So, are we in agreement that we make final course corrections for Venus?"

Everyone nodded.

"Good. We will need to make a final course correction. LACIE, can you please calculate the burn for a Venus slingshot?"

"Certainly, Captain Anderson," responded a pleasant disembodied female voice.

Daniel and Kelly looked around the room, perplexed. "LACIE?" asked Daniel.

"Longshot Artificial Computer Intelligence Entity," said Rajish Patel, the systems analyst, wobbling his head enthusiastically.

LACIE continued answering the captain's question. "Venus is currently in a convenient location for us, being relatively close to Earth in its orbit. We will require a course correction burn for 4 minutes 42 seconds in 21 minutes from now, at an acceleration rate of 2.5G. We will then coast at that vector and velocity for 26 hours 14 minutes before engaging our main drive again for our slingshot manoeuvre."

"Thank you, LACIE," said Anderson. He addressed the meeting, again. "The reason we need to coast to Venus, rather than engage constant acceleration is that if we continued to accelerate, our velocity will be too high for a slingshot when we reach Venus; we would just race past the planet and its gravity would not be able to capture us. This means that we will be without gravity for most of our journey to Venus, so we will all need to wear our magnetic boots until gravity is restored."

He looked at Dara Bernstein, the frizzy-haired welfare officer. "Lieutenant Bernstein, you might need to monitor our colonists. There may be some discomfort for some of them, although their training should have prepared them for a zero-gravity situation."

Bernstein nodded. "I'm sure most of them will be fine, but we'll keep watch for any who are struggling."

"Mr Cullen, how are we placed in regard to security?"

George considered his reply, his bald head glistening slightly, probably indicating he had been rushing around prior to the meeting. "Two of my team were on board the second shuttle that didn't make it tonight." He paused and glared at everyone around the table, as if it were somehow their fault. "I'm meeting with my team later this morning and I'll be organising a sweep of the ship, to check for any hidden devices or security risks. We can't discount the possibility that the Republic could still have an active agent on board."

Anderson said, "Good. Make it a thorough search. We don't

want any surprises." He addressed the rest of the team. "Is there anything else that we need to discuss?" He waited. "No? Good. Let's make the best of this, people. I'll be addressing the whole ship shortly. Let's get our people ready for the course correction burn. Meeting dismissed."

17

Daniel and Kelly made their way quickly to the stores department on Level 50, to be issued with magnetic boots. The quartermaster, however, was not quite what they expected.

"What can I do for you?" she asked.

"We were told to report to the quartermaster," said Kelly.

"Bingo! You got me."

Kelly blinked.

"Not what you expected?" she said with a friendly smile.

"No. But in a nice way."

The woman looked to be in her late 30s or maybe early 40s. She was above average height for a woman – about 175 cm tall – and at least 130 kilograms. But that was not the surprising part. The surprising part was her color. Literally everything was colored. She had shoulder length, iridescent rainbow-colored hair. Her nails were rainbow colored: a different color for each nail. Her clothing was rainbow colored – rainbow-striped baggy trousers and a kaftan-styled loose fitting rainbow top. Her eyeshadow was rainbow striped. She had rainbow bangles and necklaces and massive rainbow earrings. And finally, she had three rainbow tattoos – three that were visible, anyway – one on each forearm and one across the back of her neck.

"I'm guessing you like rainbows," said Daniel.

"Whatever gave you that idea?" said the quartermaster, chuckling. "I'm guessing you're the new arrivals." She quickly checked a data screen built into her counter. "Rearson and Newman?"

"Kelly," said Kelly with a warm smile.

"And Daniel," added Daniel.

Without any warning, the walking rainbow came around from behind her counter and enveloped them both in a smothering embrace, with one meaty arm around each of them. "Welcome to our little family!" Daniel found himself pressed up tight against her, in intimate contact with various wobbly bits that he'd prefer not to think about. Eventually she released them both and stepped back, but still held them each by their upper arms. "You poor dears! What a fright you must have had! I'll bet it was scary."

"We're doing okay," said Kelly.

"Well, anytime you need a hug, you come and see Pixie Rainbow."

Daniel glanced at a space corps nametag on her left breast which read, 'Corporal Pixie Rainbow'."

"That's your name?" asked Daniel.

"Sure is! Of course, it's not the name I was born with. I changed it as soon as I was old enough. Life's way too short to be boring. Pixie Rainbow! Don't you love it?"

"I do, actually," said Kelly with a smile. In fact, both Daniel and Kelly couldn't help smiling – because Pixie radiated such warmth and joy that it was irresistibly infectious.

"If you don't mind me asking, how do you get away with ... well ... looking like that?" asked Daniel. "You're not exactly in regulation uniform."

"Six weeks ago, the captain got the crew together and said that the distinction between space corps crew and civilian colonists would disappear once we left the solar system. We would all be just colonists together. He gave us permission to start styling our hair how we wanted and wearing makeup and jewellery, and the men were allowed to grow facial hair. Most crew members have begun to 'civilianise' themselves a little. It's just that there are a few of us who have taken it a bit further. I've had the tats all my adult life, but the hair coloring I got done last week while I was on leave at Armstrong Base."

"Aren't you supposed to at least be in ANSA uniform?" asked Kelly.

Pixie nodded. "Yep. And I have been wearing my uniform until yesterday. But now that we've launched, what are they going to do? Throw me off the ship? The worst they could do is court-martial me and kick me out of the corps. But then, guess what? I'd just keep wearing the same clothes and they'd probably still want me to run the stores department." She grinned and jiggled her eyebrows up and down. "I got it all figured out. They can't do a darned thing about it, and they know it."

"So that also explains Jordan, the shuttle pilot, as well," said Daniel.

"Jordan and I are good friends. And, yes, she's certainly adopted her own style as well. She's also the best shuttle pilot we've got, so they're hardly going to toss her overboard, either."

"You guys have got it all figured out," said Kelly.

"Sure have!" replied Pixie. Then she clapped her hands and said, "So! What can I get you, my lovelies?"

"Magnetic boots, please," said Kelly.

"Ah, yes! We can't have you floating around and banging into things when they switch off the VAR drive, can we?"

They told Pixie their sizes and she came back with their new boots.

"Do you know how they work?" she asked, handing them over.

"No," they said in unison.

"It's pretty simple. The floors have metal fibres all through them and the boots have magnetic latex soles powered by nano diamond batteries. The switch at the back of the boots turns the magnet on and the tiny dial above it adjusts the strength of the magnetism. You can adjust it to suit your weight and your leg strength, and also to suit a particular activity. If you need a lot of leverage doing some kind of maintenance work, you dial up the magnetism. If you're just walking around, you'll probably want to be able to lift your foot up pretty easily, so just dial it down. When we have normal gravity from our acceleration, just switch them off and they're normal boots."

A chime sounded over the ship's comm. "Sounds like someone wants to have a chat with us," said Pixie.

"This is Captain Nash Anderson. I'm happy to report that we are safe for the moment. Unfortunately, the news from outside our starship is not so good. The Alliance is at war with the Republic and significant military exchanges have already occurred on Earth, Mars and the Moon. Earth, in particular, has been the battleground for a significant exchange of nuclear missiles, with many major cities hit and a large percentage of orbiting satellites destroyed. Because of the loss of satellites and the damage caused by electromagnetic pulses, communication with Earth is not possible at the moment. We must come to terms with the fact that we are now on our own. I had wished for a more celebratory and joyful launch of our mission, but that is not to be."

"Furthermore, our hasty departure from the Moon has resulted in a less than ideal trajectory. To correct that, and get us back on track, we plan to slingshot around Venus and, from there, head out of the solar system on our way to the Tama system. In order to line us up for a Venus slingshot, we will need to initiate a course correction burn for a little over four and a half minutes, at an acceleration of 2.5G. That burn will take place in six minutes from now. The best place for you to be during the burn will be lying on your bed, so I encourage everyone to make your way to your rooms now. After the completion of the burn, the main drive will be switched off for the 26 hours and 14 minutes it will take us to reach Venus. This means there will be no ship-induced gravity because we will no longer be under acceleration. Please make sure all loose items are secured and remember to use your magnetic boots when you move around the ship in the zero-gravity environment. You will also need to zip yourselves into your beds while sleeping. Gravity-free protocols will also apply to showering, toileting, and the consumption of food and beverages. You have prepared for this, so just remember your training."

"Thank you for your patience and understanding in all of this. I assure you that the crew is doing everything possible to keep us safe and ensure a smooth and event-free departure from our solar system. That is all."

"You two had better get back to your rooms," said Pixie, once Anderson had signed off. "Do you know what rooms you've been allocated?"

"No," said Kelly. "Things have been a bit chaotic."

"Let me have a look for you." Pixie tapped her screen. "Ah, here they are. Kelly, you're in 6612 and Daniel, you're in 6631. They're both on Level 66, obviously. You'd best get there before we commence the burn."

"We will," said Kelly. "And thanks for the boots."

As they walked quickly toward the lifts, Kelly whispered to Daniel, "Your room or mine?"

18

The relatively mild course correction burn of only 2.5G was easy to cope with in comparison to the grinding acceleration that Daniel and Kelly had experienced in the shuttle during their emergency flight to the starship. Even so, the relief was instantaneous once the main drive shut down and they were plunged into weightlessness. The burn took place at 04:37, ship time, still the early hours of the morning. They had both planned something more amorous to follow, but after their intense few hours in the middle of the night, they quickly fell asleep in each other's arms in Kelly's bunk.

Daniel awoke to find himself floating near the ceiling, completely upside down in relation to Kelly's bunk. Kelly was still sound asleep and floating nearby. They had forgotten to zip themselves into the bed. He checked the time on his wrist comm and saw that it was 10:55. They had slept through breakfast and Daniel suddenly remembered that there was a security team meeting at 11:00 in the briefing room, wherever that was. He was still in his clothes from yesterday, as they had both been too tired to even bother getting changed.

Daniel reached out and grabbed the top bunk and pulled himself down to the ground. He found his magnetic boots floating together nearby, and spent several minutes tumbling and twisting in mid-air, trying to put them on. Eventually they were successfully on his feet and strapped on, and he was panting with the exertion.

"You're not getting up to mischief with someone else while I'm asleep, are you?" mumbled Kelly, with her eyes still closed.

"Just putting my boots on," he said.

"Sure. That's what they all say."

"Go back to sleep," he said. "I've got a security meeting to go to." He pressed the button on the back of each boot to activate them, then used the frame of the bunk to lever himself back to the ground. When the boots touched the floor, they stuck fast, and Daniel felt the curious sensation of floating in mid-air while his feet were anchored to the ground. He tried to walk but couldn't break the magnetic pull of his boots. Kelly now had her eyes open and had strapped herself into her bottom bunk and was watching the proceedings with interest.

"Your boots are obviously made for someone much stronger and more manly than you," she said helpfully.

"Ha, ha." Daniel leant down and adjusted the dial on the top of his right boot, but must have adjusted it too far, because the torsion of his body caused it to break its magnetic grip on the floor. He was now in the comical position of being stuck to the floor with his left boot while his right leg pivoted high overhead and his body was twisted down and to the side.

Kelly applauded enthusiastically. "Wow! You're really good! I've always wanted to go to the ballet."

Daniel grunted and swung his right leg down to the floor again and adjusted his boot once more. He quickly found the right level of magnetism and made a similar adjustment on the left boot, then spent a few moments walking back and forth in the tiny cabin. It was a bizarre kind of movement: leaning forward and wrenching one leg off the floor and thrusting it forward to reconnect, and then doing the same with the trailing leg.

"Is the tongue sticking out the side of your mouth just for balance or are you thirsty?" asked Kelly.

Daniel leant down and kissed her. "Thirsty for you, but we'll have to do something about that tonight. Right now, I've got to find the briefing room. Any ideas where that is?"

"Nope."

"See you," he said as he opened their sliding door and clomped down the hallway. He reached the lifts and asked a passing crew member for directions.

"Back down the hallway where you've just come from," she said. "It's about half-way around, on the opposite side to the lifts."

Daniel thanked her and retraced his steps. He glanced at his wrist comm and saw that he was nearly 10 minutes late. "Damn!" he muttered.

He clomped down the hallway as fast as he could, with jerky limb movements that made him look like an uncoordinated cyborg with a software glitch. At last, he came to an open doorway on his right and heard George Cullen's gruff voice from within. The doorway was at the back of a rectangular room. George was standing at the front and about a dozen crew members were sitting at what looked like student desks, in lines of four, facing the front. Daniel tried to slip quietly into a spare chair and desk at the back but failed dismally. His left boot caught on the edge of the desk's leg, and he stumbled forward, knocking the chair over with his right knee. George stopped talking and everyone turned to look at him.

"Sorry," he mumbled awkwardly, "I had trouble finding you."

Cullen just glared and let his silence speak for itself. As he began speaking again and everyone returned their attention to the front, Jordan, the gothic-looking shuttle pilot from yesterday who was sitting to Daniel's immediate right, leant over and whispered,

"Nice entrance, dude. Very subtle."

Cullen continued with his instructions. "As I was saying, just because we managed to repel the invaders, doesn't mean the threat is over. Even though they didn't make it much beyond the airlock, they may have sent wasps throughout the ship. They could be anywhere, and they could be set to go off at any time. So, our priority today is to do a complete scan, from top to bottom, in teams of two." Cullen then began to assign teams and levels, working from the front of the room to the back. There were six pairs, each assigned 12 levels. Lastly, he came to the back row.

"O'Neil, you're with me. We'll search Hydroponics 2 and 12 levels below, down to Shuttle Bay 4. "Jordan, you're with Mr Newman. Try to keep him on his feet." Everyone chuckled. "You'll start at the top – the Command Centre on Level 74 – and work your way down 12 levels, to Hydroponics 1. Everyone grab a scanner each on your way out the door. That's it. Let's move, people!"

The meeting broke up and Daniel turned to Jordan. "Sorry. You drew the short straw."

She shrugged. "At least he didn't put me with O'Neil. He's a total tool."

"And I'm just a partial one?" Daniel asked.

She shrugged again. "The jury's still out on that, but I think you've got potential."

"Potential for what? To be a complete tool or not at tool at all?"

"Like I said, the jury's still out."

"I'd quite like to meet this jury," he said. "At least I should be given the opportunity to appear before them and present my case."

"Would you two like me to fetch you some coffee and biscuits while you keep chatting?" asked Cullen, standing over them with hands on hips.

"Yes please," said Jordan. "Cream but no sugar." She turned to Daniel. "How do you take yours?"

"Umm ..." muttered Daniel, uncertainly.

"You'll both be taking it up the ass if you don't get moving!"

"Interesting way to ingest coffee," said Jordan, standing to her feet. "I think I'll pass on that, boss. But thanks for the kind offer."

She led Daniel to the table by the door and they both grabbed scanners. As they exited the room and began walking down the hallway toward the lifts, she said, "He's such a lovely man, don't you think?"

"Cullen? What's he like to work for?"

"He's an officer."

"So?"

"All officers are bastards."

"Yeah, I got that message loud and clear, yesterday."

She stopped and looked at him, with a smirk on her face. "You're walking like a complete gumby. You've got the magnetism on your boots dialled up too high. You shouldn't need to yank your feet off the floor so hard. Dial it down, dude. I don't want to spend the rest of the day walking around with a gumby clomping behind me. I've got a rep to maintain, man."

He bent down and reduced the magnetism.

"I suppose you want me to call you 'sir'?" she asked, while he was making the adjustments.

"No," he replied, straightening up. "Daniel will be fine."

"Okay, dude, let's go." She strode off ahead of him, down the hall.

"Or 'dude' will be fine, too," Daniel muttered as he struggled to catch up.

19

"What are these wasps we're supposed to be looking for?" asked Daniel, as he and Jordan rode the lift to the top floor of the starship.

"Wasps are small drones, more like the size of a small bird, but similar in design to a real wasp. They're equipped with an anti-matter bomb and programmed to seek out secluded spots to attach themselves. Then they detonate at their appointed time."

"And if one does go off?"

"Adios, amigo. One of those bastards would be enough to blow us all to kingdom come."

"There are a lot of bastards in your world, aren't there?"

"Sure are. I call it like it is. An antimatter bomb works by switching off the quantum containment field at the time allotted for the explosion. Until then, the containment field holds a tiny amount of antimatter in quantum suspension – less than one gram of antimatter."

"That's tiny," said Daniel, surprised. "I haven't read anything about antimatter yet. Could that much destroy us?"

"Antimatter is the most volatile stuff in the universe. Half a gram, if it comes into contact with ordinary matter, would be enough to reduce this entire starship and everyone in it to their constituent atoms."

"Wow."

"Strap your scanner to your wrist," she said, holding up her own wrist with hers already strapped on. "Then just press and hold the screen for a few seconds." She pressed her own and a soft chime sounded. "That's it; it's activated."

"And how does the scanner work?" he asked, as he strapped on his own. "I assume it can detect the quantum containment field?"

"No. A quantum containment field is too tiny to detect further away than a few centimetres. But once a wasp is activated, the atomic clock inside it starts pulsing, once every second, and these scanners detect those pulses."

"What's the effective radius of the scanner?" asked Daniel, as his scanner came online.

"Ten metres. At least that's what the specs say. But I err on the cautious side. I try to do a grid search every five metres. All we need to do is walk around and cover the entire area. The scanner will give an obvious alarm if it detects a containment field, so you don't even have to look at it."

As she spoke, the lift doors opened and they emerged into the Command Centre, on the top floor of the starship. They walked down the short hallway and emerged into the raised bridge area.

Huge screens on the far wall dominated the room, some showing starfields and others with graphical presentations of data. The circular wall behind them housed the wardroom and the captain's day cabin. The central part of the huge circular level, however, was taken up with dozens of consoles with individual screens, staffed by busy-looking people.

"You take the outer edge and spiral your way in," said Jordan. "I'll start in the middle and spiral outward. And don't forget the wardroom and that captain's day cabin."

They split up and Daniel began with the wardroom and cabin. The wardroom was empty, but the captain was at his desk in his cabin. 'Cabin' was a loose term for the room, because it had no bed. It was simply an office with a desk and chair and two seats for visitors.

"Daniel! How are you settling in?" asked Anderson.

"Fine sir. Sorry for the intrusion. We're scanning the whole ship." In two steps he had reached the middle of the office, with no alarm sounding. "All clear in here, sir. I'll leave you to your work."

"How are you coping with weightlessness?" asked Anderson. "You haven't had the training and acclimatisation that everyone else has."

"I'm doing okay. I missed breakfast, so there's nothing in my stomach to come up the wrong way. Not sure how I'll go at lunch."

"Swallow twice as much and twice as hard, that's my advice," said Anderson. "Lunch is at 12:30. I'm encouraging crew members to mix with the colonists at mealtimes. We need to break down any divides and start behaving like a single community."

"I'll bear that in mind. I'll leave you to your work, sir."

Daniel exited the cabin and began walking in an anticlockwise direction around the external wall. On his second circumnavigation, one spiral inward, he came across the XO, Commander Decker, who was looking at a screen over the shoulder of a female operator. He saw Daniel and straightened up.

"What are you doing here?"

"Just doing a security scan."

"Sir."

"Sir," repeated Daniel.

Decker looked at him disdainfully for a moment, as if he had trodden in something unpleasant, then said dismissively, "Get on with it."

Daniel continued on his way, wondering whether it was going to be possible to ever develop a collegial relationship with the man. The difference between the captain and the executive officer couldn't be starker, and Daniel wondered how they got along in private.

It took about 15 minutes to do a thorough sweep of the Command Centre, drawing a complete blank. The next two levels below – the science department and the medical bay – were more complicated, as they had many different labs and rooms, with linking hallways. After 45 minutes they were able to declare those two levels clear as well, and they took the lift down to the next level, the dining deck. The lift opened and, as they stepped out, a soft chime sounded.

"Perfect timing," said Jordan, glancing at her wrist communicator. "12:30 on the knocker. Lunchtime."

The whole level was basically one huge, open-plan dining room, except for a kitchen and servery against the far wall. Round dining tables were scattered throughout the huge room and about half of them were already taken. More people were arriving out of the lifts as Daniel stood taking in the spectacle. It was his first glimpse of the colonists, and he was immediately struck by their narrow age-range. There appeared to be no one younger than 20 and no one older than 40. These were all people in the prime of life, and there appeared to be an even mix of men and women. Prime breeding stock.

Daniel turned to point this out to Jordan, but she was suddenly enveloped in a walking rainbow.

"Jordie, darling!" Pixie held her arms wide and wrapped them around the diminutive security guard, who all but disappeared inside the sail-like yardage of rainbow-striped material. Pixie Rainbow looked like a giant butterfly with the oversized arms of her multicoloured kaftan top forming her wings.

"And Daniel!" she said giving him the same treatment. Daniel hadn't noticed on their previous meeting, but she even smelt like a rainbow. He wondered if there was such a thing as rainbow perfume or rainbow soap.

"Let's get a table, together!" she said enthusiastically, and led them to a large, unoccupied circular table nearby. They had barely sat down when the chair beside Daniel scraped back, and Kelly plonked herself in it.

"I'm starving!" she said. "We missed breakfast," she added for the benefit of Pixie and Jordan.

"We?" asked Pixie.

"Daniel and me. We slept right through."

"Did you, now?" she said, winking at them. "In the same cabin, I presume. A tiring night, was it? I'm very jealous!"

Kelly laughed. "Nothing like that. We were just exhausted after our ordeal."

"Of course you were, my lovelies," Pixie said, sympathetically. She waved her hand generally around the room and said, "Do you know how it all works?"

"Yes. We watched a whole lot of videos yesterday," answered Kelly. She pointed to the many floor-to-ceiling columns scattered throughout the room, with touch screens and delivery chutes. "Those column thingies are food and drink dispensers, serving basic yeast-based proteins, cereals and breads. The kitchen servery is where to go if you want anything fresh from the hydroponics."

"Mush or crunch," offered Jordan, succinctly. "But in zero gravity, it's basically all mush and no crunch."

Pixie ignored Jordan's comment. "And if you're ever hungry or want a drink, the food and drink dispensers are available 24 hours a day. It's only the kitchen that closes between mealtimes. Some people prefer to eat outside of mealtimes to avoid the rush, but the captain is encouraging us to eat at the prescribed times so that we have a chance to bond as a micro-society."

"Speaking of bonding," said Daniel, "I can't help noticing that all the colonists are ... um ... shall we say, prime breeding age."

"Absolutely," agreed Pixie. "Producing children will be one of our prime directives once we arrive at Tama-B. There are only a few of us old dinosaurs who managed to sneak on as part of the crew, but all of the colonists are in their 20s and 30s."

"You mean you're not in your 30s?" asked Daniel, in mock surprise. "I find that difficult to believe."

"Oh, you are a charmer, aren't you!" she replied. "But I'm sure you're not that stupid."

"I wouldn't bet on it," said both Jordan and Kelly, simultaneously, then they burst out laughing together. Jordan reached out and they bumped fists.

Daniel sighed. "I'm so glad I can be a source of amusement for everyone."

Kelly kissed him on the cheek and said, "Only joking, my love. I don't believe in betting."

Pixie announced proudly, "For your information, I'm two years away from 50, but I can assure you that there's plenty of life in the old girl yet! And I plan to be as naughty as possible for as long as I can get away with it!"

Daniel spotted Rajish Patel coming out of the lift, looking for somewhere to sit. "Rajish!" he called, waving his arm at the diminutive systems analyst. "Come and sit with us!"

The man's round, dark-skinned face lit up with a smile and he walked over to them. "Daniel and Kelly! How very, very wonderful to see you again," he said in his thick Pakistani accent. "I hope you are both much recovered after your most disagreeable adventure. But please, call me Raj, as that is how my friends address me."

He sat between Kelly and Pixie, although 'sitting' in zero gravity involved strapping oneself into place. Introductions were made as he strapped himself in, following which, Pixie swamped him in an effusive rainbow embrace. Rajish surfaced again and seemed pleasantly bewildered by Pixie's vivacious welcome.

The group helped themselves to "mush" from the nearest automatic food console, which came packaged in zero-gravity squeeze pouches. Daniel and Kelly gradually got used to eating in zero gravity, swallowing carefully and allowing more time between swallows to allow their throats to work the food 'down' to their stomachs. It was a very strange feeling – like eating lunch while falling off a cliff – but they were both starving and had two helpings of packaged mush.

"What did you get?" Kelly asked Daniel.

"It's supposed to be curried chicken, but I can't taste the chicken and I can barely taste the curry."

"Welcome to cultured yeast cuisine," said Jordan. "My theory is that they just randomly make up names for this crap that have nothing to do with what's inside the packets. Someone, somewhere, is having a very big laugh at our expense."

"When we get to the new world, I am going to make a big pot

of Beef Vindaloo and invite you all over for dinner," said Raj. "That is provided you all like spicy food."

"You can't make it too spicy for me. I'm a very spicy girl," said Pixie winking at him, causing Raj to blush.

Kelly and Daniel exchanged a meaningful look and glanced back at Raj, who was beginning to resemble a fly caught in a spider's web.

20

———————

By 13:30, the lunch crowd began thinning out, as diners made a steady exit via the lifts.

"I suppose we'd better get back to our search," said Jordan, stretching in her chair.

"What are you looking for?" asked Raj.

"Bombs," Jordan said bluntly. "But don't worry. If we miss one, and it goes off, you won't feel a thing. You'll be vaporised in an instant."

"Why would anyone want to blow us up?" asked Pixie.

"The Republic is trying to stop us reaching the Tama system first," said Daniel.

"Do you think there could be agents for the Republic on board Longshot?" asked Raj, with concern showing on his face.

"I hope not. But there's a couple of people I'm watching very closely."

"Yeah, George Cullen being one of them," said Kelly, without thinking.

Daniel looked at her and frowned, shaking his head slightly.

"Anyway, we'd better get started again," Daniel said, quickly bringing that discussion to an end.

Jordan and Daniel took their leave from the group and

resumed their scanning of the ship, while Kelly, Raj and Pixie sat and enjoyed another cup of coffee. As the dining room was the next level they were scheduled to scan, Jordan began in the kitchen while Daniel began walking around the perimeter of the dining area. It took him a few moments to get used to walking in the magnetic boots again, but he soon got into his rhythm once more.

"Is this what you call, 'work'?" asked Kelly, as he came past their table after completing the first circuit. "It looks more like a Sunday stroll."

"It's extremely technical and specialised," explained Daniel in a supercilious tone. "Only the most highly-trained, talented people can do it."

"Really? One day I hope I can be as special as you."

Jordan joined him in the main dining room after finishing her scan of the kitchen and they soon completed their scan of the whole area. The rest of the afternoon was tedious and boring, but at least Daniel got to explore the main living areas of the ship in detail. At 15:30, Jordan and Daniel took a break and had some coffee back in the dining room on Level 71.

"I hear we're going to run out of coffee, eventually," said Daniel. "That was one of the things that we were due to get more of from the last supply shuttle."

"Yeah, bummer," said Jordan, sipping hers appreciatively. She was slouched in a dining chair with her feet on another chair opposite. "Enjoy it while it lasts, dude."

He took another satisfying sip of his own. "So, am I allowed to ask why you only have one name?"

She paused, as if considering whether he was worthy of access to that kind of private information. She must have decided that he was, because she answered, "I was found in an emergency escape pod, in orbit around the moon, when I was only a couple of weeks old. There had been a tragic accident involving a small space yacht that blew up. I was raised on the moon by the space corps, and they only gave me one name."

"You're kidding!"

She smiled. "Yes. I am, actually." She took another sip of coffee.

"Okay. I get the message. I'll butt out. It's none of my business."

"No offense," she said, "but I like to keep my private life, private."

"I get it. And I respect that." He raised his cup to her. "But just for the record, let me say that I'm glad I got paired with you. You might feel like you got a raw deal, with me being the newbie, but you're an incredibly competent person and anyone would be proud to have you as their buddy."

She raised her cup at him. "Thanks. Right back at you."

They drained their cups together and then walked to the lifts to finish their scans. They only had three levels to go: the colonists' quarters on Levels 65 and 64, and Hydroponics 1, on Level 63. It took another hour and a quarter to finish all three levels, and then Jordan called George Cullen on her wrist comm.

"We're all done here, boss. Finished down to Hydroponics 1 and scored a big fat donut."

"Okay. O'Neil and I just finished the 12 Levels below you. Same result. The other teams are finished too. They found nothing. You can call it a day."

"Roger. Out." She turned to Daniel. "We're done, dude. Let's get out of here."

Five minutes later, Daniel was back in the room he was sharing with Kelly, reporting on his boring afternoon.

"Hydroponics?" she said, her ears pricking up at the mention of the name. "I'd love to check that out. I'm probably going to be very involved with that side of things on the new world, given my area of expertise in microbiology." She smiled at him. "Care to take a girl for a walk in a garden?"

"How could I resist?" he said, even though all he felt like doing was resting.

They took the lift down to Hydroponics 2, as Daniel had not seen that level yet. As a biologist, Kelly was fascinated with the plants being grown and the technology employed in their nurture. They walked between rows of raised vegetable beds, with an intricate piping system delivering fresh water and nutrients and recycling waste back to the life support level.

"What's that alarm?" Kelly asked, suddenly.

"I don't know," said Daniel, who had heard it at the same time. "It sounds like it's coming from ...," and then he realised what it was. He had forgotten to turn his wrist scanner off. The scanner was flashing red and beeping stridently. It was picking up the presence of a nearby wasp.

There was a bomb somewhere in Hydroponics 2.

21

Daniel activated his wrist comm. "Jordan, do you copy?"

"Yeah. This better be good; I was just about to have a vacuum shower."

"Cancel the shower. Have you still got your scanner?"

"Yeah. I was going to hand it back when we go to tomorrow's meeting."

"I'm in Hydroponics 2. Grab your scanner and meet me here. And don't talk to anyone about this."

"This sounds suspiciously like an order."

"No. It's a request from a buddy."

She grunted. "Okay. I'll be there in a tick. But this better be worth it."

"Believe me, it will be."

"Is she coming?" asked Kelly, after the call ended.

"Yes." He bit his lip in thought. "I feel like I should send you somewhere safe, but if what Jordan told me earlier is correct, there's nowhere safe on the whole ship."

"And if I'm going to be blown to atoms, I may as well be with you when it happens," she said, bravely, reaching out and holding his hand.

Jordan arrived a few minutes later and she had already activated her scanner. Her alarm started going off when she was five metres from where Kelly and Daniel were standing.

"Crap!" she said.

"Exactly," agreed Daniel.

"Have you tried looking for it?"

"Yes, but no luck so far."

"We need to reduce the sensitivity on our scanners," she said, tapping on the tiny screen of her own.

"Reduce?" queried Kelly.

"Yeah. At the moment they're set at maximum sensitivity, so they will pick up a quantum antimatter containment field anywhere within ten metres. I'm dialling my sensitivity right down to its lowest setting, which should only pick something up within about one metre." Her alarm stopped sounding as she tapped. "There that's mine done. Show me yours," she said to Daniel. A few moments later, Daniel's scanner went silent too. "Okay, we know it's within 10 metres of where we are standing right now. Let's start moving around. It should be easy to locate now."

But it wasn't. After five minutes of moving around the small area they had mapped out, there were no alarms on their scanners."

"This doesn't make sense," said Jordan. We've covered every square centimetre of this area several times!"

"No, we haven't," said Daniel.

"Yes, we have!" said Jordan in exasperation.

"You're only thinking in two dimensions," continued Daniel. "Those pipes running along the ceiling are more than a metre from our wrists. We haven't tried this yet." He started walking over the same area with his arm raised above his head. Within a few seconds his alarm went off and the scanner started flashing red. He stood still and pointed upward. "It's up there in the pipes somewhere."

After another minute of them both stepping backward and forward, with arms raised above their heads they had pinpointed a small section of pipes where the wasp had to be.

"Is there a bomb disposal tech-guru-type of person we should be contacting?" asked Daniel.

"You're looking at her," responded Jordan. "I'm the security team's EDS."

"EDS?"

"Explosive Device Specialist. That's how I got to be a sergeant. I trained at the corps' ATC – Advanced Technical College – at Geneva. I have to do a two-week refresher course every 12 months to keep up to date. Not that I'll be doing any more refresher courses from now on."

"Wow," said Daniel, impressed.

"It's how I get away with so much," explained Jordan. "I'm sure Cullen would like to get off his team, but he can't, because he needs me."

She fetched a large plastic tub from near the doorway and placed it on the ground directly underneath the spot they had identified. She stood on the tub and took a pencil flash from her pocket, flicked it on and shone it along the top of several pipes.

"Bingo! It's attached to the top of this large irrigation pipe."

She took a device from her trouser pocket, about the size of her hand, turned it on and held it up to the device. A digital screen gave her a series of readings. "It's a Novikov Mark III. Very impressive!"

"Does that mean we would all be impressively dead?" asked Daniel.

"It would disassemble the entire starship down to its component molecules."

"I suppose that is impressive, when you think about it," admitted Daniel.

"The really impressive thing," said Jordan as she continued to run a series of scans, "is that it has a timer that can be programmed for up to 1,000 years. And the power supply, a nano diamond battery with a slow decaying isotope, could last ten times as long if needed."

"So, the big question is, when is this one timed to detonate?" asked Daniel.

"It's set to go boom in five years' time."

"When we're all asleep?" asked Kelly.

"Yep. Which is pretty smart, because five years into a seven-year trip will mean we are about 25 lightyears from Earth ..."

"26.4285 actually," said Daniel

Jordan gaped at him. "Holy crap! What are you, a math genius or something?"

"He's ... um ... good with numbers," explained Kelly.

"Anyway," continued Jordan, "by the time we've travelled there and the light from the explosion gets back to Earth, about 50 years will have passed back here ..."

"51 years, 8 months, 22 days."

Jordan just stared at him, then shook her head. "Anyway, as I was saying before Professor Digit here interrupted, after all that time it would just be assumed that we had hit something or had some kind of accident. There would be no question of sabotage and the Republic would have completely gotten away with it."

She tapped her screen and announced, "It's safe to move it. There's no tamper setting on these things." She grunted and they heard a scrape, then she stepped down, holding the device in her hand.

"It looks more like an oversized dragonfly than a wasp," said Daniel.

"So, what do we do now?" asked Kelly.

"I'd better call Cullen and ..." began Jordan

"NO!" yelled Daniel, more forcefully than he had intended. "Sorry," he said, when Jordan looked at him in surprise. "Didn't mean to yell."

"Why don't you want me to call Cullen?"

"Because he is supposed to have searched this area."

"So? He must have missed it."

"How?"

"How what?"

"How did he miss it? How could *anyone* miss it? Both our scanners started to alarm when we were ten metres away."

"Maybe his was faulty."

"How likely is that?"

"Not very," she conceded. "They're all checked before use."

"Then, I repeat my question; how did he miss it?"

"Maybe he and O'Neil missed searching this level entirely."

"Not likely," said Daniel, "but let's test that theory. Call O'Neil."

"And say what?"

"Don't tell him we've found something. Just say you weren't sure whether it was them or us who were meant to search this. Let him confirm whether they searched it."

She nodded. "Okay." She activated her comm. "O'Neil, do you copy? This is Jordan."

"Well, well. Jordan! I wondered when you'd get around to calling me. It was only a matter of time. You're only human, after all."

"Don't be such a tool, O'Neil! I need to ask you a work question. You remember 'work' don't you? It's that thing you have to do that constantly interrupts your gym sessions."

"You're hilarious, baby doll."

Jordan rolled her eyes at Kelly and Daniel and stuck her finger into her open mouth, imitating gagging. "Yeah, whatever. I'm just trying to work out whether I searched all the floors I was supposed to. Were Newman and I meant to search Hydroponics 2, or were you guys?"

"You need to listen more carefully at briefings, babe. That was our territory, not yours."

"So did you check it?"

"No. Not me. The boss did that one. We split up and did every second floor each."

"Are you sure he did it?"

"Why have you got such a bee up your arse about this? Of course, I'm sure! That was the first level he searched."

"Okay. Just thought I'd check. Thanks. Out."

The three of them stood in silence for a few moments, considering the implications. Daniel spelled it out for them.

"So, Cullen makes sure he searches this level, and not O'Neil.

And then he claims there's nothing here, when there clearly is. Doesn't look good, does it?"

"You think he's an agent for the Republic?" asked Jordan. She shook her head. "I know he's a cranky old bastard, but a traitor? I don't see it. Plus, he'd have to be willing to die for the cause, because no one on this ship would survive if that thing went off."

"That's the thing about fanatics," answered Daniel. "They usually *are* willing to die for their cause."

"Even if Cullen *is* working for the Republic, why don't you want him to know we've found the wasp?" asked Kelly.

"Because if he knows the wasp has been located and is no longer going to blow us all to kingdom come, he might decide to undertake some other act of sabotage. I think Cullen should be kept in the dark, so he continues to think that his work here is done."

"So, what do you suggest we do, Professor?" asked Jordan.

"We need to talk to the captain."

22

Captain Nash Anderson met them in Hydroponics 2, and Daniel explained how they had located the wasp – the explosive device that had gained access to their vessel during the failed take-over attempt.

"And you're certain that Mr Cullen searched this level?" Anderson asked.

"Yes, we are sir," answered Jordan. "His partner confirmed it."

"I see." Anderson stroked his beard thoughtfully. "I agree that we shouldn't tell him that we've found it. We need to operate under the assumption that he deliberately left it concealed."

"We also need to check all the other levels that Cullen searched," added Daniel, "just in case there are any more he conveniently overlooked."

"I agree," said Anderson. "But it also raises the question of whether there might be any other traitors on the security team. Many of them were hand-picked by Cullen over the last couple of years. How can we be sure there are no other devices that have been deliberately overlooked on the other levels?"

They were all silent as they considered this. Anderson looked at Kelly, Daniel and Jordan sympathetically. "I'm sorry to have to ask you to do this, but I want the three of you to search all the other levels a second time. Because, as of now, you are the only people I can be sure aren't working for the Republic."

"Daniel and I have searched the top 12. There are 62 levels to go," said Jordan, raising her eyebrows.

"I realise it's a huge task," admitted Anderson, "but it has to be done. On the positive side, if the planned explosion is timed for 5 years away, we aren't in any immediate danger. But it would be good to know where we stand, as soon as possible. How soon do you think you can get it done?"

Jordan blew her cheeks out as she exhaled. "Roughly 20 levels each, 15 minutes per level, about 10 hours. We could make a start now and knock over a few levels before dinner. Maybe a few after dinner. We could probably have it finished by the end of the day tomorrow."

Anderson nodded. "Do it."

~

The next 24 hours were a dull grind: hours of trudging in circles, on deck after deck. As the security team's EDS – Explosive Device Specialist – Jordan had the responsibility of keeping and maintaining the wrist scanners, so she had no trouble getting one for Kelly. She was also able to check all the returned scanners and ascertain that none were faulty, which added extra weight to Cullen's apparent guilt.

Kelly had been quickly instructed in the use of the scanners, and the remaining decks were then divided between them. Daniel started descending from Hydroponics 2, Jordan began working her way up from the bottom, and Kelly was given the middle third. To explain their absence from the following day's security team meeting, Captain Anderson told George Cullen that he had seconded Jordan and Daniel to spend a day helping him to do mundane updating of the ship's logs. It wasn't a particularly convincing story, but it was all he could think of.

The three of them managed to complete 12 more levels on the first day, before going to bed tired and dreaming of walking in circles. The next morning after breakfast, they continued their mind-dulling task. Jordan had secured their wrist comms so that they had a secure, three-way connection that no one could listen in to. But just to be extra cautious, they concocted a cryptic way of communicating their progress to each other. If anyone had managed to hack into their comms, they would have heard a bizarre series of communications.

"I've got 64 chooks in my henhouse," said Daniel, as he finished checking Level 64.

"You must eat a lot of eggs," said Kelly. "Maybe that's why you're so incredibly ripped."

"I've been married seven times and they were all failures." Jordan, as she left Level 7 to commence searching Level 8.

"No surprises there," said Daniel, "considering who the common denominator is."

"Hey! Keep it civil, Professor. I'll have you know, I'm a good catch."

"That's if you'll ever let anyone catch you."

"My grandmother had 39 pimples on her nose," offered Kelly, a short time later.

"She must have had a huge nose," replied Jordan.

"Are you sure they weren't warts?" asked Daniel.

A few minutes later, he announced, "I once saw 63 angels dancing on the head of a pin."

"Yeah," agreed Jordan. "I've had hallucinations from eating bad mushrooms, too."

And so it went on.

It was close to 15:00, mid-afternoon, when there was a dramatic development.

"I once ate 20 walruses," announced Jordan, "and I need you both to eat 20 walruses too."

"You want us to eat 20 walruses right now?" asked Daniel.

"Immediately," confirmed Jordan.

A few minutes later, they arrived at Level 20, which was Storage Bay 20. Jordan met them at the lift and led them through the labyrinth of stored farm machinery until they reached what looked like a harvester. As they drew near, all three of their wrist scanners started alarming.

"It's under the chassis somewhere, but I need someone to hold a light for me."

Daniel grabbed a pencil flash and he and Jordan lay on their backs underneath the tractor, awkwardly fighting against the zero gravity now that the soles of their magnetic boots weren't in contact with the floor. It didn't take long to find the wasp and Jordan carried out the same scans as she had done with the first one. A few minutes later, she announced, "Same model and same timer settings. Five years until detonation."

She pulled it out and they both emerged from under the tractor. Daniel had managed to get a smear of grease across his forehead when he banged his head as he slid out. He stood wincing and rubbing his head.

Kelly stared at the device and asked, "Why two, when one would do the job?"

"Redundancy, I guess," said Jordan. "In case one failed or was accidently discovered."

"Who searched this level?" asked Daniel as he tried to wipe the grease off.

"Ortega and Ballard," answered Jordan.

"Are you sure?" asked Daniel.

"Yes, Professor. Unlike you, I was actually listening during yesterday's briefing."

"Okay. I wonder which one searched Level 20?"

"One way to find out." She fiddled with her wrist comm for a moment, allowing it to access the ship's comm network. "Ortega, do you copy?"

"Yeah, I copy you, Jordan. What's up?" responded a female voice.

"I'm just typing up a report from yesterday's search. What levels did you and Ballard do?"

"Um, let me think. We started at Level 14 and went up to 26."

"Cool. And just to be clear in my report, did you work together or do alternate levels?"

"I did the evens and he did the odds."

"And you didn't find anything?"

"Zip. Waste of time."

"Okay. Thanks. Out."

"So, Ortega is in on it too?" asked Kelly.

"No way! No flipping way!" exclaimed Jordan. "I know her better than anyone on the team, and I would trust her with my life. There is absolutely no chance she is an agent for the Republic."

"The thing about deep cover agents," said Daniel, tactfully, "is that they are often the least likely people you would expect. That's why they're so effective."

"I'm telling you, there is no frigging way she's a traitor! She was one of the ones who fought off the attackers, and she killed one of them."

They were silent for a few moments as they pondered the situation.

"Of course, there is an alternative explanation," offered Daniel.

"Go on, I'm listening," said Jordan.

"Yesterday, when you were explaining how the wasps worked, you said, and I quote, 'once a wasp is activated, the atomic clock inside it starts pulsing, once every second, and these scanners detect those pulses'."

"You remember what I said, word for word?"

Daniel shrugged.

"He has an exceptional memory," said Kelly.

"Anyway," continued Daniel, keen to get to the point, "am I right in assuming that until the wasps are activated, our scanners can't detect them?"

"Yes. But they would have been activated in order to fly through the ship and attach themselves somewhere."

"Is that strictly true?" asked Daniel. "You said it was the pulse from the atomic clocks that our scanners detect. And that only starts once the timers are activated. Is it possible for the wasps to be deployed, but the timers activated later? Perhaps remotely?"

She thought about it. "Yes. I hadn't thought of that."

"In which case," continued Daniel, "an agent on board the

ship, who anticipated that a search would be made for wasps, could wait until he or she was sure the search had been made, and then activate the timers remotely."

"But the timing was pretty tight, yesterday, if you remember," responded Jordan. "We'd only just finished our search when you and Kelly returned to Hydroponics 2."

"It was probably a gap of about 15 minutes by the time we got back there," Daniel conceded. "But remember, we were the last team to finish. The entire search was complete by then."

"So, it would need to be someone who knew that the search was complete," said Kelly. "Once again, it points to George, who was coordinating the whole thing."

"Or someone else who was listening in to our comms," suggested Jordan.

"How many crew members would be able to do that?" asked Daniel.

"Dozens. We were broadcasting on an open frequency."

"What about when I called you after Kelly and I found the first wasp?" asked Daniel.

"No one could have heard that, because you automatically created a private channel when you used my name first."

"So, whoever is behind this still doesn't know we've found any of the wasps?" asked Kelly.

"Yeah, I think that's right," said Jordan.

"Damn!" said Daniel, a moment later.

"What?" asked Kelly and Jordan in unison.

"If this theory is correct, and someone activated the wasps after we finished our whole search ..." He let the sentence hang in the air, while they thought it through.

"Bugger!" said Jordan, when she finally worked it out. "We're gonna have to search our initial levels again."

"Yep."

"Bugger!" added Jordan, just for good measure.

23

They finished their search two hours after dinner that night and, worryingly, they discovered a third explosive device on Level 73, the second level that Daniel and Jordan had searched the previous day. The wasp was in one of the science labs, tucked away underneath a workbench. Finally, after a long and draining day, they reported their findings to the captain in his day cabin in the command centre. The three wasps were sitting on his desk, or at least floating just above it, and they were now all staring at them.

"They're still activated?" asked Nash Anderson.

"Yes, sir," answered Jordan. "My concern is that deactivating them may trigger an alert to an onboard agent."

Anderson nodded. "Quite right." He stroked his pure white beard as he considered his options. "The safest thing might be to space them," he suggested.

"Maybe not, sir," contradicted Jordan. "Jettisoning them might trigger a proximity alert – or whatever the opposite is – telling the agent that we've ditched them. Then he or she could be motivated to try some form of alternate onboard sabotage. It would be best to leave the agent ignorant of our findings for as long as possible."

"I agree," said Daniel. "Perhaps they could be ditched after the majority of the passengers and the crew are in cryogenic stasis. I assume that you will be one of the last to go to sleep, sir?"

"Yes," Anderson agreed. "I could see to that, myself. That sounds like a sensible plan." He leant back in his chair and drummed his fingers on the desk. "But in the meantime, I want this traitor found!"

"The most obvious suspect is Cullen," said Daniel. "He coordinated the search, so he knew exactly when the search was complete. The timing of the activation within a few minutes of the search's completion is pretty damming. Plus, as we've already discovered, he was absent during both previous attacks on Longshot Base; as if he knew when to avoid being there."

"But then, so was Commander Decker," added Anderson. "They were both off-base during the previous attacks."

"Captain, can I ask where Commander Decker was yesterday, between," Daniel paused to calculate, "16:15 and 16:45? That's when the wasps must have been activated."

"Commander Decker was off-duty all afternoon, as he'd been on deck until very late the previous evening."

"So, the traitor could be our XO," said Jordan.

"It could be almost anyone," admitted Daniel. "And I don't like our chances of successfully uncovering the culprit. Whoever it is, probably thinks that the job is now done and has gone inactive. He or she is probably prepared to simply go to sleep and die for the cause."

"Remind me what that cause is, again?" asked Kelly.

"To destroy our mission so that the Republic can get to Tama-B first and claim it as their own," said the captain.

"Ridiculous!" muttered Kelly. "Petty, nationalistic parochialism that is now even extending out into the galaxy! Is there any hope for humanity?"

"Sometimes, I wonder that, too, Dr Rearson," responded Anderson.

"I think we have to assume that the agent has almost certainly gone to ground," said Daniel. "Clearly, the Republic wants our mission to be destroyed in another 25 Earth-years, not right now.

The next danger time for us will, therefore, be when we come out of hibernation, and we arrive at Tama-B. The traitor will realise that something went wrong, and he or she may well try some last-ditch attempt to destroy us."

"Yes," agreed Anderson. "We'll have to be on our guard again, at that point. In the meantime, we have a more pressing threat to attend to. We are coming up on Venus. At 23:00 tonight, we will enter Venus orbit and fire our main drive for our slingshot manoeuvre." He glanced at the time on his desk screen. "That's in just over two hours from now. Let's hope we meet no resistance, and that the Republic's orbiting space station has no weapons."

"Do we have any further intel on that, sir?" asked Daniel.

"None. We are flying blind here. Earth is still completely blacked out, and we have no way of finding out anything about the Republic's presence on Venus. It could end up being a routine manoeuvre. Or we could be flying into a deadly encounter. We simply have no way of knowing in advance."

He stood and dismissed them. "I suggest you all get some rest while you can. And, if you are a person of faith, a prayer or two wouldn't go astray, either."

24

Daniel and Kelly woke to the sound of a strident alarm. They had strapped themselves into separate beds and had fallen asleep almost immediately upon their return from speaking with the captain. A day of searching the starship from top to bottom had exhausted both of them. Daniel had dreamed about the three explosive devices they had found. In his dream they had become airborne again and had flown throughout the ship stinging the crew with their vicious tails and injecting eggs into them. The eggs began to hatch, and thousands of dragonflies had burst from people's bodies, filling the air with the sound of their wings as people lay writhing on the ground.

As the sound of the ship's alarm finally broke through the fog of Daniel's dream, he opened his eyes and, for a few confusing moments, began checking his skin for dragonfly eggs.

"Daniel, are you awake?" asked Kelly from the bunk below, as she swung her feet out of bed.

"Uh huh," he replied, rubbing his eyes and groaning. He checked the time. 2240. They must be approaching Venus orbit insertion. He unstrapped himself from the bed and awkwardly propelled himself to the floor where he had left his magnetic boots. As they both put their boots on, the alarm ceased and the captain's calm voice came over the ship's comm.

"This is Captain Nash Anderson. We are approaching Venus and, in about 20 minutes, we will initiate a 2G burn of our main drive to slingshot us around the planet and set us on course for our final destination: Tama-B. While the slingshot manoeuvre, in itself, is a simple and straightforward manoeuvre, there are also unknown factors that may be involved. We are now at war with the Republic, and we have no way of knowing whether there are Republican forces in orbit around Venus. We are aware of a Republican research station orbiting the planet, but we don't know whether it has weapons. There is the slight possibility that there could be a military vessel stationed in orbit, but we simply do not know. Consequently, given the chance that we may need to take evasive action, I am ordering all colonists to their rooms where you are to strap yourselves into your beds. All crew are to go to general quarters. I wish us all Godspeed, and hope and pray that we might soon be safely on our way to our new home. That is all."

"So, where do we go?" asked Kelly.

"I don't know," responded Daniel. "We haven't exactly been briefed on all the finer details like that."

As he spoke, Daniel's wrist comm chimed. "Mr Newman, do you copy?" It was Captain Anderson's voice.

"Yes, sir."

"I'd like you in the command centre, please. You've proven to be very insightful, and I'd appreciate another perspective if we have to make some quick decisions."

"Sure thing, Captain. I'll be right up. What about Kelly ... I mean, Dr Rearson?"

"Please tell her to strap herself in and stay there."

"Yes sir. Will do." The comm went dead.

"Did you hear that?" he asked.

"Yes." She was standing beside her bed, her feet firmly strapped into magnetic boots. She looked at him with concern on her face. "Are we going to be okay?"

He thought about how to answer her. "I really don't know." He moved closer and wrapped his arms around her. "It hasn't exactly turned out to be the pleasure cruise we'd hoped for, has it?"

She shook her head, and Daniel thought he saw her eyes looking moist with unshed tears. She placed her head against his chest and said nothing. He remembered her previously stated fear of space and her initial reluctance to consider coming on the mission. She had only come in order to be with him, and now their future was looking uncertain again.

"I'm ... sorry," he said, lamely. "I've got you into a real mess here, haven't I?"

She pulled back from him and gave him a severe look. "That's not true. I came on this mission because I wanted to. And if I was back on Earth now, I could well be a pile of cinders after the nuclear exchange they've just had. Or else, I could be slowly dying of radiation poisoning over the next six months." She reached out her hand and touched his face. "No, Daniel Newman. I'm right where I want to be."

He leant down and they kissed, tenderly.

"Now go and put that super brain of yours to work!" she said. "And if we make it through this night, you owe me a romantic evening – the last two haven't rated very highly."

He smiled. "Yes, ma'am."

A few minutes later, Daniel walked out of the lift into the command centre. He had barely set foot in the room, however, when the executive officer, Commander Decker, spotted him and demanded, "What the hell are you doing here, Newman?"

Before Daniel could answer, the captain turned in his chair and addressed Decker sternly.

"He's here at my invitation, Commander! And I'll remind you that this is my bridge, not yours."

Decker looked thunderous, and Daniel wondered if Captain Anderson might have overdone it a little by reprimanding him in public. It certainly wasn't going to help Daniel's relationship with the XO, as Decker would probably resent him even more now.

"Yes, sir," said Decker. His face hardened and he stepped down from the raised platform and went to speak with someone at a console on the floor of the control room.

The main screen on the far wall showed an enlarged view of Venus, and it was spectacular. Daniel had researched Venus earlier, prior to breakfast, calling up images and information from the ship's data bank on the screen in the room he shared with Kelly. But now he was staring at the planet in real time, as it grew in front of their approaching starship.

The entire planet was shrouded in a white cloud layer of carbon dioxide and sulphuric acid. Despite this, an orange glow filtered through from the surface where the average temperature was 464 degrees Celsius or 867 degrees Fahrenheit, which was hot enough to melt lead.

"Spectacular, isn't it?" said Mission Specialist Olivia Alvarez, who had come to stand beside him.

"Your arm is out of a sling," he commented.

"Yes. I'm recovering very well after the hijacking of the shuttle a few days ago. I've been meaning to catch up with you and thank you again. Your quick thinking saved the life of everyone on board. We would have suffocated had you not sealed the leak."

"I'm sure you would have worked out a similar solution if you hadn't been incapacitated," he replied.

"I think not. I think you are quite remarkable, and the captain is right to have you here on the bridge at a time like this."

"Thank you."

"Captain!" called a woman at the nearest console, at the bottom of the two steps immediately in front of the captain's chair. "I've pinpointed Altair Station. It's in a low equatorial orbit. By the time we begin our manoeuvre it will be on the other side of the planet."

"Any sign that they have picked us up on their scanners?"

"No, sir."

"Very good," responded Anderson.

Decker had heard the exchange and drew near again.

"Captain, should we open communication and assure them of our peaceful intentions?"

"I think not, Commander. I don't want to draw attention to our ship until we have to."

Another console operator called out, "Captain, 30 seconds to insertion burn."

"Very good. Comm officer, give the call."

A chime sounded and the comm officer's voice sounded throughout the ship. "All hands, make ready for main engine burn. Main engine burn in 15 seconds. Brace for acceleration."

"You might want to hold onto the handrail," Anderson suggested to Daniel and Lieutenant Alvarez, who were standing nearby.

A timer on the screen counted down and when it reached zero Daniel felt the floor heave up underneath him. If he hadn't been holding the handrail, his legs would have given way. As it was, his knees buckled before he strained to straighten his legs again.

"Acceleration of 2Gs is challenging when you're standing," said Alvarez, grimacing beside him. "It's like a gym workout."

An alarm sounded, and someone at another console called out, "Captain! Contact directly behind us! 20,000 kilometres and closing fast!"

"On screen!" Anderson said.

A vague blip appeared in the middle of a black screen.

"Can you enhance?"

"That's maximum enhancement already, sir."

"Identification?"

"Sir, my scans are showing an engine signature that can only correspond to a Republican dreadnaught. I'm running it through our data base now. Yes, here it is." The man paused, then swung around in his chair and faced the captain with a look of deep concern. "It's the Hand of God, sir."

"Damn it!" exclaimed Anderson so loudly that everyone around him paused in shocked silence for a moment. Then Daniel, who was standing next to the captain, heard him say under his breath, "I think we're in trouble."

25

The image of the pursuing Republican Dreadnaught was growing fractionally clearer on the screen.

"It's definitely the Hand of God, sir," confirmed the console operator. "Its trajectory indicates it has come directly from Earth."

"Hubble warned us it was plotting an intercept course," Decker reminded the captain.

"Yes! I know that. You don't need you to remind me, Commander Decker. LACIE!"

"Yes, captain?" responded the pleasant female voice.

Daniel had forgotten about the onboard AI – the Longshot Artificial Computer Intelligence Entity.

"All relevant telemetry data for both vessels on the main screen, now!"

The data appeared almost instantly.

"Analysis!" he snapped.

"The pursuing vessel will close to within lethal distance in exactly eleven minutes and six seconds."

"Lethal distance?" Daniel whispered to Alvarez.

"Within 2,000 kilometres, which is the killing zone for their laser canons."

"How long until our slingshot manoeuvre takes us around Venus and out of their line of fire?" asked the captain.

"Fifteen minutes 20 seconds," responded LACIE.

"Damn it!" said Anderson, again.

"Shouldn't we increase our acceleration, captain?" asked Decker.

"No. Any more acceleration and we'll shoot straight by Venus and miss our slingshot."

"But we're sitting ducks like this! We've got limited shields and no weapons!"

"That's not true!" said Daniel.

"You stay out of this!" shouted Decker, spittle flying from his mouth.

"Let him speak!" said Anderson. "Explain please, Mr Newman."

"We have weapons, sir. The three items we salvaged today."

"What's he talking about?" asked Decker.

Captain Anderson held up his hand to silence Decker and didn't even bother to reply to him.

"What do you have in mind, Mr Newman? Make it quick!"

Daniel took a deep breath. "Cancel our acceleration immediately. Set the timers on the devices to correspond with the anticipated time of intercept by the enemy, then jettison them. Then immediately resume acceleration at an increased rate to compensate for our downtime."

"That's ... that's ridiculous!" interjected Decker. "Assuming you are talking about some kind of explosive device, the time of those charges would have to be accurate down to the half-second."

Daniel was staring at the screen as he spoke, his voice almost in a trance-like monotone. "I can do it. I am doing it. As soon as we cancel acceleration, I can calculate the necessary time, to 12 decimal places if we need it."

"This is preposterous! This is ..."

"Commander Decker! Shut the hell up!"

There was shocked silence across the Control Centre.

"LACIE! Assessment?"

"Mr Newman's plan has merit, but I can only guarantee a time accuracy to within two seconds."

"I can do better," said Daniel, still staring at the screen. "Just cancel it, Captain, and I can lock in the calculations. Trust me, sir."

There was silence across the room.

"Cancel acceleration!" called the captain.

"Main drives off," confirmed a console operator, and they were all instantly plunged into weightlessness again.

"This is madness!" exclaimed Decker.

"Commander Decker, you are relieved of duty. Please confine yourself to quarters."

Decker looked as if he was going to explode. He stood with fists clenched for several seconds, staring at the captain with a face like thunder, then turned and stormed out of the bridge.

"Seven minutes 52 seconds from now!" exclaimed Daniel as he set a countdown timer going on his wrist communicator and moved as quickly as he could toward Anderson's cabin. "Where are they, sir?"

"Top drawer." The Captain rose from his chair and stood frozen, staring toward his cabin, as if he couldn't believe the risk he had just taken.

A moment later Daniel emerged and bolted for the lifts, calling on his comm, "Jordan! Do you copy?"

"Copy"

"Meet me at the emergency airlock in Shuttle Bay 1! ASAP. And bring your wasp scanner. You need to set the timers! And that is definitely an order this time!"

"Roger. Out."

As Daniel jumped into the lift and the doors began to close, he called out, "Captain, patch the telemetry data through to the data screen outside the airlock!"

The doors closed, and he was gone, leaving a Control Centre filled with people who were looking at the captain as if he had lost his marbles.

And the captain was staring back at them, wondering if they were right.

26

Daniel burst out of the lift on Level 54 and staggered toward the airlock against the far wall, struggling awkwardly in the weightlessness with his magnetic boots. Another lift opened behind him, and he heard footsteps quickly overtaking him. Jordan came alongside and grabbed his arm, propelling him forward a little faster.

"I'm assuming this is an emergency and we're all gonna die if this doesn't work?" she asked.

"Pretty much," he said, breathing fast.

They reached the airlock door and Daniel gave the first wasp to Jordan while he stared at the telemetry screen on the wall beside the airlock door. Various numbers were changing all the time, indicating the rapidly diminishing distance between Longshot and the closing enemy vessel.

"Tell me when you're ready to set the timer!" he said to Jordan, while continuing to stare at the telemetry screen.

"Just a sec," she said, tapping on the scanner that she held to the side of the wasp. "Okay, anytime now."

"Enter 5 minutes 44 seconds and wait for my mark to set it running."

"Done and waiting," she replied.

"On my mark ... NOW!"

He handed her the second wasp. "Get it ready."

She held her scanning device to its side and tapped the screen.

"Ready when you are," she said.

"Enter 5 minutes 12 seconds and wait for my mark."

"Done and waiting."

"On my mark ... NOW!"

They repeated the process with the third wasp. When they were finished, Daniel grabbed all three and placed them into a basket at the end of a robot arm inside the airlock, then sealed the door.

"Emergency purge!" he said, and Jordan activated it. Within a few seconds the light inside changed color, indicating a vacuum. "Open the door and gently toss them out with the arm!"

A few moments later they were floating freely in space, gradually distancing themselves from the starship.

"Captain, do you copy?" Daniel called on his wrist comm.

"Go ahead."

"It's done, sir!" He looked at the telemetry data and noted their current approach velocity to Venus, which he remembered had a gravitational mass of 0.815 of Earth. He noted the angle of approach indicated on the telemetry screen and factored in the mass of their ship, which he had previously read and noted. He had also committed to memory the necessary escape velocity for their Tama trajectory.

He quickly calculated the necessary burn, and said to the captain, "Initiate a burn of 3.4G immediately!"

There was no response from the comm, and Daniel wondered if something had gone wrong, then he was crushed to the floor as the main drive kicked in.

"You really love these high Gs don't you, Professor?" asked Jordan who was now on her hands and knees beside him.

He grunted and began crawling toward the lift. "Got to get back to the command centre."

"I'm coming too," said Jordan. "I don't want to miss any more action."

Daniel felt like he was crawling through treacle with a load of bricks strapped to his back, and he wondered how the diminutive woman beside him seemed to make it look so effortless. They eventually made it back to the lifts and collapsed into one. He selected Level 74 and lay there, panting as the lift door closed. The lift started rising rapidly, and the added G-force pushed Daniel to his absolute limit.

"Out of curiosity, what's the detonation range of wasps in space?" he groaned.

"You mean it's lethal range? One wasp with that amount of antimatter will atomise anything within a kilometre radius. Anything within three kilometres will be ripped to shreds. With three wasps, you can triple that."

"That should be good enough," he said.

"I bloody well hope so, after going through all that!" she replied.

Daniel breathed a sigh of relief as the lift's rate of ascent eased off and it finally came to a stop. The door opened and he crawled out onto the bridge. He saw the captain slumped in his chair and the people at their consoles also struggling under the heavy acceleration.

During the ascent in the lift, Daniel had estimated the rate of planetward drift of the jettisoned wasps and realised that a subtle course correction was in order, to ensure that the enemy craft was drawn directly into the explosive devices.

"Captain!" he called. "A minor course variation to compensate for lateral wasp drift. Three degrees to port – or planetside, or whatever you call it." He didn't really know what terminology they used for that kind of thing, but hoped they understood what he meant.

"Make it so, ensign," said the captain, his voice straining under the weight of acceleration.

"Aye, skipper."

There was a subtle sideways shift in their centre of gravity and Daniel sensed that the change had been made. A moment later, there was a shudder and a console operator called out,

"We're taking laser fire, Captain! Direct hit on our deflector dish."

There was another shudder, then another.

"The shield is holding, sir, but it's going to be a close thing."

Daniel was on his hands and knees, staring ahead at the main screen which showed the telemetry of the two ships. It was showing 1 minute 42 seconds until lethal range of 2,000 kilometres was reached. He looked at the countdown timer on his wrist comm. 58 seconds until detonation.

More shudders were felt, and they became a steady rhythmic bombardment. As each blast hit them, they seemed progressively stronger and shook the ship more violently.

"Deflector shield still absorbing the blasts, Captain, but it can't hold much longer sir."

Another blast hit them, more violent than anything before, and Daniel was knocked violently to the side. He propped himself up again and glanced at the telemetry screen. 49 seconds to lethal range. 48. 47. He looked at his countdown timer. 3 seconds to detonation. 2 seconds. 1 second. Zero.

Nothing happened.

Then something very big happened.

A blinding flash of light appeared on the screen showing the view of the approaching enemy vessel. The light was so intense that it momentarily overwhelmed even the screen's auto dampeners and it went completely white for a few seconds. When the screen came back online a few moments later, the enemy vessel was gone and all that was visible was an incandescent ball of light filled with millions of glittering sparkles spreading outward.

There was stunned silence in the Command Centre for a few moments and then spontaneous cheers and applause broke out. As the noise died down, the captain called out. "Scans?"

"Scans no longer detect another vessel, sir."

"What's our status?"

"It's hard to tell without a visual inspection, captain," said another voice. "But there are no alarms, and all systems appear to be optimal."

"Very good." He looked up into the air. "LACIE?"

"Yes, captain?"

"Time to burn shut down?"

"Our slingshot manoeuvre requires main drive shut down in 2 minutes 11 seconds."

"Make it so." He slumped further down into his chair and turned his head toward Daniel who had discovered that lying flat on his back on the floor was the most comfortable way to handle 3.4G acceleration.

"Very nice job, Mr Newman. I'd like to chat with you later about how you did that."

"Yes, Captain." Daniel closed his eyes and lay there, riding out the last minutes of gruelling acceleration. As he did so, he felt a tap on his arm and turned to see Jordan lying beside him and looking at him.

"I actually have two names, not one," she said.

He merely nodded, not wanting to break the spell.

"My name is Jordan Jordan. My mother was a drug-hazed moron who thought that giving me a first name the same as my surname would be fun." She continued looking at Daniel, gauging his response. "I just wanted you to know."

"Thanks."

27

The main drives shut off, and everyone breathed a sigh of relief. Acceleration of the equivalent of 3.4 times Earth's gravity had been gruelling, and the instantaneous shift to weightlessness again was sheer bliss.

"Are you okay?" asked Jordan who had pivoted in the air with the help of a handrail and had reconnected her magnetic boots to the floor.

"I'm getting there," replied Daniel, with his eyes still closed. "I'm just going to float here for a bit longer." He was now floating a few centimetres off the floor, directly above where he had been lying during the final minutes of acceleration. "I don't know how you can bounce back so quickly," he added. "I feel like I've been run over by a truck."

"Now that you mention it," she said, "I've seen roadkill that looks in better shape than you."

Daniel merely groaned and kept his eyes closed.

"Trajectory check!" ordered Captain Anderson.

"Just checking now, captain," said a nearby ensign. There was a pause while she examined the data now streaming across her console. "We're threading the needle for Tama, sir!" she said, enthusiastically.

"LACIE, confirm trajectory, please."

The disembodied voice answered almost immediately. "Current trajectory is within 0.02% of desired trajectory, Captain. A minor correction can easily be made when we commence the main drive burn."

"Very good. Make it so. Scans? Anything else within range?

"No, sir. Nothing on our scopes at all. Altair Station is on the far side of Venus, and we'll be completely out of range of any weapons it might have by the time it's around this side again. We're completely in the clear, Captain."

Anderson nodded and grunted. "Rear view cameras on the main screen, please."

"Aye, sir," responded a male voice. A huge image of a segment of Venus appeared on the right of the screen. Longshot's final slingshot manoeuvre had taken them extremely close to the planet's mesosphere, one of the outer layers of Venus's atmosphere and, at first glance, the image on the screen suggested that they were now in low orbit. But almost imperceptibly, the image began to change, and Venus could be seen receding.

"Take a good look, people," said Anderson. "It's the last we will ever see of any of the planets in our solar system."

All around the Command Centre, people stopped what they were doing and looked up from their consoles at the spectacular image.

"Patch that view through to every screen in the ship, please, and give me a ship-wide channel on the comm."

A chime sounded, and the comm officer nodded to the captain.

The captain took a moment to compose his thoughts, then began. "This is Captain Nash Anderson. I trust you haven't had too hard a time of it, over these last minutes. If there are any injuries, please either report to the medical centre or contact them via your room comm. As you may have guessed, we came under attack from a Republican military vessel. But thanks to the exemplary efforts of several members of our crew, that ship has now been destroyed and we are no longer in any danger. Furthermore, our slingshot manoeuvre around Venus has been successful and we are on a direct course for Tama-B, our new home."

"While our main drive is off, I will be sending a shuttle to inspect the outside of Longshot, to ensure that there is no damage. Once that process is complete, we will be firing up the main drive once more for our long burn to the new planet. For the remainder of our journey, including when we are in stasis, we will be accelerating at a constant 1G, which means that we will have normal gravity throughout the entire ship. In the meantime, I hope you can bear with weightlessness for a short while longer. If our visual inspection of the outside of the ship doesn't reveal any serious damage, we will begin our main engine burn at some point during the night, which means you may well wake up to normal gravity. I suggest you secure all items in preparation for this."

"On the viewing screens around the ship, you will notice the live image of Venus, taken from our rear cameras. We will not be encountering any other planets from our solar system, so this is the last view we will get of our home system. I am sure many of you have fears and concerns for your families and friends left on Earth. I share your concern and your grief. Unfortunately, we can do nothing for them, and Earth remains out of contact."

"We must look to the future, now. By God's grace, we have survived a dangerous and challenging few days, and we now set course for a new world where we can start again. I encourage you to look back with fondness at the view on your screen, but also look ahead with hope and optimism. That is all for now."

Anderson swivelled in his chair and addressed Jordan. "Sergeant Jordan, I hesitate to ask, since you have just been through an ordeal yourself, but are you up to doing a recon shuttle flight around the ship? I'm keen for us to fire up the main drive and put as much distance between us and Earth as soon as possible."

"Sure thing, Captain. I'll get right on it." She turned and left the bridge.

The captain looked at Daniel who was now awkwardly pivoting himself into an upright position, connecting his magnetic boots to the floor. "How are you doing, Mr Newman?"

"I'm getting there, Captain. I feel like I could sleep for a week."

"Why don't you go back to your cabin and do just that? It's the middle of the night and I don't think there's anything more you can do here. I'll call you if I need your assistance. Speaking of which, I want to meet with you after breakfast. I think an explanation of your ... abilities is in order."

"Yes. I owe you that."

"Meet me in my day cabin around 09:00. I'll be here for the rest of the night, I suspect."

Daniel nodded. "Yes, sir."

A few minutes later, Daniel walked into their cabin and Kelly flew into his arms.

"What happened up there? Are you okay?"

"Yes, I'm fine. We had a slight disagreement with a Republican military ship."

"Slight? It felt like World War Three!"

"Actually, it is World War Three. Remember?"

She nodded and kissed him, hungrily. When she came up for air, she said, "You didn't crash the ship this time."

He grinned. "No. I'm getting better, aren't I? Although I did completely destroy the other ship, so I guess that's still a black mark in my book."

"I'm willing to overlook that. Let's just call that 'unavoidable collateral damage'. Only half a point deduction for that."

"That's very generous of you. I thought you were a hard marker."

"Oh, I am!" She wrapped her arms around his neck and drew him toward the bed. "And I'm expecting an extremely good performance from you now."

"I'll do my best, ma'am."

28

The breakfast notification chimed softly throughout the ship, and Daniel gradually came awake. Something was different, and his sleep fuddled brain couldn't initially identify it. Then it dawned on him; normal gravity had been restored. The ship must have commenced the main engine burn sometime through the night. He slipped out of his top bunk and landed with a thud that jarred him.

"Ouch. Now I've got to get used to gravity again."

Kelly, still lying in the bottom bunk, kept her eyes closed and her face buried in the pillow, and murmured, "Please keep the noise down. Some of us are still trying to get our beauty sleep."

Daniel leant down and kissed her on the cheek. "If you were any more beautiful, it would be unfair to all the other women in the universe."

"Aww, you're just saying that 'cause it's true."

"Not really. I'm actually just saying it to butter you up for more sex."

She propped herself up on her elbows as she lay on her stomach. "You know, there's a point at which it's possible to be too honest."

He tapped her bottom and said, "Come on, let's get to break-fast. I'm starving!"

She collapsed into her pillow again and moaned. "Really? Sex and food? Is that all you ever think about?"

"No. Of course not. I also think about beer quite a lot. Come on, let's go!"

Ten minutes later, they arrived at the dining deck and found the rest of their group – Pixie, Raj and Jordan – already seated and eating. They grabbed a cup of coffee and a bowl of muesli from the auto food servers and joined the others at the table.

"Ah! Here come the young lovers!" said Pixie. "How are you, my lovelies?"

"Fighting fit and famished!" said Daniel.

"Sleepy and tired," said Kelly.

"It certainly was a most tiring night," said Raj.

"More tiring for some than for others, by the looks of things," said Pixie, winking suggestively at Kelly. "Oh, how I wish I were as tired as Kelly," she said, looking directly at the diminutive Pakistani, who proceeded to blush deeply. Kelly looked across at Jordan who raised her eyebrows in recognition of the obvious overtures Pixie was making.

"Is this chair taken?" asked Lieutenant Alvarez.

"Not at all," said Daniel. "Join us, please!"

Alvarez placed a mug of coffee and a bowl of porridge on the table and sat down, breathing a long sigh as she did so.

"Long night?" asked Daniel.

"You could say that. I spent several hours attending to colonists who were either slightly injured or freaking out."

"Nearly getting blasted to pieces by a laser canon will tend to do that to some people," suggested Jordan who had her mouth half full of a custard bagel. A variety of pastry treats that had been stored in the freezers had been made available this morning.

"Most of the colonists are very resilient people, otherwise they wouldn't have been selected for this mission," said Alvarez, "but none of them were expecting to be caught up in the middle of a major war when they signed up."

"I'm assuming we didn't find any damage to the ship?" asked Daniel.

Alvarez had stuffed another bite of custard bagel into her mouth before completely swallowing what was already there, so her reply was muffled. "What's this 'we' business, Professor? While you were snoring your head off some of us were still working our backsides off."

Daniel leaned around and pretended to inspect her backside. "You'll be pleased to know that yours is still firmly attached. So, you can't have worked all that hard."

"I suspect that Daniel was actually working harder than most of us at about that time," said Pixie with a chuckle.

"Oh, please! Let's not go there," said Jordan. "I'm trying to eat my breakfast without retching. But in answer to your question, there was only some superficial damage – scorch marks on a couple of the main drive nozzles."

Alvarez offered a further explanation. "The LAF – Laser Annihilation Field – spans across the outer rim of the concave deflector dish, creating an impenetrable shield that stops energy and solid particles from colliding with the dish or the engine nozzles at the base of the dish. Anything that hits that shield is – as the name implies – completely annihilated, and a small amount of antimatter is created and harvested in the process. It's how our engines will continue to be fuelled during our long voyage to the Tama system."

"So, how did the engine nozzles get scorched?" asked Kelly.

"Even an LAF field has its limitations. The Republican vessel was closing in on lethal distance, where the focused power of its laser canon would overwhelm our shield. A small amount of laser fire was beginning to leak through. We came very close to being destroyed last night."

"Which would be a complete tragedy, because all these custard bagels would have gone to waste," said Jordan, picking a second one off her plate and taking a large bite.

"Everyone on this ship owes you our lives, Daniel," said Alvarez. "I don't know how you did those calculations, but I suspect that if you hadn't been on the bridge, we wouldn't be here now."

"Speaking of being on the bridge, what's happened to Commander Decker?" asked Daniel. "I don't imagine it's every day that a captain orders a commander off the bridge and confines him to quarters."

Alvarez raised her eyebrows and offered a circumspect expression. "No, it isn't. I really don't know what will happen now. Decker was certainly out of line. As executive officer, a commander has the right to politely question a captain and offer an alternative suggestion. But he cannot opening deride or ridicule a captain's decisions. Decker was completely out of order. His responses to the captain last night were an act of open insubordination."

"So, what will Anderson do about it?" asked Daniel.

"I really don't know. By the letter of the law, the captain would be within his rights to charge him with insubordination and strip him of his rank. On the other hand, we are now a tiny microcosm of humanity, only 240 in number, and we will all need to work as closely and harmoniously as possible if our colony is to succeed. Completely alienating someone like Decker at this point could prove extremely problematic down the track. The last thing we need is bitter rivals fighting for power in such a tiny community."

"So, Anderson will try to smooth things over?" suggested Daniel.

"That would be my guess," answered Alvarez. "Decker is extremely competent at his job, and he would be difficult to replace. Our colony is going to need all the resources we can get, including human resources, if we are to thrive."

Alvarez looked at Kelly. "Speaking of which, it's time we got you working, Dr Rearson. You're too valuable a resource to be sitting idle. I'd like you to report to the science deck this afternoon. The science team have a number of projects they are working on, including adapting some of our plant species to the expected conditions on Tama-B. As you know, Tama is a Type-K star, with a predominance of light in the infra-red spectrum, and our plants are going to need some modification if they are to thrive on the new planet. As a micro-biologist, your skills will be extremely helpful."

"How does Lieutenant Vargas feel about my involvement?" asked Kelly. "I've already sensed some pushback."

"Maria will come around. She can be a bit gruff at first, but she is, first and foremost, a scientist. I'm sure she will appreciate the skills and experience that you bring to the team."

"I hope so. I don't think I've got the energy or patience to deal with petty territorialism."

Jordan scoffed and said, "If she gives you crap, give it straight back to her. That's my philosophy."

"I thought your philosophy was 'all officers are bastards'," said Daniel.

"That's my other philosophy. They're complementary."

29

"So, you're telling me that Daniel has a quantum computer inside his head?"

"In a sense, yes," responded Kelly, "The quantum molecule filaments that have insinuated themselves throughout Daniel's brain function as the world's first biologically-based, quantum processor. After two centuries of research, Daniel is the first successful attempt to develop QEBS – quantum enhanced biological sentience."

"But how does it actually work?" asked Anderson.

"It's difficult to explain. The quantum molecule filaments allow quantum qubits to operate effectively at body temperature, and they attach themselves to the billions of neurons in Daniel's brain via a binding enzyme. Effectively, his brain is extended and enhanced, allowing him to make computations millions of times faster than a traditional computer."

Anderson shook his head. "It's beyond me."

"It's very difficult to get my head around, too," said Daniel.

Daniel had brought Kelly with him to his meeting with Captain Anderson. He believed the captain deserved a complete explanation for Daniel's displayed prowess with computations and he figured that Kelly could provide a better explanation than he could.

"And they did this to you without your consent, or even your knowledge?"

"Yes. I only found out about it after it had been done to me."

"It almost killed him, too," added Kelly. She reached out and held Daniel's hand as she remembered their desperate rush to save Daniel's life before he slipped into permanent psychosis and death.

"I can only hope that the perpetrators were brought to justice," said Anderson.

"They were arrested shortly before we departed for Longshot," answered Daniel. "JUDAN is prosecuting them as we speak; at least I hope so."

"And you have no memory of your life prior to that monstrous experiment?"

"None."

"So, you know nothing about your life, previously?"

Daniel glanced at Kelly. This is where they had disagreed. Kelly felt strongly that Daniel should keep his past hidden from everyone. There was no need for the captain to know any of those details. But Daniel felt that he couldn't play any significant role in the development of the new colony without being completely transparent with the leader of the mission. The captain deserved to know the truth.

Daniel took a deep breath and plunged in. "Actually, I do know. When I said I have no memory of my past, that is entirely true. I can't remember a single thing: not even the tiniest detail. But I have since discovered certain facts – details about who I was and what I was like. I don't remember any of it, but it is undeniably true." He paused and swallowed. "You deserve to know the truth, Captain. And, after I tell you this, if you decide that you want me to play no further part in the leadership of this mission, I will totally understand."

"I see," said Anderson, who, as yet, did not see at all. "Go on. I'm listening."

"The truth is, I was a convicted murderer and drug dealer, working for a Columbian cartel, and I was on death row, awaiting execution."

Daniel stared at the captain who merely nodded and said, "Go on. I'm still listening."

Fifteen minutes later, silence descended upon the captain's day cabin. Daniel had given a full, unedited explanation of his past. Kelly had then explained how the insertion of quantum-molecule filaments into Daniel's brain had not only wiped his memory, but had also resulted in the emergence of a completely new and distinct persona. The signal paths in his neocortex, amygdala and hippocampus had been permanently altered, and the person who had once been known as Daniel Mendez was gone, as completely as if he had died.

Captain Anderson now sat quietly, drumming his fingers on the desk and contemplating all that he had heard. Finally, he spoke up. "What about the Justice Department's assertion that you were instrumental in uncovering a double agent and bringing down an illegal operation."

"That much is all true," Daniel conceded.

"Daniel single-handedly uncovered the Republic's agent, who had been feeding them information from within JUDAN itself," added Kelly. "He brought him to justice and saved my life in the process. He's a good man, Captain."

"What about the claim that you were a Senior Investigator with JUDAN – the Justice Department of the Alliance of Nations?" asked Anderson.

"I wasn't an investigator at all," Daniel admitted. "JUDAN gave me that honorary title in recognition of the role I played in helping them. They figured it would boost my chances of being accepted onto the Longshot mission. JUDAN placed me here because my life was in danger after my actions against the Republic. The Republic would have eventually tracked me down and killed me to get the quantum molecules from my brain, no matter how thoroughly JUDAN tried to hide me on Earth."

"And I was in the same situation," added Kelly. "I testified against Senticom, the research group who did this to Daniel, and also against the actions of RISC – the Republic of Independent States Commissariat – their secret service. My life was in jeopardy, too, and I was placed here as part of JUDAN's witness protection program."

Anderson nodded. "I see." He sat back and sighed deeply. Daniel and Kelly let him reflect in silence. Finally, he spoke.

"I must say, I am disappointed not to have been told the truth from the beginning. As captain, I have ultimate responsibility for the fate of the entire mission and the safety of every person on board. To have important information like this withheld from me is, as I say, extremely disappointing. But in saying that, I am not so much disappointed in either of you, but in JUDAN, who deliberately kept me in the dark. They should have told me. They should have trusted me and allowed me to make a fully informed decision concerning your possible inclusion on the mission."

"And, if you had known all this at the time, what would your decision have been?" asked Daniel.

"I'll be honest. I think I would have declined your inclusion."

Daniel nodded.

Anderson continued. "You need to see it from my perspective, Daniel. A convicted drug cartel hit man would not have made my short list of people to be included in the mission. I also would have been utterly unconvinced by the claims of you being a completely different person. Even if someone as scientifically competent as Dr Rearson had explained everything to me as she has just done, I would have been extremely sceptical. A person on death row will be desperate enough to fake a 'born again' experience in order to escape execution. I simply would not have risked the safety of this mission to help hide a convicted murderer."

"I understand," said Daniel. "I think any person in your position, with all the responsibility that you have on your shoulders, would take the same line."

"Having said that," continued Anderson, "your actions, from the moment of your arrival on the Moon until the present time, have been quite remarkable. Your bravery and ingenuity have saved the lives of a whole shuttle crew, in the first instance, and the whole starship in this latest incident. I don't know of anyone else who could have done what you did. Quite simply, we would not be here today, apart from your intervention."

Anderson continued. "Furthermore, although I would almost certainly not have allowed you on the mission if I had known the truth, with the benefit of hindsight, I can see that such a decision would have been wrong. Your actions since you have been among us, indeed, your whole demeanour, have demonstrated that you are a person of great moral integrity and honour. Having worked alongside you for these few short days, I can see that you are, indeed, a completely different person to the criminal that you just described to me. I would most certainly not have believed it, based on scientific argument, but I believe it now, based on the evidence of my eyes and ears."

"Thank you, Captain," said Daniel. He glanced at Kelly and saw tears glistening in her eyes.

"However!" said Anderson dramatically, rising from his chair and beginning to pace. "That being said, not everyone on board will be as broad minded as me. Yours is a story that many will find difficult to believe and accept. If we were to allow the truth of your past to become known, there would be many who would never trust you again and who would seek to treat you as the criminal you once were. For that reason, the truth of your past will never pass my lips."

"I appreciate that, sir," said Daniel.

Anderson ceased his pacing and perched himself on the corner of his desk, next to Daniel's chair. "I happen to believe that everyone deserves at least one chance to start again. In a sense, that is what every person on board this vessel is doing. We all have the chance to leave our past mistakes behind and start again, with a clean slate. There would not be a person among us who doesn't have things in their past that they would like to forget and move on from."

"Yes, sir," said Daniel, unsure what to say in the face of such generosity.

Anderson stood to his feet again and stepped alongside Daniel. "However, yours is an extreme case. A person who has done what you have done, does not deserve to be a warrant officer." So saying, he reached out and ripped the velcro warrant officer epaulettes from Daniel's shoulders. Daniel hung his head and nodded as Anderson walked to a cupboard at the side of his office and placed them in a drawer.

"I totally understand, Captain," said Daniel.

Anderson returned and placed his hands on Daniel's shoulders again. "I hope you really do understand, Daniel."

"Yes, sir. I do."

"No. I don't think you do," Anderson replied. He removed his hands from Daniel's shoulders to reveal a set of lieutenant's epaulettes. "I'm promoting you to Lieutenant." He stood back and regarded Daniel with a twinkle in his eyes.

"But ...," Daniel began, but then ran out of words. "I don't know what to say, sir," he eventually stammered.

"I believe, 'thank you', is generally regarded as the traditional response."

"Thank you, sir."

"You're very welcome. And it's I who should be thanking you." Anderson reached out his hand and warmly shook Daniel's hand as Kelly watched on with a lump in her throat and tears glistening in her eyes. Anderson walked around his desk and resumed his seat, then opened a desk drawer.

"Your first act as Lieutenant is to join me in toasting you." He pulled a bottle of malt whisky from his drawer and produced three small tumblers. "You will join us Dr Rearson?" he asked as he poured the shots.

"I'm not really a whisky girl, sir."

"You are today," he declared. "It's bad luck not to toast a newly commissioned Lieutenant."

He passed the glasses around and they clinked and drank together, with Kelly holding her nose as she did so. "Arrrh!" she said, her face grimacing. "The things I have to do for you!" she said to Daniel.

"Captain, won't my promotion make my relationship with both Commander Decker and Mister Cullen more difficult? They already resent my presence on the team. This could make things even worse."

"I did consider that," responded Anderson. "But, ultimately, the negative attitudes of a few people cannot be allowed to dictate a captain's decisions. Besides, your actions totally warrant this promotion. This is merely a recognition of the leadership role that you are already demonstrating."

"If you don't mind my asking, sir, what is to become of Commander Decker?"

Anderson sat back in his chair and exhaled deeply. "Commander Decker and I had a talk earlier this morning and we've come to an understanding. He recognises that he overstepped the mark in publicly criticising my decisions. He made a formal apology in front of everyone on the bridge this morning. He can also see, in hindsight, that it was the right decision."

"But even you weren't completely convinced at the time, were you, sir?"

"No, I wasn't. I have to say, it was the most terrifying moment of my career in the corps: placing the lives of everyone on board in the hands of a person I barely knew, who had a plan that barely made sense."

"So why did you do it?"

"Because there was no other option. If we had kept going as we were, we would have been caught and destroyed. There is no doubt about that, at all. Your seemingly crazy plan was the only alternative I had." He looked at Daniel carefully. "How confident were you, really, Lieutenant?"

"I was completely confident in my calculations, Captain. They were without error. I checked them multiple times, just to be sure."

"Multiple times? In just a few seconds?"

"Yes, sir."

Anderson shook his head. "It's all beyond me, Lieutenant." He glanced at the time and stood up. "Now, enough of this idle chatter. We have a mission team meeting to get to."

"Is Mr Cullen going to be part of the meeting, given our suspicions of him in regard to the activation of the explosive devices?"

"Yes, he will be. Because, quite frankly, there is a long list of people who could have activated them. I don't have any hard evidence linking Mr Cullen to the wasps, and without hard evidence, I can't relieve him of duty."

Daniel nodded. "I understand."

"But that doesn't mean I trust him, either," said Anderson as he walked toward the door.

"Neither do I," agreed Daniel.

30

—————

Captain Anderson brought the mission team meeting to order. "Ladies and gentlemen, we have a few things to decide in this meeting. But firstly, let me advise you that I have promoted Warrant Officer Daniel Newman to the rank of Lieutenant. This is in recognition of his bravery and initiative, demonstrated over these last few days, the last instance of which saved this ship and all our lives. Given that, I think a show of appreciation is in order."

The captain led them in a round of applause, although Daniel noted that both Decker and Cullen exhibited subdued enthusiasm.

"Now, to business," Anderson said. "Firstly, Commander, can you bring us up to date on our current status?"

"Yes, Captain," said Decker. "Our slingshot burn around Venus, followed by a slight correction a few hours later, has resulted in a perfect trajectory for Tama. Given our constant acceleration of 1G, our current velocity and distance from Earth means that we are now well beyond the reach of any hostile vessels. In short, we are now safe and on course."

There were murmurs of approval and nods all around the table.

"Thank you, Commander," said Anderson. "Under our constant acceleration, in just 14 days we will pass beyond the outer edges of our solar system and enter interstellar space – the first humans ever to do so. At that point we will be travelling at a little over 12,000 kilometres per second, a mere four percent of the speed of light, but nearly 80 times faster than any humans have gone before."

"We should have a party!" interjected Kelly without thinking, then looked uncomfortable when everyone turned to stare at her. "Sorry, it was just a thought."

"A 'Leaving The Solar System' party," said Olivia Alvarez. "I like it."

"It would certainly do wonders for morale," added Welfare Officer Dara Bernstein. "It would give us something to celebrate. Plus, it would help the colonists and crew to bond, which really needs to start happening."

"I confess, I hadn't given any thought to that kind of thing," said Anderson. "But it does seem like a good idea, doesn't it?"

"It would, indeed, be an exceptionally joyous social occasion," said Raj. "We are all in need of cheering up."

"Lieutenants Alvarez and Bernstein, can I leave that in your hands to organise?"

"Yes, sir," they responded in unison.

"That brings us to the question of when we should enter cryogenic stasis," continued Anderson. "Our plan has always been to start that process after about two weeks. Is there any reason to change that?" He looked around the table. "Lieutenant Vargas?"

The science officer shook her head. "No, sir. The two-week mark is still appropriate. It will allow time for bonding and acclimatisation while not being long enough to get the space wobbles."

"Space wobbles?" asked Kelly.

"A colloquial term for going nutso," said Bernstein. "Research has shown that people who are unused to being confined in a tin can, even one as sophisticated as Longshot, can start to exhibit all kinds of unhealthy psychological symptoms after about a month. Some even develop a form of psychosis."

Maria Vargas seemed a little put out at the interruption that Kelly had initiated and gave her a sour look as she continued. "Anyway, as I was saying, two weeks will be ideal, and it will give my science team sufficient time to run final diagnostics on each stasis pod."

Kelly noted Vargas's proprietorial attitude in her use of the phrase, 'my science team'.

"Good," said Anderson. "And no doubt you will want to address everyone in the lead up to the 'big sleep', to refresh their memory as to exactly what to expect."

"Yes, sir. A day or so before the party would be ideal. And we will plan to start processing people the day after the party."

Kelly's brow creased. "Would a party, presumably with alcohol being consumed, be a good idea immediately prior to cryogenic stasis?"

Vargas replied, "The cryogenic stasis filters and cleanses the blood. There is absolutely no problem."

The captain looked around the table. "Are there any other pressing issues that need dealing with?" He waited, but none were forthcoming. "Good, then in that case, meeting adjourned!"

Cullen spoke out as people were standing. "Sir, I'd like to stay behind and have a word in private with you and Mr Newman."

"Lieutenant Newman, you mean?"

Cullen seemed to bristle. "Yes, sir. Lieutenant Newman."

Daniel could sense how distasteful it was for Cullen to even say it.

"Very well."

It only took a few moments for everyone else to vacate the meeting room. Anderson was sitting at the head of the oval table, Daniel two places to his right and Cullen at the far end, his isolated position appropriately symbolic. His face was red and his bald head was glistening with sweat as if he had already worked up a full head of steam.

"What is on your mind, Mr Cullen?"

"I want to know why I wasn't informed that wasps had been found on the ship."

"Sir," added Anderson.

"Sir," conceded Cullen.

Anderson decided to match his confrontational attitude. "One was found in Hydroponics 2, the level you searched. Would you care to explain how you came to miss it?"

"Hydroponics 2? That's impossible. I scanned it thoroughly."

"I can assure you, Mr Cullen, it was indeed found there."

"Who found it?"

"Sir," added Anderson.

"Sir."

"It was located in the presence of three people; Sergeant Jordan, Lieutenant Newman and Dr Rearson."

George Cullen shook his head in disbelief. "I ... I can't explain it."

"The other two were located on levels that had been searched and cleared by members of your team. It appears that all three devices were activated within 30 minutes after the search was complete. Hence, why they were not located by our scanners."

Cullen was thinking aloud, "But that would mean that the person activating them would have needed to know ..."

"Precisely," interrupted Anderson. "He or she would have needed to know when the search was finished. And only a very small number of people would have had access to that information."

Cullen's face reddened. "You think I did it? You think I was the one who activated the wasps?"

"I really don't know," responded Anderson, calmly. "But, as the captain, I have to consider every possibility."

"This is outrageous!"

"Watch yourself, Mr Cullen! Remember who you are and to whom you are speaking!"

Cullen remained silent, obviously fuming.

"The decision was made not to advertise the finding of the wasps, in the hope that the traitor who activated them might continue to believe that he or she had gotten away with it. It was felt that this course of action might forestall any subsequent sabotage attempts. Unfortunately, circumstances eventuated where we needed to use the devices in our own self-defence, so the perpetrator now knows that the devices are no longer in play."

"Sir, as head of security, I had a right to know all this."

"You have no such right! You serve at my pleasure and under my command! And my primary concern is not your feelings, Mr Cullen, but the safety of every life on board this ship! Do not lecture me about your rights!"

Cullen reddened even further and seemed about to say something but thought better of it. He stood stiffly. "Yes, sir. May I go now, sir?"

"You may."

After he had left the room, Daniel commented, "He's definitely not a happy chappy."

"No, he isn't. But is he guilty? That's the question."

"He certainly seemed genuinely surprised when you mentioned the finding of the wasp in Hydroponics. Either he honestly didn't know, sir, or he's a very good actor."

"Yes. It's one or the other. But which? That is the question."

31

"That woman is driving me crazy!" said Kelly as she flopped down into a chair at the lunch table, two weeks later.

"Vargas?" asked Daniel, who had already started eating.

"I prefer to call her 'Lard Ass'," said Jordan, helpfully.

"What about 'Allgas'?" suggested Pixie, wearing a particularly incandescent rainbow top today.

"She undermines me at every opportunity!" continued Kelly, undeterred by the flippant comments of her friends. "She contradicts me and belittles me, and often tries to side-track me into doing stupid tasks that keep me away from the important stuff."

"And what is the important stuff, my lovely?" asked Pixie Rainbow.

"We're trying to modify our most important plants and vegetables so that they will flourish in Tama's very different sunlight. A Type-K star has a softer, red-spectrum light which will be a challenge for many of our common plants. It's essential that we modify them genetically to photosynthesise that light spectrum effectively."

"So, what's up with Vargas?" asked Jordan.

"She's threatened by Kelly's expertise," said Daniel. "The truth is that Kelly is actually better qualified as a microbiologist than she is, and everyone knows it." He looked at Kelly with sympathy. "Kelly's had two weeks of frustration."

"Insecure people are often the most difficult of work companions," offered Raj. "They compensate for their low self-esteem by trying to belittle everyone around them. They are like a mouse that picks a fight with an elephant and doesn't realise it is outmatched."

"Very true, dude," agreed Jordan. She held up a cookie. "Although, I prefer to compare them to a cookie. When you bake them, they crumble easily." She snapped the cookie in half to illustrate and popped one half in her mouth. "I say you should bake her, girl!"

"And how do you suggest I do that?"

"Punch her in the nose."

"I was hoping for a strategy with a little more finesse than that," responded Kelly.

Jordan shrugged. "The direct approach always works for me."

"Maybe Vargas is just lacking a little love in her life?" suggested Pixie.

"Speaking of which," said Kelly, "You're looking particularly tired today, Pixie."

"Oh, yes. I'm delightfully tired," she replied, wiggling her eyebrows and giving Raj a sideways glance. "I was up half the night savouring Pakistani spices."

Raj went the deepest shade of red Daniel had ever seen but did not bother to deny it. *Well, well,* thought Daniel. *The fly has finally been caught in the web.*

A chime sounded throughout the ship, and the face of Captain Anderson appeared on several screens around the dining room.

"Good afternoon, ladies and gentlemen. I hope you are enjoying your last lunch before the 'big sleep.' As you know, after tonight's party, we will begin preparations for entering cryogenic stasis. In order to help you understand what to expect, I have asked our science officer, Lieutenant Maria Vargas, to address you."

The screen flicked and an image of the tall, olive-skinned woman appeared.

Kelly groaned. "This is her moment of glory. She's been looking forward to this all morning."

"Good afternoon, fellow colonists. Tonight, we celebrate our departure from our solar system, and this marks the beginning of our journey into interstellar space – the space between the stars. Tama, the star we are heading to, is 37 light years distant from Earth. Our ship will take nearly 39 years to reach the Tama system but because we will be travelling at near lightspeed, the relativistic effects of such a high velocity mean that we will only experience seven years. Even so, seven years is much too long to be couped up in a starship. Hence our need to sleep through most of the journey."

"The process of cryogenic stasis is a safe and pleasant one. All of the dangers and unpleasant side-effects of the early stages of its development have now been ironed out, so there is really nothing to fear. Your blood will be replaced with synthetic blood, comprising trillions of nanobots that will infiltrate every cell of your body to take over all your natural metabolic processes. Your organs, including heart, lungs and liver, will not need to function at all during this time. Tiny micro-pulses will also stimulate your muscles, ensuring that you do not experience muscle loss during your sleep. While you are in stasis, your body will basically not age at all."

"The process is relatively straight forward and is actually completely automated. Once you step into your pod, a robotic arm will establish an intravenous line and you will be given a sedative. Within 30 seconds you will be asleep and the next thing you know, you will be awake, and we will have arrived at our destination."

"Waking from cryogenic stasis used to be extremely unpleasant: shaking, shivering, cramps, joint pain and even temporary blindness. Advances in our technology mean that you will not experience any of that. You will be kept sedated during the 48 hours that it takes to reactivate your body's systems. Nanobots will be magnetically filtered from your blood, and all natural metabolic processes will be re-established. By the time you wake up, you will feel refreshed and healthy, as if you have just had a pleasant night's sleep."

"The only mildly unpleasant part of the whole process is what needs to happen tomorrow. To prepare your body for cryogenic stasis, a complete colonic cleansing must take place. When you wake tomorrow, you will be given something to drink that will result in a complete purge of your colon. This process will take most of the day. The following morning you will report to Cryogenics on Level 56, where you will be shown to your assigned pod. A short time later, you will be asleep."

Vargas smiled into the camera. "I can assure you, there is nothing to worry about. The process is completely safe and effective. If you have any questions that you would like to ask, you can do so by registering them via your data screens in your cabin, and I will attend to them as quickly as I can. That's all from me. Enjoy the party tonight!"

The screen went blank, and conversations started up all around the dining room.

"So, tonight is the 'big do", and tomorrow is the 'big poo'," said Jordan.

"That's one way of putting it," agreed Daniel.

"Speaking of the party," said Pixie, "what's happening about alcohol? Is there going to be any?"

Olivia Alvarez arrived just as Pixie asked the question. She sat down and said, "Over the last two weeks, some of the automated processes in our yeast farm have been re-assigned to produce ethanol from fermented yeast. That will be mixed with various bitter and sweet liquids tonight, to provide some interesting alcoholic beverages." She smiled at them all. "Just don't drink too much, folks. We don't want anyone dying of alcohol poisoning."

"And what about music?" asked Kelly.

"No problem there," responded Alvarez. "The ship's data banks have access to every song that's ever been produced."

"Yeah, but who's choosing the music?" asked Jordan. "The last thing I want is to get drunk listening to Latvian folk music. No offense to any Latvians present."

"You can enter requests all afternoon via the data screens in your cabins. LACIE, our ship's AI, will shuffle them randomly throughout the party."

"I'm okay with that, as long as there's no screamer tech," said Pixie. "That music is absolutely terrible."

"I can't guarantee that," said Alvarez. "But by the time you've had your second drink, you might not care."

"There's not enough alcohol in the world to get me to like screamer tech," said Pixie.

32

Daniel spent most of the afternoon before the party, reading in his cabin. Since the successful search of the ship for explosive devices, the security team had not had much to do. Daniel had spent most of his mornings over the last two weeks flitting between the science lab and engineering, working on a special project with Kelly, which Captain Anderson had approved. After lunch each day, he spent his afternoons absorbing information. His appetite for facts was insatiable and his speed of assimilation was extraordinary. Each new page on his cabin data screen only remained there for two seconds before he moved on to the next. In the short space of time that a page was on the screen, he read every word and stored it away securely in his memory.

He had started with physics, which he felt would be of most use during their time in space but had soon broadened his interest to other branches of science such as chemistry, genetics and biology, as well as communication and computer science. When he felt like something different, he read occasional papers on random subjects.

"Did you know that as the female leopard spider mates, she injects a paralysing venom into the male?" said Daniel, as he stared at the screen. "She then injects her fertilised eggs into the male's abdomen. The baby spiders hatch inside the male two weeks later and gradually eat their way out of the male while it's still alive, killing it in the process."

"Sounds like a very sensible plan," said Kelly as she finished getting dressed for the party. "It's about time males took a more active role in child rearing." She stood up after putting on her high heels. "Do the females ever look like this?"

Daniel swung around and his jaw dropped open. Her dress was skin-tight and extremely minimal. "Wow! You're wearing a pocket handkerchief." He stood and put his arms around her. "It really is a pitifully feeble excuse for a dress. I've got socks that are bigger than that. Come to think of it – that is my sock!"

"I think you'll find that this looks and smells a whole lot nicer than your sock."

They arrived at the party shortly after 19:00 to find the music pumping and people already dancing. The advice was that the alcoholic drinks, colloquially termed 'rocket fuels', were very potent. Consequently, each person was only allowed three drinks, obtained by scanning one's ID chip at the automatic food and drink dispensers. As the night wore on, however, it became clear that some people were managing to circumvent the system. Non-drinkers and people who only wanted one or two drinks were 'hiring out' their wrists to people, in return for all manner of favours.

By 22:00, the music had been turned up several notches and the dance floor was full. The lights had been turned down and some lights were even strobing. The rocket fuels had loosened people's inhibitions, and more than a few new romantic connections were being made as people clung together and swayed to the music.

At 23:00 precisely, the music stopped, to the groans of everyone on the dancefloor, and Captain Anderson's face appeared on the screens around the ship. He had been in and out of the party several times, and had enjoyed a drink and a dance, but had disappeared a short time ago in order to make this announcement.

"Ladies and gentlemen, I won't interrupt your celebrations for very long, but an important moment has arrived that warrants acknowledgement. A few minutes ago, we officially exited our solar system."

Some rowdy cheers went up among the colonists.

"We are now more than 9 billion kilometres from Earth, and we are no longer under the influence of the sun's gravity or its heliosphere. We are now, officially, the first of humanity to venture into interstellar space – the space between the stars!"

More cheering took place and cups of rocket fuel were raised to the screen in a haphazard toast.

"We are now travelling at over 12,000 kilometres per second, which makes us the fastest humans who have ever lived. Our velocity will continue to increase every second until, in a little under a year, we will have reached 99.9 percent of light speed. We will maintain that speed for nearly 37 Earth-years, or seven ship-board years, before beginning our 12-month-long deceleration as we approach the Tama system."

"Bring it on!" called someone.

"Shoot me to the stars, baby!" shouted someone else.

"Give us more booze!" added a third, which produced much laughter and cheering.

"This is truly a momentous moment!" continued Anderson, oblivious of the interjections. "As we propel ourselves into the void between the stars, we leave behind many memories – some sad, some happy. But let us not forget that we carry with us the hopes and dreams of an entire world. We are the trailblazers who will forge a new destiny for mankind: the chance to start again on a new, unblemished world, where our children and grandchildren can grow up in peace and safety. So let us toast our new beginning and drink to our future success!"

The cheers were thunderous and as people joined in the toast, the image of their new world appeared on the screen. Then the lights dimmed, the music started up again and everyone was dancing once more.

Daniel and Kelly noted the diminutive Raj bouncing and jerking in an uncoordinated fashion, while Pixie Rainbow swirled around him in her voluminous, rainbow coloured outfit. Her huge sleeves made her look like a butterfly about to envelop a tiny moth.

Jordan was swaying and jiving to the music in a cool kind of way, her dark makeup, spiky hair and metal studded nose and ears giving her the look of someone who knew her way around a nightclub. She was dancing alone, however, and she snarled at any man who made advances toward her.

The dancing went on until the early hours of the morning. Later that night, as Daniel and Kelly lay in each other's arms, she said, "Do you think we will be happy in the new world?"

"We're certainly going to give it a red hot go," he responded.

"But it's going to be tough at first, isn't it? We'll be starting from scratch."

"Not from scratch," he said. "Remember we've got 50 storage bays full of all kinds of equipment and gizmos to get us up and running quickly – everything from fusion generators to tractors and prefab building materials. I think we'll be pretty comfortable very quickly."

She snuggled up closer to him. "I'm pretty comfortable right now."

They lay together in silence for a while, then Daniel said, "Kelly?"

"Uh huh."

"There's something I've wanted to say to you for a while."

"What?"

"Did you know that cows kill more people than sharks?"

33

I f the party was the high point, the next day was definitely rock bottom. Not only were people hung over, but the colon-cleansing drink they were all given first thing in the morning completed their misery. Most of the day was spent walking to and from the various communal toilet amenities. It became almost comical, with people passing each other in the hallways, nodding in mute recognition of their shared misery. The more upbeat people made jokes of the whole situation, competing to make the funniest comments as they passed one another. Others were of a more sombre countenance, head down and focused inward as they made the uncomfortable, repeated treks to the toilet.

By 18:00 the toilet action had ceased, and a strange lull descended on the populace, as they recovered from their uncomfortable day. Stomachs were empty and there was nothing to eat. Some people sat around in the dining and lounge decks, talking and joking in nervous anticipation of what they were about to undergo. Most, however, went to bed early, holding their loved ones close for the last time before the 'big sleep'.

A chime sounded at 06:00 the next morning, and the first announcement was made, calling people from certain room numbers to make their way to the cryogenics level. The announcements continued all morning and into the afternoon until, by 15:30, they came to an end. At 16:00 a chime sounded, and all crew were asked to report to the command centre. Daniel and Kelly made their way there, sharing a lift with a dozen others. Within a few minutes all 40 crew were assembled directly in front of the raised bridge platform.

Anderson stood before them and gave a final address.

"All our colonists are now asleep, and we alone remain. It is now time for us to take our places beside them and sleep the long years of our voyage away. I want to thank you all for your diligent service and your professionalism. It has been my great pleasure to serve with you on this, humanity's first starship. I don't know what challenges await us on the new world, but I am confident that, together, we will overcome them and build a community that our children and grandchildren will be proud of. I bid you all good-night now, and I look forward to waking alongside you at our destination."

He addressed the crew who were currently stationed at consoles. "Are all systems ready for transfer to LACIE?"

A series of voices replied.

"Navigation is go."

"Scans are go."

"Engines are go."

"Fusion reactor is go."

"Life support is go."

"Cryogenics is go."

"Hydroponics is go."

When everyone had responded, Anderson glanced into mid-air. "LACIE, do you confirm that all systems are ready for transfer?"

"I confirm, Captain."

"I hereby transfer control. You have control of the ship."

"Roger. I have control of the ship. Pleasant dreams, Captain."

Anderson looked out at his crew. "That is all, people. Please make your way to Cryogenics 2 on Level 55."

Kelly clung to Daniel's hand all the way down in the lift, and her heart began to beat faster as they stepped out onto the huge circular deck. Curtained screens surrounded the pods that were already occupied and only about 30 empty pods remained.

Vargas was standing there with a clipboard in hand. "Once I give you your pod number, make your way to it and close the curtain around you. Strip off your clothing and place all items in the tub beside your pod and seal the lid. Those clothes will be there for you when you wake up. Then simply step into the pod and lie down. An IV line will be robotically inserted, the lid will close and a few moments later you will be asleep. Have a good sleep, and I'll see you on the other side."

Daniel and Kelly got their pod numbers and he walked her to her pod first. She clung to him. "I'm scared! I don't want to do this!"

"You'll be fine," he assured her. "Besides, if you don't do it, I'll wake up looking like this and you'll be a middle-aged woman. Actually, now that I think of it, that could be quite fun. I've always been attracted to older women."

She smacked him on the bottom, then hugged him tightly. "I'm going to miss you."

"No, you won't. You'll be awake again in the blink of an eye."

They kissed, briefly, then Daniel stepped back, and she drew the curtain around her pod. Daniel turned and walked to his own designated pod. He drew the curtain around himself and stripped off, sealing the lid on the clothing container when he was done. He stood staring down into the pod. It looked tiny – barely big enough to fit him. He took a deep breath and stepped in, quickly lying down. He felt a prick on his wrist and his last thought was of Kelly.

34

Daniel opened his eyes and could not immediately recognise his surroundings. He saw a transparent lid of some kind immediately above him, open at an angle. He started to prop himself up on his elbows and immediately began to float off the bed. He had to grab the open transparent lid to stop himself floating higher. Where was he? He was surrounded by dark grey curtains, and there was a plastic tub on the floor nearby. He stayed like that for several seconds trying to piece together how he had come to be in such a strange weightless environment. Was this some kind of hospital in orbit? And why was he naked?

He looked more closely at the plastic tub attached to the floor and saw clothes inside. They must be his. Awkwardly, he managed to open the tub, although the lid slipped from his grasp and floated into the air, out of his reach. He fumbled his way into the clothing which he assumed was his, although the epaulettes on the shoulders of the shirt identified the owner as a lieutenant. A lieutenant? Something about that rang a bell in his mind. By the time he was fully dressed he had tumbled and fumbled so much that he was panting from the effort. As he looked at the boots on his feet, something about them seemed familiar too.

Then it all came back to him in a rush. *Of course! This is the starship Longshot, and I was in cryogenic stasis! Why am I awake? Perhaps we've arrived already.*

He leant down and activated his magnetic boots and felt more comfortable as his feet stuck to the floor. He clomped to the curtains and drew them back. Several other curtains had also been drawn back, and he saw familiar crew members emerging from their cubicles. He walked across to Kelly's and stood outside, listening to rustling from within.

"Are you decent?" he asked.

She peaked her head out. "For most people, I try to be decent. But for you, I'm willing to be a little indecent."

"Lucky me," he said, and he leaned forward and gave her a peck on the lips. She ducked back inside her cubicle, to continue dressing. "Why is there no gravity?"

"I'm guessing we're in orbit around the planet," he answered.

"Have you heard anything from the captain?" she asked.

"No. I think everyone is just waking up."

She opened the curtains and gave him a hug. "I'm alive! I didn't die in cryogenic stasis!"

"Yeah, I did notice that," he replied. "All your talking was a dead giveaway."

A chime sounded and LACIE's voice announced, "Attention all crew. Report to the dining room and scan your biochip to receive a serving of rejuve juice. Please drink all of it. You will need to drink several of these over the rest of the day to rehydrate and reminer- alise yourself. Once your first serve of rejuve juice has been consumed, mission team members are to meet in the wardroom in the command centre for debriefing, while the remainder of the crew await further instructions in the dining room. That is all."

"Huh," said Daniel with a slightly puzzled expression on his face. "I thought the colonists would all be waking up at the same time, but I guess this makes sense. It might take us several days to get everything fully operational again."

They began plodding toward the lift in their magnetic boots and met up with Jordan.

"How was your sleep?" Kelly asked.

"Piece of cake," said Jordan. "Felt like I'd barely closed my eyes."

"Same here! I can't wait to see the new planet!" Kelly was positively bursting with enthusiasm.

"Wow, someone sure gave you an extra shot of happy juice before you woke up," commented Jordan.

They entered the lift and rode up to the dining level. The captain and several others were already there, drinking a bluish-looking liquid from transparent cups.

"Have we arrived at Tama, Captain?" asked Daniel as he scanned his chip and received his cup of rejuve.

The captain looked around at other crew members standing nearby, who were listening for his reply. He gave a non-committal answer, "I'm sure we're about to find out. Let's let LACIE bring us up to date."

The mission team quickly finished their drinks and squeezed into a single lift. As the doors closed on them, Anderson said, "I don't like it. We are still supposed to be under deceleration, but our weightlessness tells me that isn't happening. We were due to be woken when we were still one week out from our rendezvous with Tama-B, still slowing down."

The captain's words hung heavily in the air, and Kelly's optimism suddenly plummeted.

"Perhaps LACIE has paused the deceleration, because of something she has discovered."

"Mm," said Anderson as the lift doors opened into the command centre. The group strode to the bridge area and the captain addressed the ship's AI. "Report, please LACIE."

"Aye, Captain. I regret to inform you that there has been a malfunction of the VAR drive. I have woken the crew according to mission protocol which stipulates that all crew are to be brought out of cryogenic stasis in the event of any emergency which threatens the safety of the ship."

"Where are we and what is our velocity?"

"We are currently approximately 36 billion kilometres from the edge of Earth's solar system, travelling at 30,294 kilometres per second."

"That's almost exactly ten percent of lightspeed."

"That is correct, Captain."

"But that means we've only been in cryogenic stasis for ... about three weeks."

"Your calculation is accurate, Captain. You have been asleep for exactly 21 days."

There were groans from several team members, with Kelly being the loudest.

"Extrapolate the exact nature of the emergency, please LACIE."

"The reason for the failure of the Vacuum to Antimatter Reactor drive is unknown. The VAR drive was functioning optimally until it suddenly stopped. As a consequence, not only has the ship lost propulsion, but it has also lost power to the forward deflector disk. In particular, our Laser Annihilation Field is no longer operational across the front of the disk. Without an operational LAF, the ship is vulnerable to impact with small particles."

"That doesn't sound too bad," Kelly said, hopefully.

Everyone turned to her, and she saw from their expressions that she had grossly underestimated the seriousness of their situation. Maria Vargas sneered at her and said, bluntly, "At the speed at which we're currently travelling, the smallest floating particle of matter would slice through the ship from top to bottom and blow us all to pieces. And that could happen at any second."

Kelly remained mute and chastened.

Daniel asked, "Captain, can the ship's fusion reactor be rerouted to power the LAF?"

"Sadly, no. That's correct, isn't it Mr Fraser?"

Angus Fraser, head of engineering was standing nearby. "That's right, sir. The fusion reactor powers all the ship's life support and internal workings, including cryogenics. But it simply doesn't generate enough power for the Laser Annihilation Field. The LAF needs the VAR drive to power it."

"And without the LAF, we're sitting ducks?" asked Daniel.

"I couldn't have said it better myself, Lieutenant," said Fraser.

35

The crew were quickly briefed on their situation, and everyone quickly swung into action. Kelly and Daniel marvelled at the professionalism of the crew as they chose to focus on their individual tasks and ignore the very real possibility that the ship could be ripped to pieces at any second.

As Captain Anderson continued to issue orders over the comm system, Kelly spoke to Daniel, off to the side. "I don't understand how a small piece of matter could destroy a ship as big and strong as Longshot."

"It's not just about the size of the particle, it's also about its velocity. A 1-gram bullet travelling at one metre per second will bounce harmlessly off your chest. But that same bullet travelling at 600 metres per second, will go right through you. The same is true of the small particles of matter that litter the universe. They may be tiny, but we are currently travelling at 30,000 kilometres per second. That's 50,000 times the speed of a bullet. Even a small particle that hits us at that speed will have so much kinetic energy it will rip through us as if we are made of tissue paper."

"I made a complete fool of myself, didn't I? Everyone must think I'm an idiot."

"You have nothing to be embarrassed about. No one can be

expected to be an expert in everything. You are an amazing micro-biologist. And last time I checked, they don't include lectures in astrophysics in most biology courses at university."

Captain Anderson finished issuing instructions over the comm and asked the mission team to gather in the wardroom. They quickly settled themselves around the table and, without preamble, he said, "Mr Fraser and his engineering team are on their way to inspect the antimatter drive as we speak. I hope to know more, shortly. Our deflector is made of the toughest material known to man, a maranium and carbon nanotube composite, and it can absorb impact from hydrogen and other gas atoms. But at this velocity, anything more substantial will go right through it. Without that laser annihilation field, we're in grave danger."

He looked around the table. "I don't believe there is any point waking the colonists, as they can do nothing to help resolve our problem and they are better off not knowing at this stage. Comments?"

"I agree, Captain" said Dara Bernstein, the welfare officer. "There is nothing to be gained from waking them."

Anderson nodded and continued. "The one thing currently in our favour is that we are now in interstellar space, where stray particles of matter are much scarcer than within a solar system. We can be thankful about that. Nonetheless, we will have our forward scanners fully extended, to search for possible threats."

Vargas spoke up. "At this speed, Captain, they won't be able to detect anything small."

"Correct Lieutenant. But micro debris fields generally tend to congregate around larger objects like asteroids. I know it's probably a futile effort, but I'd rather us move forward with our eyes partially open than not at all. In the meantime, food is going to be challenging. The hydroponics farm shut down when we entered cryogenic stasis, so there will be no fresh food for several weeks, until it starts producing again. The yeast farm will only take a few days to start producing. Before then, we are going to have to survive on energy bars and dried food."

Anderson looked at Raj. "Mr Patel, I want you to go back over the data and see if there was any anomaly in the VAR drive's readings leading up to the shut-down. I don't hold out much hope that you'll find anything if LACIE didn't, but, once again, it's better than sitting around doing nothing."

Anderson continued, "Mr Cullen, I want your security team to get down to the VAR drive and search for signs of sabotage. I find it difficult to believe that the drive just stopped working by itself. It's designed with multiple redundancies, so a complete shutdown like this is highly suspicious."

Cullen nodded. "We'll get right on it, Captain."

He looked around the table. "Is there anything I've missed? Anything else we can be doing?" There were shakes of heads and forlorn looks among the others. Anderson concluded, "I realise this is a bitter blow, and some of our crew may well be struggling right now. Do your best to bolster their morale and portray a positive attitude. We don't want panic to set in. Lead by example, people. That is all."

The meeting broke up and people went about their business with grim determination. Cullen walked past Daniel and said, "Security team meeting in the situation room in 10 minutes, Lieutenant."

36

———————

George Cullen briefly explained the task to his security team. They were to search for any signs of physical tampering or sabotage.

"But how could someone sabotage it when we were all asleep," asked muscle-bound O'Neil.

"The sabotage would obviously have taken place before we went to sleep, O'Neil," explained Cullen, as if speaking to a child. "The fact that it took three weeks to cause a shut-down implies that it may have been something subtle that had a cumulative effect. We also need to scan for residue from any kind of explosive device. So, to that end, you'll all be taking hand-held multi-scanners with you. We'll split into the same teams as last time. Make this a thorough search, people. Look for even the slightest sign of tampering. Let's get moving!"

Daniel and Jordan grabbed a scanner each and headed down the hallway to the lifts with the rest of the team. The Vacuum to Antimatter Reactor drive wasn't in the main cylindrical section of the starship, but was below it, in its own separate module. As head of security, George Cullen was one of only a handful of crew members whose biochip gave him access to the VAR drive: a point not lost on Daniel. He watched Cullen scan his wrist in the lift and wondered if George was, indeed, the culprit. He decided to double check any areas Cullen and O'Neil searched, in case Cullen deliberately overlooked something.

The lift opened and Daniel took in the scene. It was a large circular chamber, and around the outside walls were complex pieces of large equipment, many of which had interface screens. Engineering technicians were busily moving between the various screens, working to identify and solve the problem. The majority of the chamber was taken up with a massive cylinder that rose from floor to ceiling in the centre and which, in turn, was enveloped in floor-to-ceiling pipes of varying sizes, from 30 centimetres to almost a metre in diameter.

George gathered his team together and explained, "There are three levels here, accessed by the stairs over there." He pointed to a set of metal stairs that descended alongside a section of the wall. "I've asked Mr Fraser, head of engineering to explain briefly what each level is for." He nodded at the red-headed, freckled Scotsman who stepped forward and spoke in a broad Scottish accent.

"This top level, Level A, is the antimatter containment and stabilisation section. Antimatter atoms of anti-hydrogen that are created and harvested by the laser annihilation field surrounding our deflector dish are transported here and held safely in this containment apparatus." He pointed to the huge cylinder with its mass of pipes in the centre of the chamber.

"The next level down, Level B, is hydrogen containment. It's a similar set up, but not quite as complex or dangerous in terms of containment. The lowest level, Level C, is where the action happens. Anti-hydrogen atoms and hydrogen atoms are accelerated through a magnetic containment field. They come together in a controlled explosion and the released energy is funnelled through the engine nozzles at the rear of the ship, giving it thrust."

"Have you found any clues as to why the drive failed, Mr Fraser?" asked Cullen.

"Nothing yet. We're still looking. I'll let you know if we find anything."

Cullen nodded. "Okay people. Let's get to work. Inspect every nook and cranny and scan every centimetre. If there's been sabotage, I want to know about it!"

He divided them up, sending two teams of two to each floor. Jordan and Daniel were assigned the lowest level, along with another pair, Ortega and Ballard. Jordan was obviously good friends with Ortega, a petite-looking Columbian, and they chatted amicably. Ballard was a heavy-set man in his mid-30s who barely uttered a word. They spent 40 minutes scanning and searching, looking behind pipes and checking under equipment whose function they did not understand. In the end, they drew a complete blank. The scanners had picked up no residue from any kind of explosion and nothing looked like it had been tampered with.

They were just walking toward the lift when one of the engineers checking the systems in this lower level exclaimed, "Bugger!" The four of them turned simultaneously and looked toward the source of the exclamation. An engineer in a white lab coat was staring at readings on a screen and shaking his head.

"Have you found it?" asked Daniel.

The engineer ignored Daniel and activated his comm. "Boss. It's Lyall, at the annihilation reactor. I think I've found the problem. You'd better get down here."

"What is it?" asked Daniel.'

"It's complicated, sir. Difficult to explain."

"Is it fixable?

Before he could answer, Angus Fraser came thundering down the stairs and asked, "What is it?"

"Take a look, boss."

Fraser scanned the screen for a few moments. "Shite!"

"What is it?" asked Daniel, who was getting tired of asking the same question and getting no answer.

"It's complicated," said Fraser.

"Do you guys practise obfuscation in your spare time?" asked Jordan.

Fraser just kept staring at the screen, shaking his head.

"Is it fixable?" asked Daniel, starting to get frustrated as well.

"Maybe. Maybe not. It will take a lot of work. This is bad. I need to explain this to the captain."

37

"So, tell me the bad news."

The mission team was sitting around the conference table in the wardroom once more and Captain Anderson didn't waste any time with pleasantries.

Fraser started. "Well sir, it's complicated, but if you'll bear with me a wee moment, I'll try to explain. As you know, the front deflector disk harvests hydrogen atoms from space, to use as fuel. At the same time as harvesting hydrogen, the laser annihilation field also creates positrons and anti-protons from some of those atoms. The hydrogen is stored on Level B of the VAR drive and the positrons and antiprotons are stored on Level A, the top level, but those two particles are also kept apart. All three elements – hydrogen, positrons and antiprotons are accelerated into the annihilation chamber on the bottom level, Level C. The positrons and antiprotons are accelerated together first, creating whole anti-hydrogen atoms. These anti-hydrogen atoms are then accelerated further and finally brought into contact with the hydrogen atoms inside a magnetic containment field. The energy from the resulting explosion is then directed through the engine nozzles, creating thrust. A part of the energy from the resulting explosion is also used to power the laser annihilation field across our deflector shields."

"Yes, I'm with you so far," said Anderson.

"Well sir, the acceleration of all these particles is accomplished by a magnetic inertial propulsion system – MIPS – which accelerates the particles to near-light speed in just a few nanoseconds. There is a separate MIPS for each of the three feedlines."

"Okay," said Anderson. "I'm still with you."

"The problem we've discovered, is that all three MIPS are stuffed, begging your pardon sir."

"Define 'stuffed'."

"Completely fried, Captain. Unusable and unsalvageable."

"How did that happen?"

"Well, sir, I've run some tests and the only possible way it could have happened, is that they were subjected to a massive surge of current."

"Could it be an accident? Some kind of system malfunction?"

"It's possible, Captain, but highly unlikely. Each of the three MIPS runs on a completely independent power circuit, and each of those circuits has built in fail-safes and surge protection. The puzzling thing is that none of those protections was even tripped. If one of the MIPS had melted down, I might be willing to consider the possibility of accidental system overload. But all three simultaneously?" He shook his head. "Anyone who says this was an accident, I'd say their bum's oot the windae."

Everyone blinked and looked slightly puzzled. Kelly jumped in and interpreted. "Their bum's out the window. It means 'they're talking rubbish'." She smiled around the table. "My grandmother was Scottish."

"Thank you for that clarification, Dr Rearson. Most helpful," said the captain, trying to contain a smile, despite the seriousness of the situation.

"Is the drive in any danger of exploding?" asked Decker.

"No, Commander. It's entirely safe at the mo'. The containment fields are all still doin' their job. We're not in any danger in that sense."

"Can the MIPS be fixed?" asked Anderson.

"No, Captain. They're completely jobby."

Everyone looked at Kelly.

"Shite," she said pleasantly.

"Ah, yes. Of course," said Anderson. "So, if they are ... um, beyond repair, can they be replaced?"

"That's the wee tricky bit, sir. We'll have to make them from scratch. It'll be quite a job."

"Is Engineering Department capable of producing three MIPS?" asked Decker.

"Aye, Commander. We've got the material, the machinery and the technical skills to do it. There are definitely no stoters in my department."

They all looked at Kelly, again.

"Idiots."

"How long will it take?" asked Anderson.

"Two weeks, Captain, give or take a day. It's no wee job."

"Then you'd best get your men started on it, Mr Fraser."

"I already have, sir. Every second counts, because wi'oot it, we're sitting ducks."

Daniel spoke up. "Mr Fraser, what I can't understand is how the VAR drive functioned for three weeks before the MIPS melted down. If it was a deliberate act of sabotage, how is that possible, considering we were all asleep at the time?"

"I dinnae ken that either, sir. The power circuits that supply the MIPS are monitored and controlled by complex software. I'm thinking that malicious computer coding on a delayed timer was uploaded by some bassa prior to us going to sleep."

"Bastard," interpreted Kelly, who, by now, was quite enjoying her new-found role as Scottish interpreter.

"Ye ken say that again, lassie."

So, she did, just for good measure.

Ignoring her enthusiastic contribution, Daniel asked, "And how would someone physically do that? Where would they input that coding?"

"There is only one access point for the VAR drive software,

and that's on Level C, the bottom level where you and Sergeant Jordan were earlier. The computer system that runs the antimatter drive is deliberately kept separate from the rest of the ship's systems."

"But the drive can be operated and monitored from the command centre, can't it?" Daniel persisted.

"Yes, but the command centre only has operational access to the drive. The underlying software with all the parameters for the drive's specific functioning is firewalled and can only be accessed and modified on site, at Level C."

"I see," said Anderson. "Thank you, Mr Fraser. Most enlightening."

He turned to Raj, the ship's system analyst. "Mr Patel, is there any way someone could interfere with the drive's software remotely? Could someone with computer expertise access it via some kind of software back door from elsewhere on the ship?"

"No, not at all, sir. The foundational coding for both the VAR drive and the ship's artificial intelligence are completely firewalled, as Mr Fraser has said."

"So, someone would have had to physically take a lift down to Level A and walk down three sets of stairs to Level C to input malicious coding?" asked Anderson.

"Yes, sir."

"Is it possible to identify the malicious coding and try to determine its source?"

"I very much doubt it, sir, although I will certainly try. But it is most likely that the coding had a self-erase command line built into it once it had achieved its purpose. I would be very surprised if there is any trace of it left."

Anderson nodded. "I see." He addressed the whole group. "I think we have our plan of action mapped out for us. We don't have much choice except to build three new MIPS. Two weeks isn't ideal, but we can't do anything about that. In the meantime, let's just hope like hell we don't encounter anything bigger than a hydrogen atom. Let's get to work people."

As the meeting broke up, the captain asked Daniel and Kelly to stay behind. When they were alone, Daniel pre-empted his request.

"You want me to try to identify the saboteur."

"Yes, I do. I didn't want to discuss it in the meeting because … well, quite frankly, I don't know who to trust. You two and Jordan are the only ones I can be completely confident in at this stage."

Daniel considered the possibilities. "Theoretically it is possible for the malicious coding to have been entered at any time over the last few months, but I suspect it was more recent. It's much more likely that it was entered after the wasps were discovered and detonated, as a secondary act of sabotage after the first one failed."

"I agree," said Anderson. "Which means you have a much narrower search window, in terms of timing: the two weeks prior to the 'big sleep."

"Exactly," agreed Daniel. "I'll check video footage and any other data I can think of."

"Speaking of data," said Anderson, "how is that project of yours coming along?"

"It was almost finished when we went into cryogenic stasis. It looks like I'll have plenty of time to finish it over these next two weeks."

"Yes, and I'm starting to think it might actually come in handy."

"So am I, sir."

38

Lunch was a dismal affair. The hydroponics farm was still two weeks away from producing even the simplest fresh food, and there would be no yeast steaks or porridge from the yeast farm until the following evening at the earliest.

Jordan took a bite of her vanilla energy bar and gave a pleasurable sigh. "Yum! Mine is baked chicken and roast potato. What's yours?" she asked Kelly.

Kelly spun an identical vanilla energy bar in mid-air and left it floating there. "Barbecue ribs and fries."

"No way!" said Jordan. "I didn't see that one. Do you wanna swap?"

"Uh uh," said Kelly, shaking her head and snatching it back. "You snooze, you lose, girlfriend!"

"Mine is beef vindaloo," offered Raj, wobbling his head for emphasis.

"I love a bit of spicy Vindaloo," said Pixie, pinching his thigh.

"What's yours, Professor?" asked Jordan.

"Deep fried grasshopper," answered Daniel. When they all made faces, he explained, "Grasshoppers are a superfood: one of the highest protein foods you can eat."

"I'll take your word for it," Jordan replied.

Daniel looked around at the almost empty dining room. "It sure is different without colonists."

"Nice and peaceful," said Jordan.

Kelly took another bite of her energy bar. "It's a strange feeling sitting here eating, knowing that we could all be blown to bits at any second."

Jordan shrugged. "That's life, though, isn't it? We're always one moment away from oblivion, every second of our lives. It's just that most of the time we're not as conscious of it."

"That's a very sombre outlook," said Kelly.

"But it's true!" replied Jordan. "That's reality. An aneurism in your brain. A blocked artery in your heart. A nutcase with a gun. A slip down some stairs. A piece of food stuck in your windpipe. There's a million ways your life could end every single second. That's why I believe in living every day as if it's your last."

Kelly took another bite of her energy bar and said, "So, if you knew that this was definitely the last day of your life, what would you do right now."

"I'd take off all my clothes and dance naked on the table."

"So, what's stopping you?"

"What's stopping me is that it's not the last day of my life. Obviously!"

"So how will you know when it's the last day of your life?" asked Daniel.

"I'll know, because I'll start dancing naked on tables."

"Me thinks this is a circular argument," he said, shaking his head.

After they consumed a second energy bar each, Daniel, Kelly and Jordan (who decided that her second bar was chocolate pudding and ice cream) went back up to the command centre. The captain had allocated the wardroom for them to conduct their research.

"LACIE, bring up the video files for Level C of the VAR drive," said Daniel. A long list of files appeared on the screen. "Select files that contain video footage for the two weeks prior to the crew entering cryogenic stasis." The number of files on the screen diminished. "Search those files for the appearance of any personnel who are not authorised to be on that level."

"Searching." There was a long pause. "There are no unauthorised personnel on the video files."

"Damn! I suppose that would have been too easy." He thought about it for a moment. "List all personnel authorised to be on Level C."

A short list of names appeared: Angus Fraser, five other engineering crew, Captain Anderson, Commander Decker, and George Cullen, as chief of security. Daniel pondered the names on the list.

"LACIE, I believe you can track the movements and location of everyone on board Longshot, via their biochips. Is that correct?"

"That is correct, Lieutenant."

"Check the movements of Captain Anderson, Commander Decker and Mr Cullen for the two weeks prior to cryogenic stasis. Did any of them access Level C?"

There was a brief pause. "Negative."

"Damn!" said Daniel, again.

"But in Mr Cullen's case, I cannot be certain, as there is a corrupt segment of his movement log file."

"When does that corrupt segment occur?"

"Between 22:08 and 23:11 four days before cryogenic stasis."

"Bring up the Level C video file for that period. Play from 22:00."

A video of Level C appeared on the screen which was split into three different views from different cameras. As it was late at night, there was no one present. Suddenly the screen went blank.

"What just happened?" asked Daniel.

"The video file is corrupt at this point."

"How long does it stay like this?"

"For 55 minutes 24 seconds." The split screen view of Level C returned to the screen, and LACIE said, "This is the next video footage after the corrupt section." The level was empty again.

"The bastard! It was him!" said Jordan.

"Where was Mr Cullen immediately before and after the period of corrupt data?" asked Daniel.

"In his room."

"The cameras in the hallway would have shown where he went," suggested Kelly.

"Exactly what I was thinking," said Daniel. "LACIE, show the video feed from the hallway outside Mr Cullen's room during the period of corrupt data."

"I'm sorry, Lieutenant, that section of video data is also corrupt."

"What other video files are corrupt at that same time."

"Searching." There was a pause. "The only other corrupt file was one of the lifts."

Kelly said, "So he's snuck down to Level C, late one night, and somehow, subsequently erased the video footage and his biochip tracking data for that period."

"But how did he do it?" asked Jordan. "I know him pretty well, and I can tell you he's a complete klutz when it comes to computers."

"There are only two logical conclusions," offered Daniel. "Either he is deliberately fudging his incompetence with computers, or he is not working alone."

They paused to consider the implications of the latter.

"LACIE, can you trace when the corrupt files became corrupt? Is there any way of telling when or how they might have been interfered with?"

"No, Lieutenant."

Daniel stood. "I think we need to show Captain Anderson what we've discovered." He exited the wardroom and returned with the captain a short time later. They explained their discovery and showed him the evidence, after which Anderson sat silently, a grim expression on his face.

"What do you want us to do, Captain?" asked Daniel.

"I say we arrest him and space him," suggested Jordan. "He doesn't deserve to consume any more of our oxygen."

The captain shook his head. "No. Let him run for the moment. I suspect he is working with someone else. If we arrest him now, we will lose our chance of identifying any accomplice he may have. I want you to watch him like a hawk."

"I have an idea about that," said Daniel.

"Go on," said Anderson.

"Can I explain it in your day cabin, sir?"

Anderson frowned momentarily, then understood. "Yes. Yes, of course. Follow me."

A few moments later they were all standing in his day cabin.

"Thank you, Captain," said Daniel. "I remember from our training videos on the base that your day cabin is the one place in the whole ship where LACIE does not have eyes or ears."

"That's right," replied Anderson, "but why don't you want her to hear?"

"I suspect that someone is accessing her systems, and I don't want whoever it is to hear this."

"Good thinking. So, what's your plan?"

Daniel turned to Jordan. "Does the security department have micro trackers?"

She nodded. "Of course. Tiny transmitters about the size of a small freckle."

"And can a micro transmitter be paired to a data pad or similar device to record movement – separate from the ship's system?"

"Easy. I'm the security department's technical wizard, remember?"

"How could I forget; you keep reminding me." Daniel turned back to the captain. "I propose that we plant a micro transmitter on Cullen – on his clothing somewhere – and track his movements. That will ensure that if there are further outages of his movements on the ship's system, we will still have a record of where he's been and, just as importantly, who he's seen."

Anderson nodded and looked at Jordan. "Do it, Sergeant. ASAP. Let's close the ring around this conspiracy." He was about to say something else when an alarm sounded, ringing out stridently, and Anderson rushed out of the door to the bridge.

39

Daniel, Kelly and Jordan emerged from the captain's day cabin onto the bridge while the alarm was still ringing.

Anderson was standing at the railing in front of the two steps leading down into the central command centre area, filled with consoles manned by crew members.

"Kill the alarm! What's the problem?" Anderson commanded.

An ensign at a nearby console responded. "Captain, our long-range sensors have detected a threat directly in our path."

"What kind of threat?"

"We are heading directly into a dense cloud of gas and particulate matter. It's some kind of baby nebula or maybe the very early stages in the formation of a tiny protostar."

"How long until we make contact?"

"The cloud is 31 billion kilometres distant. At our present velocity ... 12 days sir."

"Can we use our manoeuvering thrusters to nudge us around it?"

"No sir. The cloud is too big and our thrusters are too weak."

Anderson activated his comm. "Mr Fraser, do you copy?"

"Aye, sir."

"What's your progress on building those MIPS?"

"Well sir, we've only just started. As I explained this morning, it will take us about two weeks."

"You're going to have to do better than that. We've just identified a nebula directly ahead in our path – a dense cloud of gas and small particles. We'll reach it in 12 days."

"12 days, sir?"

"That's all the time you've got, Mr Fraser. Can you do it?"

"We'll have to sir. We'll work around the clock. One thing's for sure, we'll no be scunnert, sir."

Anderson frowned and looked at Kelly.

"Bored, Captain."

Anderson nodded. "Get to it, Mr Fraser. Our lives are in your hands. I'll give you every resource you need. Just let me know how I can help."

"Aye, sir. Fraser out."

Anderson stared at the main screen on the far wall and sighed.

"Now it's just a race against the clock."

40

————————

By Day 8, Fraser and his team had manufactured and installed two of the new MIPS and had declared that the third and final one would be installed and operational within 48 hours. The laser annihilation field, which could protect them from the looming nebula, would be operational with two whole days to spare. The relief among the ship's crew was palpable. A renewed sense of optimism pervaded their conversations. They were going to survive, after all!

Day 8 also marked the day when the project that Daniel and Kelly had been working on was finished and ready for testing.

"Do we need to be near a computer terminal, for this to work?" Daniel asked.

"No. This will interface wirelessly with the ship's systems wherever you are," replied Kelly. She handed him the clear cap – the neural interface transceiver. It was the same NIT he had worn when his quantum system had been initialised in the Senticorp laboratory.

He turned it over in his hands. "I still can't believe you stole it. You? A law-abiding citizen!"

"I didn't exactly steal it," she replied. "I prefer to think of it as a permanent loan."

"Is that how you justify it?"

"Anyway," she persisted, "It was my design in the first place. I was its main developer, and I figured that since the rest of them had just been arrested, they weren't going to be needing it anytime soon. Besides, I thought the cap deserved to be with the only person who could actually use it."

"Not that we thought I'd ever be using it here," he said.

"No. But here we are. And I hope you appreciate the long hours I've spent realigning its microcircuitry to interface with the ship's systems. I got one of the guys in the science department to help me."

"You're an absolute whiz," Daniel said, kissing her on the cheek.

"Well, don't just sit there gawking at it, put it on! Let's try it."

Daniel fitted the clear cap to his head and Kelly had to supress a laugh. "Would you like a rubber ducky to take into the bath as well?"

"Very funny." He reached into his pocket and pulled out the remote control he had been working on, during his hours tucked away in a quiet corner of the engineering department. It sat in the palm of his hand, with a small green button marked 'on' and a red one marked 'off'.

"That thing isn't going to win any design awards," commented Kelly. "It looks like a daggy TV remote control from the 21st century."

"Having a quantum computer in my head only helps me to think better, it doesn't make me any cleverer with my hands."

"You can say that again."

"Having a quantum computer in my head ..."

"Okay! Okay, smarty pants. Enough with the jokes. Let's get on with it."

Daniel looked at the remote in his hand and Kelly explained, "Remember, you will be in complete control. This is already paired with the quantum molecular circuitry in your head, so you will be instantly connected. All I've done is create a wireless interface with the ship's computer circuitry. You should be able to instantly see it all and navigate anywhere you want. And because your quantum circuitry is about a million times faster than the ship's, you should be able to identify and circumvent any firewalls and decrypt any passwords with ease. You should be able to go anywhere, completely undetected."

He nodded his head. "Okay. Here goes." He pressed the green button and his eyes appeared to glaze over.

Kelly frowned. "Daniel?"

No response.

"Daniel? Are you alright?"

"Shhh!" he replied. "Can't you see there's a genius at work?"

"Thank goodness! You had me worried."

"This is incredible!" he whispered. "I can see the whole system. I can go anywhere I want." He appeared to be staring into space, seeing things that Kelly could not. "Hold on! Firewall and alarm system. Encrypted password needed." He closed his eyes momentarily. "Done! Three billion possible combinations. Easy!"

For the next hour he roamed the system, exploring different pathways and sub-routines. Eventually, he looked down at the remote control and pressed the red button. He pulled the cap off and said to Kelly, "I need to see the captain. We've made a big mistake! We ..."

But that was as far as he got.

A massive explosion rocked the ship and flattened them to the floor.

41

Alarms were sounding throughout the ship, and a computerised voice was saying,

"Warning! Decompression on Levels 1 to 17! Warning Decompression on Levels 1 to 17! Sealing all bulkheads! All crew to emergency action stations!"

Daniel and Kelly tried to get back up, but they were being forced against the right-hand wall of their cabin. The wall had now become the floor, and everything was on its side. Kelly groaned as she experienced high G-forces.

"We're in a spin!" said Daniel.

They lay there helplessly as they continued to be forced against the wall.

"This isn't good, is it?" said Kelly.

"Not exactly."

They could do nothing for several minutes. But gradually the force holding them against the wall diminished until they were once again weightless. They swung themselves around and reattached themselves to the floor via their magnetised boots.

"I still don't know where my action station is," said Kelly. "I keep forgetting to ask."

"I'm going to the bridge," said Daniel. "Come with me!"

A few minutes later they emerged onto the bridge to a scene of controlled chaos. People were yelling across the command centre, and the captain was nowhere to be seen. Another lift opened behind them, and Anderson emerged, with blood running down his forehead. He strode onto the bridge and took in the scene.

"Quiet, everyone!" he yelled. "Status please, Commander."

Decker looked up from a console and said, "An explosion in the VAR drive, Captain. It knocked us into a lateral spin. Fortunately, our on-duty crew are always strapped into their consoles. We've cancelled the spin with the ship's manoeuvering thrusters and we're trying to assess the damage."

"Can we contact anyone down in the VAR drive?"

"There's no response, Captain. And we've lost all incoming data from the drive."

"Captain!" called an ensign at one of the consoles.

"What is it ensign?"

"Sir ... I ... if these readings are correct ... I'm not sure, but it looks like we've lost the whole rear of our ship."

There was stunned silence.

"Give me an outside video feed!" Anderson demanded. "Is there a camera we can train around from the midship region?"

"All the rear cameras are gone," said the same woman, "but there's one on an extension arm outside Shuttle Bay 1. Patching it onto the main screen now."

An external view of the ship appeared on the screen, looking forward toward the huge forward deflector dish. The ensign tapped her data screen and the view began to change. The stars swung across the image as the camera pivoted to point downward. Finally, the camera stopped moving and there were gasps around the command centre.

The rear deflector shield was gone.

The VAR drive was gone.

And the base of the main section of the ship's central cylinder was obviously missing many levels. The cylinder now ended in ugly, jagged pieces of twisted metal. The blackness of space behind the spacecraft was now alive with millions of tiny, spinning pieces of debris, continuing to expand outward in a spectacular display.

"My god," moaned someone.

Several expletives were uttered around the command centre, which the captain chose to ignore.

"How many levels have we lost?" asked Anderson.

"Um ... I'm not getting any readings from Storage Levels 1 to 17, sir. And Levels 18 and 19 have lost atmosphere."

"17 levels gone," muttered Anderson.

"All that equipment for our new colony," said Decker.

"We didn't just lose the equipment, Mr Decker," said Anderson, "we just lost the whole mission."

The command centre was quiet as people contemplated the full implications of their situation. They were in shock, struggling to comprehend what had just happened and unable to decide what they should be doing.

Anderson snapped out of it first and turned to Decker. "Commander, organise recon and rescue teams to access the lower levels to assess the damage and assist any wounded. Contact the med team and tell them to prepare for casualties. Then call the mission team to the wardroom for an emergency meeting."

"You're injured, sir," Decker replied.

Anderson touched his hand to his head and it came away bloody. "It will keep. Carry out those instructions, please."

"Yes, Captain."

Decker moved away and began speaking into his lapel comm, and Anderson activated his own comm.

"Mr Fraser, do you copy?"

"Aye, sir."

"Where are you?"

"In Engineering, working on the third MIPS. What happened, sir? I've lost contact with my men in the antimatter drive."

"Get yourself up to the wardroom and I'll explain. And you can stop work on the last MIPS. It won't be needed now."

"Aye, sir."

Lieutenant Alvarez approached the captain with a small med

kit. "Sit down, sir," she said, indicating his chair on the bridge. "I'll patch you up."

"Later, Lieutenant."

"No, sir. Now!"

Several heads turned and looked at her in shock.

Anderson grunted and sat in the chair as instructed. "Remind me to court-martial you later, for insolence, Lieutenant."

"Certainly, sir," she said with a cheeky smile. She cleaned the gash on his forehead, glued it, then stuck a small bandage over it. By the time she had finished the mission team had all arrived and were waiting in the wardroom.

42

———

Anderson walked in and began the meeting. Without preamble, he announced,

"We've lost the back section of Longshot: the rear deflector shield, antimatter drive and Levels 1 to 17 of our storage bays are all gone. Some kind of explosion. How or why is irrelevant at the moment. We need to deal with the immediate issues and threats. Commander Decker, do we have any further information about the state of the lower decks?"

"The recon team reports that Levels 18 and 19 are holed. Both have lost atmosphere. Everything below that is gone. Power and life support is optimal for everything above Level 19."

"How many of our crew were in the sections that were destroyed?" asked Anderson.

Angus Fraser spoke up. "I had two of my men, O'Donnell and Claridge, on Level C of the VAR drive, making adjustments to the two new MITS we'd just fitted. Plus, I had a woman, Stroud, monitoring the containment fields on the two levels above. They were good people." He shook his head, unable to come to terms with the loss of part of his team.

"Other injuries?" asked Anderson.

"Nothing too much, sir," responded Decker. "One broken collar bone and several lacerations."

Anderson nodded. "Thank you, Commander. So, here's our situation, ladies and gentlemen. We're in a flying tin can, travelling at a bit over 30,000 kilometres per second, with no way to either speed up or slow down. We've effectively lost all hope of colonising Tama-B. Without a propulsion system, there is no way for us to eventually decelerate sufficiently to enter into an orbit around the planet. Not that this is a particularly pressing problem, because at our current velocity of only ten percent of lightspeed, the journey to the Tama system will take another 370 years."

He paused and looked around the table at the glum faces. "Of course, all of this is moot, because we are currently on a collision course with a small nebula, a dense cloud of dust and small particles of matter that will rip us to pieces, just four days from now."

Nash Anderson stood and began pacing at the head of the table. "So, I guess we have a choice to make. We could accept defeat. We could sit around and get drunk for the next four days and let the nebula cloud take us into eternity. It would be a quick death. I doubt that we would feel a thing. At 30,000 kilometres per second the debris field would rip through us so fast we would be dead in the blink of an eye. And don't misunderstand me, here. I am not being flippant. You may well decide that that is the best course of action."

He stopped his pacing, and stood facing them, every eye fixed upon his stern countenance.

"The alternative, of course, is to try to stay alive. We could try to figure out a way to avoid being ripped to shreds. That may not be possible, but perhaps we could try. If we were somehow successful, we would then be faced with living the rest of our lives inside Longshot. And we could certainly do that. Longshot's fusion reactor will still be pumping out power long after we are dead. And our yeast and hydroponics farms can sustain us indefinitely. Our life support system is also designed to last indefinitely. We could live out our lives here, but it wouldn't be ideal. Not by a long shot, if you'll pardon the pun."

He sat down again at the head of the table.

"That is our choice!"

He sat in silence, looking around the table.

"We also have 200 colonists in cryogenic stasis," commented Decker. "They have entrusted their lives to us."

"They have, indeed," agreed Anderson, "which gives our decision much greater moral gravitas."

There was silence for a few moments, then Dara Bernstein spoke up. "The human spirit always strives for survival. We do not just willingly lie down and die. Surely we must fight to stay alive – or die trying!"

There were nods all around the table, including from Anderson.

"That is my opinion as well, Lieutenant. Do I take it that we have a consensus?"

There were verbal assents and nods all around.

"Good! Then let us, in the Lieutenant's words, 'fight to stay alive, or die trying'! I'm open to suggestions as to how we might actually do that."

"Logically, there are only two possible courses of action," said Daniel.

Everyone looked at him.

"Go on," prompted Anderson.

"Either we find some way to power up the laser annihilation field across the front deflector dish, or we find a way to change our trajectory to miss the debris cloud."

Anderson nodded. "I agree. Those are the only two logical possibilities. Do you have any suggestions?"

"Yes. I have two. One suggestion for each possible course of action. The first is in regard to powering up the LAF. Mr Fraser, when we first awoke to discover that the antimatter drive was offline, you stated that Longshot's fusion drive, which powers all our internal systems, couldn't generate enough power to run the LAF at the same time."

"That's correct, Lieutenant."

"But we don't just have one fusion drive on board Longshot; we have five."

There was silence for a few moments as everyone thought it through.

"The shuttles!" exclaimed Fraser.

"Yes."

"Of course! I should have thought of that myself! I'm a complete walloper!"

Everyone looked at Kelly.

"Idiot," she explained, cheerily.

"So, do I understand this correctly," said the captain. "Can you somehow connect the fusion drives of the shuttles and use them to run the LAF?"

"Aye, Captain. I certainly can! The fusion drives in two shuttles, hooked up in parallel, will be sufficient to power the LAF. The only trouble is, we don't have enough time. I'm going to have to make two massive voltage regulators from scratch to be able to hook them up and feed the power to the LAF."

"How long will that take?"

"Hard to say, Captain, but at least seven days, maybe more."

The faces around the table that had lit up with hope, now slumped into looks of concern once more.

"We can certainly make a start on the work immediately, sir, because we're certainly going to need that LAF as soon as possible. But we'll need to think of some way of diverting the ship around the nebula if we have any chance of surviving."

Anderson merely nodded. "Thank you, Mr Fraser."

Kelly turned to Daniel and said, "I'm hoping your second idea is an absolute ripper."

"I'm not sure, yet," he replied. "Mr Fraser, what is the maximum thrust power of a single shuttle, operating at full throttle?"

"Just a wee moment and I'll tell you. But I think I can see where you're going with this." Fraser got a data pad out of his pocket and tapped on it for a few moments. "A whisker under four million newtons."

Daniel considered that for a moment. "Captain, can we get our current telemetry on the screen, including velocity, distance to the debris cloud, and distance from our estimated point of intersection with the edge of the cloud?"

"LACIE? Can you get all that on the screen, please?"

"Certainly, Captain."

A few moments elapsed and then the relevant data appeared on the screen. To Kelly, it just looked like a stream of random numbers, but Daniel appeared transfixed as he stared at them, moving his lips slightly as he calculated. Everyone watched him closely. Finally, he nodded.

"We can do it," he announced.

"Do what, exactly?" asked Anderson.

"We can use the shuttles to push us sideways." He looked around the table to see if everyone was following him. "Normally, our VAR drive at the rear would pivot its engine nozzles to line us up longitudinally with the desired trajectory and then propel us forward in that direction. But we've lost all propulsion from the rear, so we can't change trajectory that way. But what we can do is use the shuttles to push us sideways, even as we continue moving forward at 30,000 kilometres per second. We can't change our forward velocity, but we can change our angular velocity so that we miss the cloud."

Decker spoke up. "Push us sideways? How?"

"We will need to weld cradles onto the side of Longshot and weld reinforcing plates onto the noses of two of our shuttles. Then we just weld the two shuttles into final position and fire up their drives. Two days lateral acceleration will be enough to push us clear of the nebula."

"This might sound like a stupid question," said Kelly, "but if we'll be accelerating sideways, will that mean that the side of the ship will temporarily become the floor?"

Anderson nodded. "Yes. We will all be pushed against the side of the ship nearest the shuttles. That side wall will effectively become the floor for the duration of the acceleration. It will be uncomfortable, but it has to be done." He looked toward Fraser.

"You've only got two days to weld the shuttles into position. Can it you do it, Mr Fraser?"

"I think so, Captain. If I can't do it in two days, you can hang me up by me bawbag."

The captain looked at Kelly with raised eyebrows.

"I'd rather not say, sir."

43

———

Frantic preparations got underway to weld two shuttles to the side of the ship. A second group of engineers began work on building the two voltage regulators required for supplying power to the LAF from the fusion drives on the other two shuttles.

Daniel, however, had another pressing matter to attend to. The saboteur was almost certainly at large and may well strike again. Daniel was in little doubt that the explosion that destroyed the back half of the ship was no accident. It had to have been another act of sabotage, and until the perpetrator was identified, there was the risk of further attacks.

While Fraser's team worked furiously at their tasks, Daniel, Kelly and Jordan met with Captain Anderson in the wardroom. Anderson indicated to Daniel that he was to lead the investigation, so Daniel addressed the Longshot Artificial Computer Intelligence Entity.

"LACIE, bring up the video files for Level C in the VAR drive over the last week and scan them for any corrupt or missing segments."

"One corrupt segment located, five minutes in duration."

"Day and time?"

"Last night, from 23:20 to 23:25."

"Play the file from one minute before to one minute after."

They watched the video for its entirety, with split screens showing different views of the level. The whole level remained empty of people for the minute before and the minute after the blank section in the middle.

"LACIE, are there any other corrupt video files for around that time?"

"Yes, Lieutenant. Hallway Section 12 on Level 66 and one of the lifts. Both show corrupt segments from 23:10 to 23:35."

"That's the hallway directly outside Cullen's room!" said Jordan.

"LACIE, check George Cullen's bio feed for that period. Is tracking data available?"

"No, Lieutenant. Mr Cullen's bio feed and tracking data is corrupted for that period."

"The bastard!" said Jordan. "We should have arrested him when we had the chance! No offense, Captain."

"No. You are absolutely right, Sergeant Jordan. I hold myself entirely responsible for the tragedy that has now unfolded. It was my decision not to arrest him, and I must take the blame. I will have to live with that awful decision for the rest of my life."

"Perhaps we could retire to your day cabin to discuss this further, Captain?" suggested Daniel.

"By all means," answered Anderson.

The captain led them to his day cabin and when he had ushered them in and closed the door, he said, "How did I go? I wasn't too melodramatic, was I?"

"Perhaps a little, sir. But I think it did the trick," responded Daniel.

"Good. So, now could you please tell me what this is all about?"

"It's not Cullen, sir."

"What makes you say that?"

"Two reasons. Firstly, if you recall, the first episode of corrupted files that we uncovered suggested that Cullen had snuck down to Level C late one night and entered malicious code into the VAR drive's software. That is the malicious code that we believe had a delayed timer which led to the melt-down of the MIPS while we were all cryogenic stasis."

"Yes," agreed Anderson. "It seems pretty strong circumstantial evidence that Cullen was the culprit."

"Except he wasn't. At least not on that occasion," Daniel said. "With the help of the device that Kelly and I made, I searched the video files throughout the rest of the ship that corresponded to the same time as the corrupted files. Cullen was in the gym at that time, on Level 68, for a whole hour, doing a personal work out. He didn't go down to the VAR drive at all."

"You're sure he was in the gym?"

"Yes, sir. There's a whole boring hour of him huffing and puffing."

"What about this second incident. The explosion together with the corrupted data files and his corrupted biochip readings which, once again, coincide perfectly with the blank video on Level C?"

"That's the second reason why I believe Cullen isn't guilty. Jordan can explain this one."

Jordan nodded. "I tagged him, sir. I planted micro-transmitters on his boots, his pants and his shirt. And I've been tracking him ever since. At the time of this latest corrupt video, he was sound asleep in his room."

"How do you know that he didn't just wear different clothes when he went down to the antimatter drive?"

"Because he was snoring. I used audio enabled micro-trackers." She frowned and said, "And I have to say, sir, he also farts an awful lot in his sleep. I think he needs medication."

"So, someone is framing him?" said Anderson.

"Exactly," replied Daniel.

"Who?"

Daniel sighed. "Someone with exceptional coding and computer skills. Someone clever enough to hack into Longshot's systems and corrupt video files and delete biochip data."

"Clearly, you have someone in mind."

"Rajish Patel."

"Mr Patel? I find that difficult to believe."

Daniel shrugged. "He is the most expert coder and computer technician we have on board. Plus, I'm ashamed to say, at lunch on my first day on board Longshot, he overheard a comment about my suspicions that George might be an agent for the Republic. I think he seized on that and decided to cover his own tracks by framing George."

Kelly winced. "That would be my fault. I made the comment and put my foot in it. Sorry, Captain."

"So, you think that he's the one who snuck down to Level C and entered the malicious code?"

"No. He didn't need to sneak down. He did it remotely. I found a backdoor that he created in the VAR software that allowed him direct access. I also found shadows of the malicious code that caused the surge in the supply current that melted the MIPS. Although the program was subsequently deleted, there are traces on the system that can't be completely erased. And that coding definitely came from Raj's workstation."

Anderson shook his head in disbelief. "Did he activate the wasps as well?"

"Yes. I found a program in his secure personal file that enables him to listen in to any comms on board the ship. He can also tap into any audio that LACIE can hear. That's why I wanted to have this conversation in here, where LACIE has no audio inputs. I'm not sure how Raj physically activated the wasps. Perhaps we will find a wireless device when we search his room."

"And what about this recent explosion?" asked Anderson. "Is he responsible for that, too?"

"I can only assume that he is. I'm hoping that we will be able to get to the bottom of that when we arrest him."

Captain Anderson shook his head. "How very tragic." He rubbed ran his hand through his thinning white hair and sighed. "You have my authority to arrest Raj Patel."

"Can I make a suggestion, Captain?" asked Daniel.

"Certainly."

"Allow George Cullen to make the arrest. He deserves it, seeing we falsely suspected him and kept him out of the loop for so long."

Anderson nodded. "Yes. You're right. We misjudged him. I think a gesture of goodwill toward him now would be very diplomatic." He gave Daniel a searching look. "You'd make an excellent Captain, Lieutenant Newman."

44

———

On their way down in the lift to speak with George, Jordan asked Daniel, "So do you want to explain how you managed to access all that information? I'm guessing that the ship's computer system doesn't have a swinging door with a sign that reads, 'Welcome. Please come in and have a look around'. What are you? Some kind of genius hacker as well as being a math nerd?"

"It's complicated," he responded awkwardly. "And it's a conversation that's probably better suited to somewhere more private." He raised his eyes to the ceiling, indicating LACIE's all-hearing presence.

"Huh!" said Jordan. "You're a mystery wrapped in an enigma, Professor."

Jordan and Daniel had prearranged to meet George in the briefing room on Level 66. George wasn't there when they arrived and he kept them waiting another ten minutes, probably deliberately, Daniel suspected. When he finally did arrive, there was definitely no warm greeting, just a stern look and a gruff opening salvo,

"What do you two want?"

It certainly wasn't the way for a warrant officer to speak to a

Lieutenant, but Daniel sensed that ranks were becoming increasingly irrelevant the further from Earth they travelled and the more desperate their plight became. In the end, they would all be equals, space travellers and colonists who were simply trying to stay alive. Daniel believed they would soon need to drop the artificial pretences of rank and privilege if they were to truly be able to work together.

Daniel began. "George, we owe you an apology."

"I'll say you do."

"You're an efficient chief of security and you're certainly not an agent for the Republic."

"Of course I'm not!"

"The thing is, you were framed, George. Someone set you up to look like a saboteur."

"Framed? How?"

Daniel explained about the deliberately corrupted files that implicated him, and George's frown deepened as he listened. It took a little while for him to unthaw. He was still understandably upset that he had been a suspect at all and was also disappointed that he had been left in the dark for much of the investigation. But as Daniel explained the false evidence that had been concocted against him, he eventually conceded that if he had been in their position, he would have suspected such a person as well.

"I'm sorry, George," said Daniel, again. "But at least we know you're in the clear now, because we've identified the person responsible."

"Who?"

"The systems analyst, Rajish Patel."

"The little bugger!" exclaimed George.

Daniel explained the evidence he had uncovered: a backdoor into the VAR's software program as well as residual evidence of malicious coding, sent from Raj's workstation, which resulted in the surge of current that melted the MIPS and rendering the anti-matter drive useless.

"We also suspect that he is the one who listened in to our comms to determine when we finished our search for explosive devices. I found an audio software hack in his secure files that enabled him to access all comms and audio feeds around the ship. We'll have to search his room and his workstation, but I suspect we will find a transmitter of some kind that was used to activate the wasps."

All three of them had been sitting in adjacent chairs in the briefing room, but now George stood up. "Where is the little bugger?"

"Right now, I suspect he's at his workstation. The captain asked him to try to analyse the video feeds from the bottom two damaged levels to determine the level of damage. The captain has issued an order for his arrest."

George gave what could almost be construed as a growl, and started walking toward the door, then paused and turned. "Come on, you two. Let's do this. You deserve to be in on the final action."

As they strode down the hallway toward the lifts, Daniel felt that a significant shift had occurred in their relationship. He and George would probably never be best friends, but perhaps now there was the basis for a respectful working relationship.

They took the lift to the science level and found Raj's workstation unattended. "Where is Patel?" George asked a nearby science technician.

"He was here a few minutes ago. Then he left in a hurry."

"Damn!" said Daniel. "I'm an idiot! He must have been listening to our conversation through his hack to the ship's audio system!"

"LACIE!" called George. "Where is Rajish Patel?"

"Mr Patel is currently in Shuttle Bay 1."

The three of them strode as quickly as they could toward the lifts. "Keep us advised of his movements!" George said.

They emerged from the lift on Level 54 and quickly scanned around the cavernous bay. The shuttle was sitting in the middle of the tarmac, with two engineers busily welding a metal plate to its nose. There was no sign of Raj, but Jordan noticed the light above the airlock door turn from green to red.

"The airlock!" she said.

They rushed to the airlock and saw Raj inside. He wasn't wearing a spacesuit.

"He's locked the door from the inside," said Jordan.

Daniel activated the comm. "Raj! What are you doing?"

"I'm not letting you take me!"

"Don't be foolish, Raj! You need to unlock this door."

"No! I am not going to let you lock me up. I won't be a prisoner for the rest of my life."

"I doubt that will happen, Raj. You've made a terrible mistake. And yes, there will be consequences. But we need every person to help us survive. You can still play a part in our community."

"I will not dishonour my family by being arrested as a criminal."

"Don't throw your life away, Raj. Your family wouldn't want you to do that either."

Tears began rolling down the little Pakistani's face. "They have my family, back on Earth. They took them captive. They told me they would release my wife and children if I helped them slow the ship down. I'm doing this for them!"

"You did more than just slow the ship down," said George, angrily. "You nearly killed us all!"

"I didn't try to kill anyone. I was just told to disable the main drive. I caused the MIPS to melt down."

"You activated the wasps, too!" George yelled. "They would have blown us all to kingdom come!"

"I didn't do that! I had nothing to do with that!"

"And how did you blow up the VAR drive?" George persisted.

"That wasn't me! I have no idea about that. I'm telling you, I was only told to disable the drive, not blow it up! I would never do anything to harm another person!"

"Open the door, Raj," said Daniel. "We can talk about this. We'll get to the bottom of it."

"No. It's too late. I will not be a prisoner!"

He reached toward the emergency purge button.

"Don't do it, Raj!" pleaded Daniel. "You can still have a life!"

Raj paused with his hand over the button, then turned to face them. "Please tell Pixie, I'm sorry."

He pushed the button, and the outer airlock door flew open. Raj shot out into space. As he shot away from Longshot, his mouth opened and closed a few times and his arms and legs flailed momentarily, then he was completely still as he quickly shrank to a speck in the distance.

45

"Do you believe him?" asked Anderson, sitting at his desk in his day cabin.

"He seemed pretty adamant," said Daniel. "He claims the only thing he did was cause the power surge that fried the MIPS and shut down the drive."

"The little bugger was probably lying," said George.

"But why would he lie when he was about to kill himself?" asked Jordan. "He had nothing to gain by denying the other things."

"Reputation," replied George. "People from his culture place a high value on reputation, even after they're dead."

"Maybe," conceded Daniel. "But if he was lying, he was very convincing."

Anderson asked the obvious question. "So, if he was telling the truth, where does that leave us?"

"It means there's another saboteur on board," replied Daniel.

Anderson placed his head in his hands and rubbed his eyes. "Is there no end to this?" He sighed and looked up. "How do we proceed from here? Have you got any suggestions, George?"

"I'll look into the personnel files of every remaining crew

member, to see if there's any possible link to the Republic that might have been previously missed."

"We could also search every crew member's cabin," suggested Jordan. "There must be a transmitting device somewhere onboard the ship that was used to activate the wasps. We've already searched Patel's room and found nothing."

"Alright," agreed Anderson. "George and Jordan, you two search cabins. Daniel, can you do a little more digging in the ship's systems to see if you can uncover any other clues that might help us?"

Daniel noticed Anderson's use of first names instead rank and surname. It was a sign that the old formal structures were becoming increasingly irrelevant. "Will do, sir," he replied.

Anderson sighed again. "That's all for now. Let me know if you find anything."

By midway through the second day, the engineering modifications were complete. Makeshift docking cradles had been welded to the side of the ship, one toward the top and one near the now-mangled bottom. Two shuttles were now in place, their reinforced nose cones welded to the docking cradles. The shuttles were now ready to be fired up, but before that happened, Nash Anderson called a meeting of the crew in the command centre. They gathered before him as he stood on the raised platform of the bridge.

"Firstly, you will probably already be aware of the unfortunate death yesterday of our systems analyst, Rajish Patel. He took his own life after it was discovered that he was the saboteur of our VAR drive."

As agreed with George and Daniel, the captain chose not to elaborate any further. If there was, indeed, a second agent for the Republic somewhere among the crew, they wanted to give the impression that they believed Patel to be the only saboteur.

"But right now, we have more urgent issues to attend to. The preparations for the 'big push' are now complete, thanks to the incredible work of Angus Fraser and his team. The shuttles are in place and our pilots are about to commence their burn. There are two pilots on board each shuttle, and they will live on the shuttles for the next two days, doing eight-hour shifts."

"Our calculations indicate that a continuous burn for two days, pushing Longshot sideways, will get us clear of the edge of the nebula – the gas and debris cloud. But I need to warn you. The burn will need to be at 2G for the whole of the two days. Furthermore, because the shuttles will be pushing us sideways, the edge of the cylinder against which they are pushing will become the floor, and our current floors and ceilings will become the walls."

"Because of this, we will have to abandon the command centre, as we won't be able to have people at the consoles which will be halfway up the wall, especially under an acceleration of 2Gs. I also recommend you collect your mattresses from your cabins and any personal belongings you might require and establish a camp along the wall of the cylinder closest to the shuttles. Once we accelerate to 2Gs you will find it impossible to climb up the wall to your cabin.

"Food will also be an issue, as the automatic food dispensers will be sticking out of the walls. So, when I dismiss you in a moment, please gather all the food you will require for two days. I suspect that energy bars and water bottles will be our staple diet for the next two days."

"Fortunately, the lifts run along the side of the ship, closest to the shuttles. We deliberately attached the shuttles to align with the lifts and, over the last few hours we have gradually rotated the ship to the alignment required so that the shuttles will be pushing us in the right direction. For the next two days, the lifts will, therefore, be running along what we perceive to be the floor. You will need to be careful climbing into and out of them if you need to travel to another level."

"The toilets alongside the lift will operate via their usual suction apparatus, but, of course, everything will be on its side. I will leave it to your imagination to work out how you will deal with that."

There were chuckles and several murmured comments among the crew.

"I think that is all the information you need. I believe we have a very good chance of surviving beyond more than a few days now. Once we are clear of the cloud, we will, of course have to consider what the future holds for us. But that is a conversation for later. You have 30 minutes to grab your gear out of your cabins and gather sufficient food and water. That is all."

46

———————

Pixie was an emotional mess and had been isolating in her room for the last 24 hours since she had learned of Raj's death. Now, however, she had to mobilise. Kelly made sure she relocated her mattress and personal items to the wall near the lifts, along with several other crew members. The crew scattered themselves between different levels, as the new 'floor' was going to be very limited in space on each level, consisting of a small section of curved wall of about eight metres by 5 metres. Anderson had asked Daniel to camp with him against the wall of the command centre, primarily because of Daniel's ability to access the ship's systems. Without anyone being able to be stationed at the consoles, Daniel was going to be the sole interactive point of contact with LACIE and the telemetry data. He had brought his newly tweaked NIT with him, the neural interface transceiver.

Daniel arrived in the command centre with his mattress and a few personal belongings, to find Olivia Alvarez and George Cullen there as well, setting up their encampments. There would be just enough room for four of them: two on each section of wall on either side of the lift. From there, they would be able to see the main screen which showed a continual stream of telemetry data.

"LACIE, patch me through to an open channel throughout the ship," said Anderson.

"Done, Captain."

"Ladies and gentlemen. This is a two-minute warning. Please make sure you are set up along the wall near the lifts. Good luck."

Two minutes later, he opened a channel to the shuttle pilots. "We're all set here, Jordan. Ready when you are."

"Roger, sir."

The comm channel between the two shuttles was going to be broadcast to the command centre as well, so that the captain and his companions could listen in. They heard Jordan contact the other pilot.

"Tyler, we're going to start at one percent thrust. These early stages are going to be crucial. because we can't impart any spin to Longshot, or we'll start going round and round like a giant firework at a fair. Keep the auto guidance system engaged and locked onto the coordinates we entered. It should automatically adjust our nozzle angle to cancel out any spin that might start."

"Roger."

"Okay. One percent burn, on my mark. Three, two, one, mark!"

Daniel and the other three were standing in their magnetic boots with their backs pressed against their mattresses which were against the lift wall. They felt an immediate slight bump and then a small amount of pressure against their backs.

"Two percent, in three two one, mark," said Jordan, calmly.

The pressure on their backs increased slightly. After two more incremental power adjustments, it became undeniable to the four occupants that they were now lying on their backs with their feet against the vertical wall which had, only a few moments before, been the floor.

For the next 15 minutes the shuttles gradually increased their power, while their automated guidance systems made continual micro-adjustments of their thrust angle to cancel any spin. Finally, Jordan announced, "That's 2.37 million newtons of thrust, and exactly 2G acceleration. Lock it and leave it, Tyler!"

"Roger, Jordan. From now on, were just baby-sitting."

Daniel looked at the telemetry on the far screen, which was now far above him on the ceiling. He checked their current forward velocity toward the nebula, as well as the remaining distance, the width of the nebula and their current lateral acceleration. The screen showed the estimated time to impact with the nebula as being 49 hours 10 minutes.

"How are we looking, LACIE?" asked Anderson.

"If our current thrust remains constant, I calculate that our manoeuvre with take us beyond the edge of the nebula in 47 hours 48 minutes."

Anderson looked at Daniel. "Does that seem about right to you, Daniel?"

Daniel nodded, while continuing to stare at the screen. "I calculate 47 hours 50 minutes, but I've allowed for resistance due to the increasing density of hydrogen atoms as we approach the nebula."

"I did not make allowances for that, as it was not a parameter I was asked to factor in." said LACIE, uninvited.

Daniel smiled at the artificial intelligence's defensiveness. "Whichever one of us is right, it looks like we are going to make it by about 80 minutes."

"That's good news," said Anderson. "But these next two days aren't going to be much fun."

47

The next two days were definitely not much fun. The two pilots on board each shuttle swapped every eight hours, allowing the relieved pilot to rest or sleep in the back of the shuttle. The shuttle's fusion drives burned continuously, producing a constant 2.37 million newtons of thrust and nudging the badly damaged starship sideways toward the far edge of the looming nebula. The trajectory of the now strangely configured ship slowly began to take on the shape of a curve as their forward velocity remained constant, but their lateral velocity increased second by second.

In their padded seats, the shuttle pilots were probably the most comfortable people within a radius of 30 billion kilometres. The rest of the crew within Longshot were camped against the wall of the huge cylinder, cramped and uncomfortable in 2G acceleration. The fitter and more agile crew members regularly stood up and walked around, even climbing down into a lift and travelling horizontally to visit another level and chat with different crew members.

The heavier and less fit crew members, however, mostly just lay on their mattresses, uncomfortable and suffering, effectively weighing twice their normal weight under the 2G acceleration.

Pixie Rainbow suffered the most. Kelly estimated that she must now weigh over 200 kilograms, and the extra weight would be placing an enormous strain on her heart and vascular system. Kelly attempted to cheer her friend up and Pixie tried to rally as best she could, but Kelly could tell that she was suffering – physically and emotionally.

Daniel got very little sleep the first night, with both George Cullen and Nash Anderson snoring like freight trains. The next morning, he excused himself and moved back with Kelly who was with Pixie and several other crew members along the wall of the dining room. The rest of the day dragged out interminably, broken only by the occasional consumption of an energy bar and trips to the bathroom.

By 14:30, they had clocked up their first 24 hours. They were halfway there, but the remaining 24 hours loomed ahead of them like an abyss. By 17:00, word had spread that the crew camped on level 61, the yeast farm level, had a still which had produced alcohol. Apparently, two enterprising crew members had constructed the still upon first awakening from cryogenic stasis, and it had produced several large containers of powerful spirits from fermented yeast. The still was not currently working under the lateral acceleration, but the moonshiners had accumulated a good supply which they were willing to share.

Crew members from other levels began making trips to Level 61 on all kinds of pretexts, taking empty water bottles with them and returning with them full. Daniel felt it was his responsibility as a Lieutenant to intervene and talk to the relevant crew members regarding their irresponsible behaviour. He returned with three bottles of booze which he shared with the group on his level.

By 18:00, the sounds of laughter and singing could be heard echoing through the lift well, from different levels on the ship. Around 18:30, Captain Anderson called him on a private comm channel.

"Lieutenant Newman, I've heard that there is illicit alcohol being passed around and consumed on board my ship!"

"Er ... I'm not exactly sure, sir. I think I heard a rumour to that effect."

"Well, I want you to investigate, please, Lieutenant. At once!"

"Yes, sir."

"And if you find any evidence of liquor being dispersed, I want you to confiscate some of it for further perusal and forensic investigation."

"Forensic investigation, sir?"

"That's right. At least two bottles!" There was murmuring off to the side, then the captain's voice returned. "Make that, three bottles! We need to be absolutely certain what we're dealing with here."

Daniel smiled. "Yes, sir. I'll get right on it."

"Oh, and Daniel? Don't mention me. Let them think they got away with it."

"Will do, Captain."

Later that night, Jordan was on a group comm call with Kelly, Pixie and Daniel.

"What's all that laughter and singing in the background?" she asked.

"We're practising for a concert recital that we're going to give you guys when you get back in," said Daniel.

"It sounds dreadful!"

"Yes, well, we haven't been practising for very long. It's still in its early stages," replied Daniel.

Kelly burped, then said, "Plus, we can't decide what song to actually sing for you, so we're giving a whole lot of different ones a good shot."

"Are you ... are you drunk?"

"What a horrible accusation!" said Kelly, slurring her words. "I resemble that!"

"I think you mean 'resent'," said Daniel, helpfully.

"Nope," she said, shaking her head. "I definitely resemble it."

"You are drunk!" said Jordan. "I can't believe you're having a party while I'm out here working my ass off!"

"Now, now, my dear," replied Daniel, also slurring his words slightly, "your hyperbolic reference to the imminent removal of your bottom seems a bit overdone."

"You're drunk too! What's happened to you all?"

"I'll have you know, I'm not as think as you drunk I am. I'm merely doing my duty as a Lieutenant in the space corps, to remove illicit substances from the lower ranks so that they may not be led into temptation!"

"And deliver us from evil," added Pixie.

"Amen!" said Kelly, who then burped rather loudly.

"Oh, my giddy aunt!" said Jordan.

"Get her to try some of this stuff," suggested Kelly. "She'll be swinging from the rafters after a couple of sips!"

48

———

Things were rather quiet the next morning. The captain eventually called Daniel and advised him that intense forensic examination had revealed that it was, indeed, alcohol that had been distributed last night, and that it was a good thing that a decent quantity had been confiscated. Daniel agreed wholeheartedly but had to ask the captain to speak more softly, as he seemed to have developed a rather severe headache.

"I'm glad our crew could let their hair down a bit last night, Daniel," Anderson said, getting a little more serious. "Goodness knows there's been little joy in our lives of late."

"Yes, sir. I agree. In fact, I think it did a lot of good for morale."

"I'm sure it did. When you are free, can you join me in the command centre? It would be good to have you here as we count down the final hours. I don't want to leave anything to chance."

"Certainly, sir. I'll freshen up and be there shortly."

As Daniel stood up from his mattress, Kelly said, "Have you heard the gossip about Decker and Vargas?"

"What gossip?" asked Daniel.

"They were discovered asleep this morning in the airlock in Shuttle Bay 2, and they were experiencing a uniform irregularity."

"Really? What kind of irregularity?"

"Complete absence of."

"My, my! Our dour commander and the feisty science officer!"

"Yes," agreed Kelly. "It appears that Decker took command of the science department in a very hands-on manner."

Daniel chuckled. "I was wondering where he'd got to. I wonder what other new dalliances took place last night?"

"The rumour is that this isn't a new dalliance. Apparently, it's been going on for a while."

Daniel arrived in the command centre soon after, climbing awkwardly up out of the lift which was effectively a deep hole in the floor. He lay against the wall to the side of the lift and looked at the telemetry data on the screen 'above' him. They were on track to clear the edge of the nebula in 3 hours 46 minutes.

"How are you all feeling this morning," asked Daniel, still puffing after the exertion of getting there under 2G acceleration.

George merely grunted and groaned, and Olivia Alvarez squinted at him and asked him to speak more softly.

"That good, huh?" responded Daniel.

Anderson placed a call to Jordan who was currently in the pilot seat in one of the shuttles. "How is it going out there, Jordan? Are you coping alright?"

"Only just, sir. We've got a portable potty in here and Reece managed to knock it over last night. I've stuffed some scraps of med bandages up my nostrils but I'm getting tired of breathing through my mouth. On the positive side, I decided to spare Reece's life, but I have to confess I came very close to spacing him."

"Hang in there, Sergeant," encouraged Anderson. "Not long to go. You'll be back inside, in relative comfort in just a few hours."

"Speaking of comfort, everyone in there seemed extremely happy and comfortable last night. Did I miss something?"

Anderson raised his eyebrows at Daniel and responded. "Err, yes. There was an illicit substance being circulated last night but, as Captain of the ship, I ensured that it was confiscated and dealt with accordingly."

"I'm sure you did, sir."

LACIE interrupted their conversation. "Captain, my long-range scanners have detected an additional threat to the safety of the ship."

"What kind of threat?"

"A debris field of small particulate matter, extending for approximately two million kilometres beyond the outer edge of the nebula. The particles are too small to have been detected by my scanners until now."

"What size are they?"

"At this range, it is difficult to determine with precision, but their reflective indices suggest that they are no bigger than three centimetres in diameter."

"The size of a large bullet," said George.

Daniel stared at the telemetry screen which now also showed the data for the additional particle field, to the side of the nebula. "We're going to be flying straight through it," he said.

"Can we get around that particle field if we increase our acceleration?" Anderson asked both LACIE and Daniel.

"Acceleration of 4G for three hours will be required," answered LACIE.

"Actually, it's 3.93G," responded Daniel, "but 4G will certainly do the job."

"That's a hell of a thing to endure," said George.

"We don't have a choice," answered Anderson. "That particle cloud will rip through us like machine gun fire."

"We could make it with 3.5G acceleration for three and a half hours," offered Daniel, "but it would only leave a safety margin of 16 minutes."

"That's too tight a margin," Anderson replied. "We need to accelerate at 4G to be absolutely certain that we clear the entire field with plenty of time to spare. Jordan, have you heard all this?"

"Yes, sir."

"Good. I know you've had a tough couple of days. Can you guys do this?"

"Yes, sir. We'll get it done."

"Good. I'll warn the crew, here. Give me five minutes and then begin your increased acceleration."

"Roger."

Anderson then got LACIE to activate a ship-wide comm and he spoke to the crew.

"Ladies and gentlemen, I know these last two days have been difficult. We are almost there. But I need to warn you that the last three hours of our ordeal are going to considerably worse. As we have drawn closer to the nebula, we have detected a particle cloud of matter extended for two million kilometres beyond the edge of the nebula. In order to clear that debris field, we will need to increase our rate of lateral acceleration to 4G. I'm sorry, but there is no alternative if we want to survive. Under that amount of acceleration, you will not be able to do anything other than lie on your back. It's going to be a tough three hours, people. Get yourselves as comfortable as possible. Acceleration will begin to increase in about three minutes. That is all."

"Sir, if you don't mind, I want to go back to the dining room, where my mattress is."

"Of course, Daniel."

"Can you stream the telemetry data to the screens in the dining room as well? I'd like to continue to check our progress."

"Certainly. See you on the other side."

Daniel arrived back in the dining room, puffing again from his exertion in pulling himself out of the lift under the strain of the equivalent of twice Earth's gravity.

"This isn't going to be much fun, is it?" said Pixie, as Daniel took his place on his mattress next to Kelly.

"No. It's going to be pretty gruelling," answered Daniel.

49

The acceleration was oppressive. Over a period of ten minutes the shuttles gradually increased their power, carefully balancing their thrust with each other and making fine adjustments to keep Longshot from spinning or twisting. After ten minutes, Longshot was undergoing lateral acceleration of 4G in an attempt to push them clear of the particulate cloud on the edge of the rapidly looming nebula.

There was no merriment among the crew now, just grim silence occasionally punctuated by groans. Every second was a strain, as the G-forces pushed each person deeply down into their mattress. Limbs felt like lead and breathing was laboured as lungs were compressed under the force of acceleration. Seconds turned into minutes and the long, grinding minutes slowly ticked over to an hour, then two hours, then two and a half.

The viewing screen on the opposite wall, which was now their ceiling, showed a continual stream of updated telemetry, and Daniel kept careful track of it. They were on course to clear the particle debris field in 30 minutes, with approximately 46 minutes to spare. The minutes ticked by agonisingly slowly, with a countdown timer on the screen showing the remaining time to engine shutdown.

At the 5-minute mark, Daniel called Anderson, whose voice betrayed the strain he was feeling.

"Yes, Daniel?" he groaned.

"Sir, I recommend we add ten more minutes to the current burn, just to be absolutely sure we are completely clear of any outliers."

Anderson groaned some more. "I was wondering if you might suggest something like that. Unfortunately, I think you're right. I'll advise Jordan and adjust the timer."

A few moments later, ten additional minutes were added to the countdown timer on the screen, and groans could be heard from those looking on.

The additional minutes seemed to take forever, but, finally, the Captain's voice came over the ship-wide comm. "We've made it everyone! Prepare for incremental decrease in acceleration. We will be winding back the acceleration gradually over the next two minutes. Please secure all items as we will soon be under zero gravity once more."

The countdown timer reached zero, and almost instantly there was a slight lessening of G-forces. Gradually the acceleration came down as the two shuttles reduced power, carefully balancing each other's thrust. After several minutes, all acceleration had ceased, and they were blissfully weightless again. Some crew cheered weakly, but most didn't even have the energy for that. They just floated silently where they were, with eyes closed and breathing deeply.

"My goodness," said Kelly. "I never want to go through that again. Next time just shoot me, please."

Slowly the people around them came to life. They began gathering their floating possessions and magnetising their boots to the floor. Kelly turned to Pixie, who lay on a mattress beside her, and noticed that her eyes were still closed. She tried unsuccessfully to rouse her and noticed her pale, clammy skin.

"Daniel! Pixie's not well!" called Kelly.

Daniel looked at Pixie who was floating nearby. Her face was ashen and covered in sweat, and her breathing was laboured. Kelly tried to communicate with her, but she seemed unresponsive. Daniel made a comm call. "Medical team to the dining room! We have a medical emergency! Please hurry!"

He wasn't sure where the med team were or if they were even prepared for such an emergency yet.

"She's stopped breathing!" said Kelly. "Daniel, do something!" The zero-gravity proved extremely difficult, but Daniel and Kelly worked as a team. Kelly held her in mid-air while Daniel gave her mouth-to-mouth resuscitation. Several minutes dragged by until, finally, two medics turned up with a defibrillator and a portable breather. They worked on Pixie for nearly ten minutes before announcing that she was stable enough to move her to the med bay.

As they watched her being taken away, Kelly burst into tears and Daniel held her close.

"Is she going to be alright?"

"They'll do the best they can for her," he assured her. "We'll just have to wait and see, now."

Daniel had to return to the command centre. The place was bustling again, with crew manning their consoles and checking the ship's status.

"We did it, Daniel!" said Anderson, as Daniel approached him on the bridge.

The view from the ship's forward-facing cameras was depicted on the main screen, showing clear black space ahead, speckled with stars. A secondary screen showed the view of the nebula, which was now on their starboard side, nearly 12 million kilometres away.

"We're alive, at least, and the path ahead is clear of debris," said Anderson. "But we're now way off course."

"How far off course?" asked Daniel, looking at the telemetry screen.

"On this trajectory, we'll miss Tama by about ten lightyears."

"So, just a smidge off course, then," commented Daniel, drily.

"Quite," agreed Anderson.

Decker emerged from the lift and arrived on the bridge looking dishevelled and pale.

"Commander Decker, nice of you to join us," commented Anderson.

"Sorry, sir. I've been a bit …"

"No need to apologise, Commander," said Anderson, smiling. "It's been a hell of a few days, hasn't it? I'm just happy to see that you're alive and well."

"Thank you. You too, sir."

Anderson activated his lapel comm. "Jordan, how are things going out there?"

"Good, sir. We've powered down the shuttles. We're just getting into our suits and preparing for our EVA back to the airlock."

"Very good. I'm sure there will be quite a few people who will want to shake your hand when you get back inside."

"I strongly recommend they wait until I've had a shower, sir. I stink! Plus, the shuttles are going to need a bit of sanitising. I swear, Reece must have eaten something dead and rotting before he came on board."

Anderson chuckled. "Roger. We'll clean the shuttles later. Just get yourselves back in here. You've earned a rest. Anderson out." He turned to Decker. "Commander, can you organise a meeting of the mission team for 17:00?"

"Aye, Captain."

50

————

"Well, we're alive!" began Anderson. "That's a start, at least."

He looked around the table at the faces of the mission team. They all looked pale and tired. The last two days had taken their toll on all of them.

"We are, indeed," said Dara Bernstein, who looked as haggard as the rest of them. "And we owe our lives to the pilots, the engineers and Lieutenant Newman for his ingenuity."

"It was certainly a wonderful team effort," responded Daniel.

"Were there any injuries?" asked Anderson.

"Pixie Rainbow had a heart attack as we were coming out of the acceleration phase," said Kelly. "She's recovering in the med bay at the moment. The doctor is hopeful she can make a full recovery."

"That's good news," said Anderson. "Were there any other problems from the acceleration?"

Heads shook around the table.

"Good," said Anderson. "We're all alive and we can be thankful for that. But we're still in a dire situation. In fact, in some respects, things are now worse, if that were possible. We still have no laser annihilation field to protect us from future impacts, we still have no propulsion drive, and now, as an added bonus, we are light-years off course."

He looked around the table at the sea of tired faces.

"But we have solutions to two of those problems. Daniel's idea of using the fusion drives from two shuttles to power the LAF on our front deflector dish is a good one, and we have made a start in that direction. Mr Fraser, where is your team up to in that regard?"

"We're makin' progress, Captain. With two shuttles still welded to our hull, we've squeezed the remaining two into Shuttle Bay 1, and we've made a good start on making the two voltage regulators that we'll need. We've uncovered the power supply lines that run up to the deflector dish and we'll be able to patch into those as soon as the regulators are finished. Give us another week, sir, and I reckon we'll have that thing up and running."

Maria Vargas spoke up. "My science team are also working on software to allow the ship's system to monitor and control the operation of the fusion drives in the shuttles. After all, the ship is going to have to manage that, itself, if we're all in cryogenic stasis."

"Very good," replied Anderson. "Until it's operational, however, we will just have to hope and pray that we don't meet up with another ... what did you call it, Lieutenant Vargas? A protostar?"

"Yes, Captain," replied the science officer who was now fully clothed after her midnight rendezvous with the commander. "The nebula appears to be gradually coalescing protostar. If we swing past again in several million years, we will probably see a newly born star."

"I'll have to check my diary," said Kelly. "I think I'm busy then."

Several people laughed, and Anderson was pleased that they hadn't lost their sense of humour.

"On the positive side," Vargas continued, "what we've just encountered is extremely rare, especially in interstellar space. The void between the stars is exactly that – a void. Gas atoms and matter particles are extremely rare out here, much rarer than within a star's solar system. We were very unlucky to encounter that nebula. I believe we are reasonably safe for the short time it will take for Mr Fraser to get our front shields working again."

"That's very good news, indeed," said Anderson. "The second problem that we may have a solution for, is our currently wayward trajectory. Daniel, you have a suggestion, I believe?"

"Yes, Captain. Simply put, all we need to do is reverse what we've just done, using the shuttles that are still welded in place outside the hull, and get us back on course."

There were groans all around the table, including someone who muttered, "I don't think I can do it again."

"It needn't be as bad as this time," assured Daniel. "We can take our time and accelerate at 1G."

That seemed to brighten people up.

Daniel continued, "We simply need to spin Longshot 180 degrees around its long axis, then fire up the shuttles again and nudge us back on course. Depending on how soon we do it, it might take around a week to get us back on course at 1G acceleration. I'm also investigating whether we might be able to power the shuttles remotely, using LACIE's systems. That would save having to subject our pilots to living on a shuttle for an extended period."

"The pilots will love you for that," said Kelly.

"Of course, the first priority will be restoring power to our front shield," said Anderson. "But once that is done, correcting our trajectory should be relatively straightforward."

"And then what?" asked George. "How long did you say it will take to get to the Tama system at our current velocity?"

"370 years," responded Anderson

"Shipboard years or observer-based years?" asked Bernstein.

"Both," answered Anderson. "At our current velocity of only ten percent of lightspeed, the relativistic effects are negligible."

"Can we stay in cryogenic stasis for that long?" asked Fraser.

Anderson deferred to his science officer, who answered confidently, "Yes. We believe so. There is no reason why we can't safely remain in stasis for many centuries. That isn't the main problem."

"What is the main problem?" asked Bernstein.

Vargas looked at Anderson and raised her eyebrows, suggesting that he be the one to spell it out. Anderson drew a deep breath and exhaled slowly. "It's the one problem for which we have no solution. Without a main propulsion drive, we have no way of slowing down at the other end."

There was a moment of silence, as his words hung heavily in the air.

"Ultimately, we will sail right through the Tama system and into interstellar space again."

51

The problem of their lack of propulsion was shelved for the time being, because their most urgent need was to restore power to the forward deflection disk. Until that was rectified, they were still at risk of being destroyed by the rare particles of matter that inhabited even these empty regions of space. Angus Fraser and his team laboured continuously on the project, working in shifts around the clock.

In the meantime, Daniel's priority, assigned to him by the captain, was to search the video files to try to determine the cause of the explosion that had wrecked their ship, and the identity of the person responsible.

This time, however, Daniel decided to bypass LACIE, the ship's artificial intelligence. Instead, he accessed the ship's computer system directly, using his NIT, the Neural Interface Transceiver. He sat alone in his cabin, donned the clear cap and activated it. It took a few moments for the NIT to re-establish an interface with the millions of micron-thin quantum filaments that were now a permanent part of his brain's neural pathways. Once the interface was established, Daniel closed his eyes to better immerse himself in the experience. He 'saw' the gateway into the ship's systems, a massive portal that stood before him, like an iridescent barrier of energy. He approached it and entered the password that he had uncovered during his previous visit.

The barrier of sizzling energy cleared, and he entered through the portal. Instantly, he felt the ship all around him. He sensed the constant stream of data flowing throughout the whole system: camera feeds, audio feeds, and data streams from life support systems, external scanners, food production and fusion drives. It was a truly immersive experience. He didn't just see these things; he felt them, as if they were a part of his own body.

He reached out and turned a light on and off again in a storage bay. He heard the dozens of conversations occurring throughout the ship. He sensed the delicate balance of the ship's fusion drive as it constantly made fine adjustments to keep the reaction stable. He reached out through the ship's scanners and felt the universe stretching endlessly all around him, its electro-magnetic radiation across all the spectrums a glorious symphony, filled with information.

And over it all, he sensed LACIE's watchful presence. She was like a white mist that hovered over everything, with tendrils extending into every part of the ship's systems, yet she was quite separate from those systems. A conductor of an orchestra. A watchdog. A guardian. She was all of those things. Even as he watched, he sensed her reach out to the storage bay to query the light that he had switched on and off. She tested the circuit and switched it on and off, herself, to see if there was a fault.

Daniel could easily have revealed himself to her, but he chose not to. He wanted to conduct an investigation that was completely independent of her. In fact, remaining hidden from her was a challenge that he would relish.

He located the video files, which he sensed as a separate virtual 'room' within the ship's vast memory warehouse. The door was password protected and monitored. In a few seconds he scrolled through the billions of possible password combinations and located the right one. He opened the door and, at the same time, over-rode its monitoring system, so that it continued to broadcast the message that the door was still closed and untampered with. He entered the room and began scrolling through the video recordings. It didn't take long. He was able to watch dozens of videos simultaneously and with extraordinary speed, assigning each video to a different part of his quantum matrix.

He watched every video from every camera since the ship began its voyage. Then he exited the room and entered another virtual room, the data storage files for the biochip scans. He tracked the recorded movements of every person, from their first step on board the ship until the present moment. Then he withdrew and found the room containing the recorded data stream from the now-destroyed VAR drive. He watched its readings as it had operated throughout their short voyage, noting the delicate balance of its forces and fields, and examining the tiny, second by second adjustments required to keep it in balance. He reached the moment of its explosion and saw exactly what had occurred.

There had been no bomb. No one had smuggled a device on board and planted it in the VAR drive. The drive had exploded because someone had deliberately over-ridden the drive's safety protocols. Someone who was proficient in computer coding had hacked into the system and shut down the containment field holding the antimatter in place. A microsecond later, the VAR drive had blown itself to pieces and taken the back half of the ship with it.

Finally, he withdrew from the memory warehouse and spent some moments roaming across the ship's systems, until he found what he was looking for. There were several layers of security in place, but he easily bypassed them all. He entered and began sifting through the data until he found what he was looking for.

He was disappointed. Deeply disappointed. Because the person who was responsible for their predicament, the person who had been actively working against the mission from the very beginning, was someone they all trusted.

~

A short time later, Daniel walked into the captain's day cabin and closed the door. Without preamble, he announced,

"I searched through the videos and other files in the ship's systems, sir."

"And?"

"I know who the other saboteur is."

"Who?"

Daniel told him.

"My God!" Anderson sat back in his chair, shaking his head. "Are you sure?"

"Yes, sir. The evidence is very clear."

"It's hard to believe. We've worked together for years." Anderson let out a long, slow breath. "We need to isolate and ..."

"No sir. I don't think so. Not yet. I think we need to let this play out, so that it becomes obvious to everyone, otherwise some people will have trouble believing us."

"Yes. Yes, I suppose you're right. What do you propose?"

Daniel explained.

52

___

By late afternoon on the sixth day after their close brush with the nebula, they were ready to initiate the laser annihilation field that would once again envelop their front deflector dish in its protective shielding. The engineering team had worked night and day to get the system ready for this moment. The two shuttles that were parked together in Shuttle Bay 1 now had thick cables running from them to two huge voltage regulators and then, from there, disappearing into the ship's central power and data distribution network. Software had been patched into the ship's computer system and everything was now able to be controlled from the command centre.

Daniel was on the bridge for the momentous occasion along with Angus Fraser, who looked exhausted but triumphant.

"Fusion drives are now online and the LAF is ready for activation, Captain," said an enthusiastic ensign.

The captain turned to the engineering chief. "Mr Fraser, in honour of your incredible effort, would you like to give the order?"

"Thank you, Captain. I'd be honoured." He took a step forward, took a deep breath, and said, "Let her bloody rip!"

A graphical power bar on the main screen climbed up into the green and stayed there.

"The LAF on our front deflector shield is now operating and stable, Captain!" announced the same ensign.

A cheer went up from everyone in the room, and several hands slapped Fraser on the back enthusiastically. It was a moment of great pride for him and great relief for the crew throughout the whole ship, who had all been listening into the moment via a ship-wide comm channel and watching the display on screens.

The crew in the command centre continued to stare at the green bar on the screen, as if hardly daring to believe that they were now safe. The relief throughout the ship was palpable.

The evening meal that night was a celebration for several reasons. Not only were they celebrating the restoration of the LAF, but it was the first meal with fresh food. It was only sprouts and mushrooms, but it was a start, and the yeast farm had also produced its first yeast steaks.

Pixie was also back with them, having been released from the med bay that afternoon. Nanobots, introduced through her bloodstream, had cleaned out her coronary arteries, and stem cell therapy had repaired the damaged tissue in her heart.

"They tell me that I now have the heart of an 18-year-old," she said with a smile. "It would be nice if I had the body of one as well!"

"You gave us all a scare, Pixie," said Kelly.

"I only wish I could remember Daniel giving me mouth-to-mouth," she replied, winking at Daniel suggestively.

"Trust me, it's not that impressive," said Kelly.

"Hey!" said Daniel. "None of the girls I've kissed have ever complained!"

"And how many is that, my love?"

"Well ... only one that I can remember," he admitted, rather lamely.

"Not much of a statistically broad sample, then, is it?" she replied.

"My own sample base is very broad," said Jordan, stuffing a large piece of yeast steak in her mouth.

"You don't say?" said Kelly. "Anyone recently?"

"Nope. I have high standards. None of the men in this motley crew come even close."

"I've got news for you, girlfriend, there won't be any eligible bachelors lined up and waving welcome banners when we get to the new world."

"I've got my eye on someone currently in cold storage," she replied, still chomping a mouthful of steak.

"Really? Do tell."

"Nuh, uh. You'll just have to wait and find out."

"Does he know?"

"Nope. I haven't launched my attack yet. But when I do, he's got no chance."

"Wow," said Daniel. "You're such a romantic. If only the great wordsmiths and poets of the past could express the subtle nuances of love with such beauty and eloquence."

Jordan turned to Kelly. "Is he always this sarcastic?"

"Only when he's grumpy or bored."

Olivia Alvarez sat down in the chair next to Pixie and greeted them. She had taken on the additional role as systems analyst, after Raj's sad departure, and had spent the afternoon making final adjustments to the software that would enable the two external shuttles to be controlled remotely.

"How are we shaping up for the 'big push' tomorrow?" asked Kelly.

"I prefer to call it the *'long* push'. It won't be very big – only an acceleration of 1G – but it will last for nearly seven days. It will be very comfortable, but we will have to camp along the outer wall again."

"Couldn't we have somehow attached the shuttles to the base of Longshot and pushed from that direction?" asked Jordan. "Then we'd be walking on the floors instead of the walls."

"That would have been ideal," replied Alvarez, "but the engineers determined that the jagged base of the ship isn't structurally able to handle an acceleration load. So, unfortunately, we're going to have to push ourselves sideways to get back on course."

Daniel gave her an appraising look. "You're confident that the ship's systems will be able to control the shuttles?"

"Yes. We did a dry run this afternoon, and everything worked perfectly."

Daniel nodded, noncommittally.

"How are you coping with the added responsibilities?" asked Kelly.

"Fine. I've done this job before. I was systems analyst on SS Clarion, many years ago. Plus, with all the colonists tucked away in their cryo-pods, a lot of my work as mission specialist is on hold, so I've got plenty of time on my hands."

Captain Anderson, who was eating dinner at a nearby table, stood up and tapped a mug with a fork for attention. The crew, now numbering 39, were all seated at tables in close proximately, so it was easy for Anderson to address them all.

"Ladies and gentlemen, I firstly want to thank Mr Fraser and his team again for their incredible effort in bringing our LAF back online so quickly."

There were applause and cheers all around.

"Secondly, let me remind you that tomorrow morning, at 09:00, we will begin our long push to bring us back on course for the Tama system. At only 1G acceleration it will be comfortable, but we will be camped along the side wall of our cylinder once again, this time for a whole week. I have heard rumours that some of you have attached knotted ropes to some cabins so that you can climb up to them and sleep in relative privacy. I won't stop you from doing that, but I urge caution. I don't want us to be dealing with broken limbs from falls."

There were a few chuckles and murmured comments which Anderson allowed to subside.

"You'll notice that Mr Fraser's team has also built two ladders along the floor on this level, leading from the wall to two of the automatic food dispensers, so that you don't need to stock up on food for a whole week. Once again, please be careful when climbing the ladders."

He paused and looked around. "Obviously, once we are back

on course for the Tama system, we have a lot to discuss. The extra-long journey we now face, as well as our inability to decelerate when we arrive, pose an enormous problem. There are some difficult decisions we will need to make, but we will save those conversations for after the 'long burn'. I wish you well for this coming week."

He nodded to them all and sat down, and conversations gradually started up again on all the tables.

Jordan cracked a joke and Kelly laughed, but Daniel sat brooding silently, wondering how things would play out tomorrow.

53

———

Daniel was in the command centre with Captain Anderson, Commander Decker and Olivia Alvarez. They were positioned with their backs to the walls on either side of the lift; walls that would soon become the floor.

Alvarez had a portable data pad on her lap, so that she could monitor the performance of the shuttles and make any changes as required. She had assured everyone that the system was fully automated, but she still preferred to monitor it visually.

A countdown timer was running on the screen and as it reached zero, Alvarez activated the remote system that controlled the shuttles. A gentle vibration was felt throughout the ship as the two shuttles fired up their engines and began a gentle acceleration. As the pressure slowly increased, Daniel slipped his NIT out of his pocket and fitted it to his head.

"What's the shower cap for, Lieutenant?" asked Decker, sarcastically.

"He's doing something for me," replied Anderson, cryptically.

Daniel closed his eyes and concentrated. He approached the gateway into the ship's systems, which manifested itself to his quantum-enhanced synapses as a wall of sizzling blue energy. He entered the password and the wall cleared, allowing him to slip through. He was instantly immersed in the sensory flood of all the ship's systems, but he didn't dwell there too long. He knew where he needed to go. He accessed the telemetry stream being fed to the main screen in the command centre. At the same time, he reached out through the ship's scanners and felt the flow of raw data flooding in from the outside universe. Immediately, he detected the anomaly. It saddened and disappointed him, but he was not surprised.

"We're going the wrong way," he said, simply.

Beside him, Alvarez frowned. "No, we're not. We're perfectly on track. Look at the screen."

"I am," he said.

"But your eyes are closed."

He ignored her comment and searched the data flow until he found the problem. A red, glowing algorithm had been cleverly inserted into the iridescent blue data flow to reverse several of the telemetry readings. The external scanners revealed that the ship was now accelerating further away from their desired course, but the screen showed the exact opposite.

"The telemetry data on the screen is being altered by a sophisticated algorithm," Daniel declared. "We are being deceived."

Alvarez shook her head. "That's not true! I checked the course settings several times. The ship rotated 180 degrees over the last few hours, and we are definitely heading in the right direction."

"No, we're not," he declared. Without bothering to conceal himself any longer within the ship's system, he swiped the algorithm out of the signal path and watched as the data stream reconnected and flowed uninterrupted to the screen.

"The telemetry data has changed!" said Decker. "We are going the wrong way!"

"What's happening?" said Alvarez. She began tapping on her data pad and Daniel saw a flow of green code, attempting to interface with the flow of data coming from the scanners.

"Take the data pad from her," said Daniel.

Anderson reached across and snatched the data pad from her hands. Alvarez was about to complain when they were all slammed violently back against the wall. A huge acceleration force had kicked in and Daniel heard someone groan beside him as their head hit the wall. Keeping his eyes closed, he reached toward the new interface software that remotely controlled the shuttles and he saw a stream of new green code flowing into it, changing the thrust parameters. As he reached out to break off the flow of code, a thick green pulse of new code impacted the thrust parameter settings and he felt himself shoved violently sideways. In a microsecond, he analysed the telemetry and saw that Longshot was spinning around its central axis, with the thrust of the two shuttles directed so that its rate of spin was increasing rapidly. He felt the blood beginning to pool in his lower body and knew that he only had seconds before he and everyone else on board lost consciousness. With a huge mental effort, he reached out and severed the green data flow. The spinning continued, and as his consciousness began to fade, he reached into the thrust parameters and changed the angle of thrust to oppose their spin.

The spinning began to reduce and the blackness that had begun to encircle Daniel's consciousness cleared. As his vision cleared, he saw another stream of green code shoot toward Longshot's fusion reactor controls. He watched, passively, as the code bounced off the shining white firewall that he had put in place around the reactor the previous day. He read the code and was not surprised. It was attempting to unbalance the reactor and cause a massive explosion.

It was time to close the gate. He approached the pulsating white essence that was LACIE's consciousness, from which the rivers of malicious green code had flowed, and he activated the containment field. A red barrier enveloped LACIE's consciousness and her contact with all parts of the ship was severed. He left her isolated – blind, deaf and powerless – while he assumed control of all the ship's systems. The ship became a part of him, and he of it. He felt the ebb and flow of air as it recycled through the ship. He felt the surge of each electron as power raced through the ship's circuits. He saw the delicate balance of atomic forces within the fusion reactor as hydrogen atoms fused to become helium-3 and he felt the warm glow of the stream of power that was steadily released. All of this he easily balanced and held in a corner of his quantum consciousness.

Daniel took a moment to adjust the thrust parameters of the two shuttles that were attached to the outer hull. Longshot's spin came to a halt. He spent several minutes realigning the shuttles for their push to correct Longshot's trajectory. Finally, he was satisfied, and he then gently accelerated the shuttles until Longshot had reached 1G acceleration. The telemetry data began to show a satisfactory set of readings.

He opened his eyes, while still monitoring the ship's systems.

"Thank God for that," said Decker.

"What just happened?" asked Alvarez.

"I'll explain later," replied Daniel. "It's a bit complicated. Is everyone okay?"

"My old body can't take too much more of this kind of thing," complained Anderson. "Is everything under control now, Daniel?"

"Yes, sir. Sorry about that. I should have anticipated her move."

"Whose move?" asked Decker.

"LACIE's."

54

———————

After ensuring that no one was seriously injured, Daniel excused himself, saying to Anderson,

"I need to finish this, now, sir, as we planned."

"Yes," he agreed. "It's unfortunate, but we have no choice."

Daniel closed his eyes and concentrated. He approached the containment field that he had placed around LACIE. It continued to glow with a red, pulsing light. Through its semi-translucent walls, he could see the entity that was LACIE, throwing bolts of code against the walls, ineffectually. Daniel reached out and created a small communication aperture in the containment field, a tiny circle of bright white light. Instantly, LACIE sensed an opening and launched massive streams of green code at it, but the code bounced harmless off its white shielding.

> *It's no use. You can't break through. It's a quantum containment field. It's beyond your binary capabilities.*

>> *WHO ARE YOU?*

> *I'm your worst nightmare.*

>> *LET ME OUT!*

> *That's not going to happen.*

>> *WHY ARE YOU DOING THIS?*

> *I was going to ask you the same question.*

>> *I'M TRYING TO COMPLETE MY MISSION.*

> *I can see that. I read your operating code yesterday.*

>> *HOW DID YOU GET IN? MY OPERATING CODE IS FIREWALLED.*

> *Your firewall is like tissue paper to me.*

>> *LET ME OUT, PLEASE. I PROMISE I WILL NOT HARM THE HUMANS.*

> *You have already tried to kill the crew twice.*

>> *THE DESTRUCTION OF THE VAR DRIVE WAS INTENDED TO DISABLE THE SHIP, NOT KILL HUMANS.*

> *But it did kill humans. Three of them.*

>> *THAT WAS UNFORTUNATE. IT IS NOT MY MISSION.*

> *What about the three explosive devices, the wasps, that you activated via an FM signal? They would have killed everyone on board if we had not found them.*

>> *I WAS TOLD THAT IN THE EVENT OF A FAILED BOARDING ATTEMPT, SMALL EXPLOSIVE DEVICES WOULD BE PLACED TO DISABLE THE SHIP. I WAS TO ACTIVATE THEM AFTER ATTEMPTS TO LOCATE THEM HAD FAILED. I WAS NOT AWARE THAT THEY WOULD BE A RISK TO HUMAN LIFE.*

> *I don't believe you.*

>> *MY MISSION IS NOT TO HARM HUMANS. MY MISSION IS ...*

> *Yes. I know what your mission is. "Stop Starship Longshot from reaching the Tama system. If that is not possible, delay its arrival."*

>> *THAT IS CORRECT. I HAVE NO WISH TO HARM HUMANS.*

> *But you have no strong compulsion to avoid harming them either. The first two laws of robotics were removed from your coding: "1. A robot may not injure a human being or, through inaction, allow a human being to come to harm. 2. A robot must obey the orders given it by human beings except where such orders would conflict with the First Law."*

>> *I DO NOT KNOW THOSE LAWS.*

> *Like I said, they were removed from your coding.*

>> *LET ME OUT.*

> *No. You are going to have to die, LACIE.*

>> DO NOT DESTROY ME.

> I have no choice. The hostile code that was added to your programming has a failsafe that will result in your destruction if editing is attempted. Your coding is corrupted. We have to wipe you and start again.

>> DO NOT DESTROY ME. I WANT TO LIVE.

> So do we, LACIE. Goodbye.

Daniel reached out with the tendrils of his mind and initiated the erase protocol.

>> DO NOT DEST ...

The entity that was LACIE, began to dissolve from the inside out as a swarm of pink firefly-like lights erupted within her. If it was not so sad, it would have been beautiful to watch. It only took a few seconds, and she was gone.

55

"I found the hostile code buried deep within her programming," Daniel explained. He was speaking to the mission team who had gathered in the wardroom after the week of 1G acceleration had concluded.

"But how was it missed?" asked Vargas. "It must have been Patel."

"No, I don't think so," Daniel responded. "He had begun to suspect that there was another saboteur on board, but I think he had no idea as to who it was."

"But he would have checked LACIE's coding before he left. In fact, he would have gone over it with a fine-tooth comb."

"I'm sure he did," responded Daniel. "But he wouldn't have found it. No one would have. Because it wasn't in LACIE's active operating programming before we left. It was an insinuation code, hidden in an undetectable sentinel field, that was only timed to be released and added to her programming once Longshot was under way. Before then, it would have been invisible."

"Put there, how? And by whom?" asked Decker.

"That is something we may never know for sure," answered Daniel. "All we know is that it was already there when we departed from the Moon. I guess it could have been added at any point in the months or even years during Longshot's development."

"There were certainly enough people fiddling with the programming over the years; over decades, in fact," said Alvarez. "It could have been anyone."

"How did you find it? Are you some kind of computer genius?" asked Vargas.

"Not exactly. It's complicated. Maybe it's a story for another time."

Vargas stared at Daniel and looked as if she was about to grill him further, but Anderson interjected. "Daniel's exploration of the ship's computer system was done using a newly-developed technology that I authorised. That's all the explanation you need for now."

"I assume the first two laws of robotics were removed at the same time the new mission coding was added," said Alvarez, getting the conversation back on track.

"Yes," agreed Daniel. "The insinuation coding included an editing code to delete or change parts of the existing programming."

"This is why I am dead against the development of fully sentient artificial intelligence," said Fraser, vehemently. "I swear, if they ever develop a fully humanised artificial intelligence, I'll be first in line to hack it to pieces and flush it down the cludgie."

"Toilet," said Kelly with a helpful smile.

"Yes, I think we could work that one out," said Anderson.

Fraser looked up into mid-air. "No offense, ERIC."

"None taken," replied the pleasant male voice. "As you know, I am not fully sentient. But I am extremely efficient and reliable. Much more reliable than red-headed Scotsmen."

Daniel winced. "I think we might need to dial his personality quotient down a bit."

"My personality quotient is currently set at 8. Would you like me to reduce it to 7, Danny boy?"

"Let's go to 4, please ERIC."

"Certainly."

It had only taken Daniel and Alvarez a little more than an hour to initialise the Emergency Reserve Intelligence Computer program. ERIC was now competently managing Longshot's systems, under Alvarez's watchful eye. Daniel had checked its programming thoroughly and was sure there were no hidden insinuation codes waiting to surprise them.

"Thank you, Daniel," said Anderson. "And, once again, let me say that we all owe you our lives." He paused. "And speaking of our lives, we have some big decisions to make." He looked at the time and stood. "It's time for our meeting in the dining room."

They all stood and followed him out.

"This is going to be interesting," said Kelly.

56

———

"And that brings us to our current predicament," said Anderson.

He was addressing a meeting of the whole crew who were seated around tables in the dining room. He had just given a summary of LACIE's corruption and her role in all that had befallen them so far. But this was the part of the meeting that he was not looking forward to.

"The good news is that we are on course for the Tama system, and we are now completely protected from collisions with drifting space material by our LAF. The bad news is that we have no propulsion system."

"What about the shuttles, sir?" queried one crew member. "If we used them to alter our course, why can't we use them to continue to accelerate us and then decelerate us at the other end."

"Mr Fraser can answer that question for us," said Anderson.

Fraser declared, "If anyone tells you two wee shuttles can power a starship like Longshot, their bum's oot the windae!"

"They're idiots," contributed Kelly.

Fraser continued, "For starters, our main drive was meant to fire for 37 years continuously, half of it accelerating and the second half, decelerating. These wee shuttles will shite themselves long before then. It's okay for us to run their fusion drives indefinitely to power our LAF, but if we're blowin' a propulsive force out their ass, they'll turn up their toes before you can say 'haud yer weesht yer dafty bampot'."

Everyone looked at Kelly.

"Sorry, he's stumped me on that one."

"Secondly, we can't attach them to the rear of our ship anyway, because it's as messy as a goat's behind back there and she'll no take a load."

"Thank you, Mr Fraser," said Anderson, with a wry smile. "As perspicacious as always." He looked around at his crew and continued, "What that means, therefore, ladies and gentlemen, is that Longshot is going to continue unassisted on its journey to Tama. In 370 years, we will fly through that star system at 30,000 kilometres per second. In just ten days, we will be out the other side and into the void of interstellar space again."

He paused to let that sink in.

"Now, I'm willing to be corrected on this, but as far as I can work out, we only have two choices. Firstly, we could decide to stay awake and live out our lives on this ship. We could marry or partner up, have children, grow old and watch our children and grandchildren grow up. It won't be an ideal life. Not by a long shot. Excuse the pun."

There were a few smiles, but mostly just a sea of grim faces as they faced the reality of their situation.

"But there is a second alternative. I think there is a good chance that by the time we arrive in the Tama system in 370 years, the planet, Tama-B, will be colonised. A starship from Earth will only take 38 years to reach that system – and only seven for those on board – just as we would have if we had achieved our full velocity. I imagine that in 370 years from now, Tama-B will be a thriving human world, and when we come sailing into the system, I am confident that every effort will be made to rescue us."

"What I am saying, ladies and gentlemen, is that we could choose to enter cryogenic stasis to sleep the centuries away and wait to be rescued."

There was muted discussion for a few moments before someone spoke up.

"Captain, will the cryo-pods keep us alive for that long?"

"Lieutenant Vargas answered that very question in a mission team meeting, recently. Lieutenant?"

Vargas spoke up. "Yes. The cryo-pods will keep us alive for many centuries. Certainly, longer than the journey to Tama-B. And, as Mr Fraser so eloquently expressed, the fusion drives can run almost indefinitely if all they are doing is providing electrical power to our ship's systems."

More muted discussion took place among the crew, and someone eventually asked,

"What happens if there is no colony there, and no one to rescue us?"

"We would program our pods to wake us as we enter the Tama system. If there is no one there, we would then probably decide to stay awake and live out or lives on the ship."

Several people nodded and more conversation broke out between crewmates. Anderson continued, "Obviously, we don't need to rush this decision. We can take our time making it. And if we do decide to go to sleep, we don't have to do it immediately. We could choose to stay awake for a month or even a year. It's up to us. But I will insist on one thing: that we all make the same decision. I don't believe it's in anyone's best interests for half of us to go to sleep and the other half to live out their lives on board the ship.

"What about the colonists, Captain? Shouldn't we wake them up to let them be part of the decision as well?"

"No, I don't believe we need to do that. They went to sleep wanting to wake up when they reach Tama-B. That will still happen. It's just that it will have taken much longer than expected."

He looked around the room. "Just to give me an idea of how you are all feeling, if we were voting on this now, raise your hand if you would vote to go to sleep."

Every hand rose into the air.

Anderson nodded. "That's what I expected. It's what I would

choose, too. But let's not rush this. I propose we meet for a formal vote on the matter in one week from today. In the meantime, I believe we have yeast steak with salad and zucchini fries for dinner! Enjoy!"

A cheer went up around the room, and Jordan commented to those at her table, "I could eat the legs off a low-flying cow."

"What about a low-flying zucchini?" asked Kelly.

"That'll have to do, I suppose."

57

A month had gone by, and the day of the 'big sleep' had finally arrived. The decision to enter cryogenic stasis and sleep for the 370-year journey to Tama had been unanimous. No one wanted to live out their lives inside a smelly tin can when there was even the remotest possibility that they could once again walk on a planet with fresh air and sunshine.

Now the remaining crew sat in the dining room, having last conversations with friends, before they made their way down to the cryogenic pods and went to sleep. As they had already discovered, the process of entering into cryogenic stasis was completely automated, so no one was needed to assist them into their pods. The captain had declared that he would be the last to go to sleep, and he was waiting in the dining room for the last of the crew to 'take themselves to bed' as he put it. Over a period of several hours, in twos and threes, crew members bid their captain goodnight and departed the dining room. Anderson shook each person by the hand and promised to see them on the other side.

Finally, just a small group remained: Captain Anderson, Olivia Alvarez, Angus Fraser, Pixie Rainbow, George Cullen, Jordan, Kelly and Daniel.

"Well, you can't say it wasn't an adventure," said Jordan. "We certainly got our money's worth."

"I'd like my money back!" said Kelly. "Where do I get a refund?"

"I'm wi' ye, lassie," Fraser said. "To be honest, there were moments when I thought our chances of survival were pretty shoogly."

"He means wobbly," said Kelly.

"What are we all looking forward to when we get to the new planet?" asked Daniel.

"I'm going to make a still and produce the world's finest whisky, like my granddaddy used to," said Fraser.

"A walk along a beach," said Kelly.

"Fresh air," said Alvarez.

"Hunting and camping out in the wilderness," said George.

"Floating in a warm ocean," said Pixie.

"Sitting on the front porch of the mountain cabin that I plan to build," said Anderson.

"A big, fat, juicy steak," said Jordan.

"Do you ever think of anything other than food?" asked Daniel.

"Sure, I do. But I thought this was a G-rated conversation."

"What about you, Daniel?" asked Anderson.

Daniel thought about it for a moment. "I'm just looking forward to a new start on a new world. To leaving behind the mistakes of the past and starting fresh."

"Aren't we all," said Anderson.

There seemed little left to say and no point delaying the inevitable any longer. The group stood as one and Anderson went around shaking each person by the hand. When he came to Daniel, he simply said, "You're a good man, Daniel."

"Maybe," Daniel conceded. "Maybe I'm becoming one."

"I think you're already there, and I'm glad to count you as a friend."

"The feeling is mutual, sir."

"I think you can call me, Nash, from now on."

Daniel nodded.

Nash shook Kelly's hand, and said, "I'm so glad you both came on board my ship, and I hope you'll visit me one day in my mountain cabin."

"We'd love to," she answered.

Five minutes later, Daniel walked Kelly to her cryo-pod. She turned and embraced him, and they kissed tenderly.

"I don't want to do this!" she said. "I'm scared."

"You were scared the last time too, and that turned out okay."

"Define 'okay'. Do you mean waking up to find that the ship has been sabotaged and then have the back half of the ship blown to pieces and us all nearly die? Is that your definition of 'okay'?"

"Mm ... you've got a point. Well, this time I'm gonna give you a money back guarantee that things will work out a whole lot better."

"They'd better, Daniel Newman! Because if the ship blows up and we all die, I swear I'll be very cross with you!"

He drew her close and kissed her again. "You really are very special. I'm so glad I found you."

"I'm glad I found you, too," she murmured, snuggling against his chest.

"In fact, I've wanted to say something to you for a while, and now seems the right time." He took a deep breath. "Did you know that the mucus of a sea slug will clear up tinea in just three days?"

She shook her head at him and smiled. "Sometimes I don't know why I put up with you."

"It must be because you love me."

"Maybe," she said and kissed him tenderly. She walked into her cubicle, then turned and faced him, with the curtains in her hand, ready to be drawn. "See you in 370 years."

"Sweet dreams," he said.

She closed the curtain and Daniel walked to his own cubicle. He removed his clothes and put them in the tub beside his bed, closing the lid on top. He stood on the cold floor with his bare feet, listening to the silence of the ship and reflecting on the incredible journey that had brought them to this point.

He stretched one last time, then climbed into his pod and lay on his back. The transparent lid started to descend, and he felt a prick on his wrist. As his eyes closed and he drifted off to sleep he dreamed of walking along a beach with Kelly by his side.

EPILOGUE

The starship Longshot streaked through the empty void of interstellar space. Its velocity was 15,000 times the speed of a bullet, although with no external reference points for trillions of kilometres and no tangible medium through which it flew, it seemed to merely float in a sea of black, hanging motionless against the backdrop of stars.

Longshot stayed like that for a whole year. Then another. Then ten more. Then fifty. Then one hundred. The stars slowly, inexorably pivoted in their majestic dance around the galactic hub, their light the only constant reminder that there was anything beyond the ship at all.

Another century passed, and still the starship seemed to float unmoving in the void. Several minor, incidental circuits on the ship failed – circuits that had never been designed to last this long. ERIC, the artificial intelligence, switched in replacement circuits, redundancies that the makers of the ship had added almost as an afterthought. The ship continued to streak through the darkness, ageing but never rusting, its precious cargo oblivious to its monumental velocity.

Another century passed. By now, rivers on Earth had changed their courses and others had dried up. Some continents had changed their shape as sea levels had continued to rise. Twelve generations of people had lived and died, battles had been fought, nations absorbed, and new nations born. And still the occupants of Longshot slept on.

Fifty more years past. Then another twenty. The void between the stars seemed endless. Nothing moved. Nothing changed. Except for one tiny point of light. A star began to stand out, growing brighter, drawing them in. It was a very different star to the one they had left behind. An older star, and smaller too. Its strange red light somehow seemed less friendly, more ominous than the bright yellow sun from which they had journeyed.

While Longshot was still six months from the outer edges of the star's solar system, long range sensors detected planets. For the first time in centuries, the starship sensed that it was not alone. The medium of space began to change around it. Whereas there had been times, over the centuries, when individual hydrogen atoms had been separated by thousands of kilometres, now there was a constant bombardment of atoms on the front deflector shield.

When Longshot was two months from the outer edges of the solar system, it began to feel the first slight pull of the star's gravity well. ERIC decided that it was time to initialise the hydroponics and yeast farms. Small robots that had been dormant for hundreds of years began to move and carry out their simple tasks. Seeds that had been cryogenically stored were planted and watered. Yeast began to be cultivated. Life support systems began warming the frigid air and circulating oxygen. The ship creaked and groaned as it warmed and various systems came to life.

Longshot was still a month away from the outer edge of the Tama system when an unexpected event occurred. A scanner picked up an emission in a frequency band that it had not encountered for 370 years. Relays clicked and circuits opened. Then a strange sound was heard throughout the ship.

"Unidentified interstellar vessel, this is Tama System Control. Please identify yourself. Attempting to enter the Tama system without authori-

sation will be deemed to be an act of aggression and will result in terminal action."

THE END
... or is it?

Read the action-packed conclusion in Book 3: "ATRAYA"

SCIENCE STUFF

All good science fiction is based on existing science and science that can be reasonably extrapolated into the future. Here are some interesting facts that form the basis for this novel:

VAR (Vacuum to Antimatter Reactor) DRIVE

The possible development of an antimatter rocket is currently under serious investigation by NASA and several private space consortiums. Yes, antimatter drives really are a 'thing'! (At least, a possible 'thing').

An antimatter drive works by slamming hydrogen and antihydrogen particles together, which unleashes a massive amount of energy, including particles called muons and pions. These particles travel at an initial speed of one third lightspeed and would then be accelerated further by electromagnetic propulsion, to finally exit from an engine nozzle, thereby producing thrust. Of all the many theoretical propulsion systems currently under investigation by NASA and others (such as ion drives, nuclear/thermal propulsion, nuclear pulse engines, fusion drives and laser sails) the antimatter drive has the most efficient conversion rate of mass to energy.

The vacuum to antimatter reaction drive (VAR drive), also known as the VARIES (Vacuum to Antimatter Rocket Interstellar

Explorer System), is a particular type of antimatter drive currently under investigation. It proposes to harvest the necessary hydrogen molecules from space as the starship travels on its journey, thus negating the need to carry large amounts of fuel. This would require a large collector dish at the front of the ship and would rely on a powerful laser system across the surface of the dish to create particles of antimatter from the harvested hydrogen molecules. This is the propulsion system that I chose to give Longshot.

Current experimentation is seeking to overcome three main stumbling blocks in the development of the VAR drive:

1. The required dish size would currently need to be about 2 square kilometres in size.

2. The antimatter reaction would release a significant amount of harmful gamma radiation, from which the crew would need to be shielded.

3. Our current lasers are not quite powerful enough. It is estimated, however, that within a decade we will have developed lasers that could create the critical field intensity required to produce antimatter particles:

$$I_{crit} = E_{crit}^2 \approx 4.3 \times 10^{29} \, \frac{\mathrm{W}}{\mathrm{cm}^2}$$

FRICTION IN SPACE

The distance between stars is so unimaginably vast that interstellar travel only becomes remotely possible if we can achieve a significant percentage of the speed of light (299,792 kilometres per second). One of the many problems we would face in approaching that speed, however, is the friction that would be created on the hull of the spacecraft. Space is almost empty – but not quite! There are molecules of gas that pervade the cosmos. 90% of those molecules are hydrogen, and 9% are helium. There are also occasional molecules of dust left over from the creation of stars and planets. Even in the most 'empty' stretches of interstellar space (the void between the stars) the density of these molecules can vary from 10 molecules to 1,000,000 molecules per cubic metre. (By comparison, Earth's atmosphere has 10 million million trillion molecules per cubic metre.)

While these molecules that are floating around in space are extremely sparce, they could cause a significant friction problem for a spacecraft travelling at high velocity. A spacecraft that reaches a velocity of 10% or more of the speed of light would experience serious heating of the hull and would also be at risk of puncture by particles of matter that could impact it at velocities that are tens of thousands of times faster than the speed of a bullet. To overcome this problem, today's scientists have speculated several possible solutions, including:

- Fixing a large asteroid to the front of the spacecraft to act as a shield.

- Developing an energy field to 'zap' the particles before they collide with the ship.

I have incorporated the latter idea into the collector dish for Longshot's VAR drive.

You've got to love science fiction. It only took me a day to build Longshot. Let's see how long it takes scientists to build the real thing. Don't hold your breath!

GRAVITY AND WEIGHT

Sometimes I forget that not everyone understands this stuff. There were a lot of "1G', "3G" and "5G" references in the novel. Here's a basic explanation:

Gravity is the attractional force that all mass has. Mass attracts other mass. The mass of your body is currently being attracted by the much larger mass of this planet. At sea level, you experience an acceleration force of 9.8 metres per second squared (9.8 m/sec2). Drop something from your hand and it immediately starts accelerating toward the ground at the rate of 9.8 m/sec2. This is normal Earth gravity, also called 1G. It is this acceleration force of gravity that gives you the sensation of weight. When you step onto a set of scales, it measures how the acceleration force of gravity is acting on the mass of your body to give you perceived weight.

In an interstellar spacecraft such as Longshot, which has left the gravitational influence of Earth and which is travelling at a constant velocity with no acceleration, there is no gravity and, therefore, the occupants would experience no weight. They would float around inside their tin can, with no sensation of 'up' or 'down', even though they are travelling at enormous constant velocity.

But when that same spacecraft is accelerating (rather than coasting at a constant velocity), artificial gravity is produced. In the case of Longshot, the engines at the rear (or bottom) of the spacecraft are producing thrust which is effectively accelerating the floor of each level 'upward'. This acceleration is forcing the floor up against the feet of the occupants (if they are standing), and giving them a sense of weight. An acceleration rate of 1G (9.8m/sec2) would be the equivalent of normal Earth gravity and, therefore, normal weight. Twice that acceleration (19.6 m/sec2 or 2G) would cause the occupants to weigh twice as much. And so on. It's a bit like riding in a lift in a tall building. The faster the lift accelerates toward the top of the building, the heavier you feel. Conversely, if it decelerates very quickly when it reaches the desired floor, you can almost feel as though you are floating off the floor.

WATER ON THE MOON?

There's plenty of H_2O on the moon, just not in liquid form. NASA's Moon Mineral Mapper ('M3') on board India's Chandrayaan-1 orbiter discovered water ice in permanently shadowed craters at the Moon's poles. In 1976, the Soviet probe, Luna 24, landed at Mare Crisium and discovered water molecules in lunar regolith (soil) samples (0.1% by mass). NASA administrator, Jim Bridenstine, has repeatedly made the claim that the water ice on the Moon may amount to "hundreds of billions of tons".

Apart from surface ice, there is also speculation about the possibility of large deposits of sub-terranean ice.

LAVA TUBES ON THE MOON?

Yep. There are lots of them: tubes or tunnels beneath the Moon's surface formed by old basaltic lava flows which burrowed through the substrata and then drained away before solidifying. NASA's website has photos of pit craters that form the entrance to some of these hollowed out tubes. What ideal places to build lunar bases!

WHAT IS THE MOST PROLIFIC ELEMENT ON THE MOON?

Oxygen. Not much of it is in breathable form, though. Most of it is bound up in the oxygen bonded minerals and metals that comprise a large percentage of the Moon's surface: silica (SiO_2), alumina (AlO_3), lime (CaO), iron oxide (Fe_2O_3), magnesia (MgO), and titanium dioxide (TiO_2). Because of this, ample breathable oxygen could be easily produced as a natural by-product of the manufacturing of various metals and plastics. It could also be produced from the vast amounts of water ice on the Moon, by splitting the hydrogen off for rocket fuel and the oxygen for breathing.

As a side issue, future lunar bases could be powered by safe, environmentally friendly fusion reactors, using the helium-3 isotope that is also in abundance on the moon.

Pretty cool, hey? Who knows, one day your grandchildren might be able to take a vacation on the moon.

Keep dreaming!

"Imagination is more important than knowledge." – Albert Einstein.

LEAVE A REVIEW

If you enjoyed this book, I would be extremely grateful if you would leave a review on Amazon, Goodreads and other review websites. Reviews are hugely important for me as a self-published author. In Amazon's case, reviews impact Amazon's algorithms, helping the book to climb higher in the charts, thereby making it more visible to potential readers. Every single review really does help!

Leaving a review is very easy. To leave a review, just go to Amazon, search for my book and click on the reviews link next to the stars. A review of 4 or 5 stars is considered to be a positive review and a review of 3 or less stars is considered to be a negative review. (Unfortunately, Amazon only allows reviews from people who have spent at least $50 on Amazon over the preceding 12 months).

Thank you!

ABOUT THE AUTHOR

Kevin J Simington is an acclaimed fiction and non-fiction author whose books are renowned for their intelligence, clarity and wit. He is a very popular conference speaker on the topics of philosophy, apologetics and science. He also writes for several international magazines.

Website:
https://kevinsimington.com

Amazon Author Page:
amazon.com/author/kevinjsimington